AT ROPE'S END

AT ROPE'S END

A Dr. James Verraday Mystery

Edward Kay

CROOKED
LANE

NEW YORK

Copyright © 2017 by Edward Kay

Published in the United States by Crooked Lane Books, an imprint of The Quick Brown Fox & Company LLC.

Crooked Lane Books and its logo are trademarks of The Quick Brown Fox & Company LLC.

Library of Congress Catalog-in-Publication data available upon request.

ISBN (hardcover): 978-1-68331-000-6
ISBN (paperback): 978-1-68331-001-3
ISBN (ePub): 978-1-68331-002-0
ISBN (Kindle): 978-1-68331-003-7
ISBN (ePDF): 978-1-68331-004-4

Cover design by Melanie Sun
Book design by Jennifer Canzone

Printed in the United States.

www.crookedlanebooks.com

Crooked Lane Books
34 West 27th St., 10th Floor
New York, NY 10001

First Edition: January 2017

10 9 8 7 6 5 4 3 2 1

PROLOGUE

Ray Kerkhoff paused, pushing his baseball cap up to wipe away the sweat rolling down his forehead despite the cool October air. A heavy, gray herringbone cloud cover hung above him, stretching all the way across Puget Sound to the Olympic Peninsula. He had grown up here and was used to these moody West Coast skies, so he didn't find them oppressively dark and claustrophobic the way that transplanted easterners did.

Besides, the sea of crimson now spreading out beneath him in every direction more than made up for the lack of color overhead. He wiped the last of the sweat away from his eyes and put his handkerchief back in his shirt, resuming the arduous work of hauling the boom through the waist-deep water.

Gripping the end of the boom, he traced a circle around the perimeter of the bog so that the berries would be trapped within its arc. Tomorrow morning they would be pumped by water jets onto a conveyor system that would load them into the old International Harvester truck that had been in Kerkhoff's family for almost as long as they'd owned this bog. Then he would shepherd the year's harvest to the Ocean Spray plant down the coast, just south of Aberdeen. There his cranberries would be pulped, sweetened, cooked, and transformed into sauce, then shipped out to be served alongside turkey at Thanksgiving and Christmas dinners throughout the country.

He gazed across the scarlet lake, and as he had liked to do ever since he was a kid, when his father ran the operation, he wondered about the scenes that would play out when "his" cranberries reached their final destination on the tables of tens of thousands of people he would never meet. He imagined who they might be: homesick college kids who had flown back to be with their families for the holidays; couples taking their children from big cities back to small towns to spend a long weekend with elderly parents thrilled to see their grandchildren; men and women in uniform whose military service prevented them from spending the holidays with their loved ones but for whom the ritual of a turkey dinner with cranberry sauce, shared with their comrades-in-arms, would take the edge off their loneliness. His cranberries might find their way into shelters or Salvation Army halls, served to homeless people for whom families were a distant memory, or maybe no memory at all.

Kerkhoff liked to think that for all these people— most of whom would taste cranberries exactly twice a year—the distinctive flavor was infused with meaning and memories. He took pleasure from the knowledge that no matter what other troubles they faced, the ritual consumption of his berries would give comfort and a sense of continuity to their lives.

Those reveries were Kerkhoff's own ritual and gave his mind somewhere to go while he was slogging through the grunt work that was an unavoidable part of the harvest. He changed course to close the loop and began dragging the heavy boom back toward the shore. He plucked one of the floating cranberries off a stem and raised it to his lips. Testing it against his teeth, he found it firm, with just enough give to let him know it was ready. He bit down. The astringent tang flooded his mouth. The balance between fruit and tannin was perfect. This was one of the best crops ever.

Heartened by this, he pulled the boom with renewed energy, legs pushing hard against the resistance of the water. Suddenly he felt a heavy tug that stopped him midstride, almost tearing the boom out of his hands. *That shouldn't be possible*, he thought. The bog was clear of roots and branches. He pulled on the boom again. Kerkhoff was a muscular man, but it barely budged. He brushed away the berries floating on the surface so that he could see what the problem was. They parted momentarily, giving him a glimpse into the peaty water. A few feet below the surface, at the edge of visibility, he caught a flash of white. Then the berries closed over the gap.

He leaned down close to the water and cupped his hands to block the reflected light that was obscuring his view. Then he saw it again. Something curved and white. He rolled up his sleeves and reached down to grasp whatever it was. That's when he felt it. Soft and smooth as the belly of a salmon. And then something else, thin and rough to the touch. A length of rope. He tugged on the free end of it. A metallic taste flooded Kerkhoff's mouth as he realized what the shadowy shape ascending from the murky depths was. A moment later, the naked body of a young woman broke the surface, pushing the cranberries aside.

Small fragments of stem and leaves clung to her breasts and forehead. Her face was smooth and white, framed by long black hair that spread out across the surface of the water like a dark halo. Her lifeless eyes, red with burst blood vessels, stared past him. Her lips were parted slightly, revealing a chipped incisor. Tattooed in neat cursive under her left breast were the words "If you don't live for something, you'll die for nothing."

Her belly was arched forward at an unnatural angle, and as Ray Kerkhoff looked closer, he saw why: the length of rope he had pulled on had been used to hogtie her. A brown line traced an ugly circle around her neck. Fighting to control his breath, which was coming fast and shallow now, he backed away from her body toward the shore, almost tripping as he pulled his cell phone out of his shirt pocket and called 9-1-1.

CHAPTER 1

James Verraday stood behind the podium and looked out at the faces of the second-year students filling the lecture hall for his cognitive psychology class. Projected above and behind him on a retractable screen was a panoramic photo of Seattle's University of Washington campus, looking north along West Stevens Way. In the background was Guthrie Hall. It was, thought Verraday, a hideous example of New Brutalist architecture that would look more at home as the headquarters of a secret police agency in a failed socialist workers' paradise like Bulgaria or Albania than as the building in which he was at this moment teaching his class.

In the photo, happy-looking students were going about their business on the campus. Many of them wore the sort of outdoor gear popular in the Pacific Northwest—down-filled vests and rainproof outer shells over sweaters and jackets. In the foreground, a pair of pretty girls—one blonde, the other African American—were laughing over a shared joke as they made their way to class. Farther along the sidewalk, a smiling young man with a gray backpack was gesturing to a fellow student to emphasize a point. In the background, a man in his midthirties was climbing out of a taxi, his face partially obscured by the pillar of the sedan. A trio of students lounged on the grass nearby. One of them, a young woman with shoulder-length brown hair, was taking a sip from a travel mug.

It was the sort of pleasant but forgettable photograph you'd see in a university brochure, an effect heightened by a cheery-looking script, superimposed at the top of the frame, that read "Welcome to the University of Washington!" It appeared to be some sort of placeholder image in Verraday's PowerPoint presentation, and none of the students were paying much attention to it.

Without a word, Verraday hit a button on his laptop and the PowerPoint image disappeared, leaving a blank white screen in its place.

"So the last thing I want to talk about today," he said, "is something called the short-term memory decay theory. In that image that was just up there behind me, what color was the down-filled vest of the girl taking a sip from the Starbucks travel mug?"

As usual, no one in the hall volunteered a response. Even with second-year students, Verraday almost always had to pry an answer out of them.

"Okay, let's just have a show of hands instead. How many people think that the girl was wearing a maroon vest?"

He waited and in response received a small, tentative show of hands.

"Okay, how many of you say it was purple?"

More hesitation, then a larger number of hands went up.

"All right. So more of you think it was purple than think it was maroon. Anybody notice if it was red?"

There was silence in the room.

"Come on, you were all eyewitnesses," he said archly. "You must know what color it was. Who thinks it's red?"

A few students raised their hands hesitantly.

"Okay, so a small number of eyewitnesses think the girl was wearing a red vest. And some of you, a few more, think that it was maroon, right? You sure about that?"

There were embarrassed, uncertain grins.

"So clearly, most of you remember the vest as being purple."

He observed the nods of the students who voted purple, confident at being in the majority.

"So those of you who said maroon or red, do you want to change your mind? Be with the majority?"

There was more nervous laughter, and a couple of hands went up.

"All right, so you thought it was something else, but now that all these other eyewitnesses said purple, you're not so sure. Do you all recall seeing the man getting out of the taxi?"

There were more nods throughout the room. This was something they all felt much more certain about.

"Good. Looks like everybody remembers that," said Verraday. "So now I want you to pick that man out of a lineup, or, as our friends in the police department like to call it, a six-pack."

He clicked a button on his computer and the screen lit up with mug shot–style photos of six men. All were in their mid-to-late thirties. All of them had similar medium-length brown hair. One was on the thin side of average. Another was slightly heavyset. The rest were variations in the middle. Verraday smiled at the groans and laughter as the students realized the difficulty of the task he'd given them. He went through the men in the photos one by one, again asking the students to raise their hands to select which of the men they thought they had seen getting out of the taxi. When he was done, he noticed that one student, a mousy-looking girl in a bulky sweater and baggy jeans, hadn't responded to any of them.

"Now, I believe there is someone who didn't raise her hand," said Verraday. He looked at the girl. "Am I right?"

The girl shook her head affirmatively.

He challenged her, using a mock-bellicose tone of voice: "But I just showed you a lineup of six men and told you to pick one. Are you going to let some crook get away with murder because you can't be sure of what he looks like? Why aren't you picking one?"

"Because it wasn't any of them," the girl replied, gazing at him through nondescript, wire-frame glasses. "It was you."

"It was *me?*" asked Verraday, acting like it was the most absurd notion he'd ever heard.

He mugged to the rest of the class.

"She thinks the man in the taxi was *me.* Can you believe it?"

His comment, his stifled laugh, and his comically skeptical expression elicited snickers of disbelief throughout the lecture hall. He turned back to the girl.

"You really think it was *me?*"

"Yes, I do," she replied.

"And if I told you that I'd deduct ten percent of your term grade if you were wrong, would you still say it was me?"

"Yes, I would," she responded, quietly but still without hesitation.

"Ooooh, a risk taker," said Verraday, getting a rise out of the other students. "Well, let's find out then."

Verraday clicked forward on his presentation and the original image came back up on the screen, except that now everything but the man and the taxi had been blacked out.

There was a gasp of surprise, then more laughter from the students.

"What do you know," said Verraday. "You're right. It *is* me. And everybody else in this room just falsely identified six innocent people as suspects."

He paused.

"Now let's take a look at the girl in the vest and see what color it was."

He changed the slide so that the entire original scene was now visible.

"Anybody care to tell me anything about the girl in the vest? What color was it?"

Verraday turned around and looked at the screen.

"What do you know? She's not wearing a vest at all! And it's not a Starbucks travel mug. It's just a plain old generic travel mug."

There were more embarrassed groans and laughter.

Verraday smiled indulgently. He didn't have to rub it in. His demonstration was making enough of an impression on its own.

"Now, the point of this exercise was not to torture or embarrass you. I'll save that for the midterm exam next week. Rather, it was to demonstrate something called the misinformation paradigm. There are numerous documented instances in criminal investigations where police have led witnesses exactly the way I just led you, with the result that they either contradicted their original testimony or added in seeing other things that they did not in fact see, either because they weren't in a position to see those other things or because those other things never actually happened. In a number of cases, this has led to the conviction and sometimes execution of innocent people—all because the police played fast and loose with the evidence and eyewitnesses to get the verdict they wanted."

He glanced over at the mousy girl. In truth, he was surprised that anyone would have paid enough attention to pick him out of the photo after the fact. Verraday ruefully realized that if the situation were reversed, he would not have been able to identify the student who recognized him. Five weeks into the beginning of the fall semester, he didn't know most of his sixty-odd students' names, only the ones who had come to his office to discuss the course material or who were talkative in class. This girl in the big sweater and baggy jeans was neither of those things, though she was clearly more observant and confident than he would have given her credit for. He had only ever noticed her at all because he remembered thinking that her surname—something Scandinavian sounding like Jensen or Janzen or Johansen—didn't seem to match her black hair and olive skin.

Just then, Verraday noticed someone hovering outside the door of the lecture hall. That usually meant another professor was waiting to use the room. He checked his watch and saw that it was only a couple of minutes until the end of the period. As if on cue, he heard the telltale shuffling of books and papers and the zip of Velcro. He recognized their Pavlovian response. They'd interpreted his glance at his watch as the end of the class. He knew from experience that from this point on, they'd barely hear anything he said. He decided not to fight the tide.

"Okay, we will wrap it up there for today. The readings for next class are on the course outline, but just to remind you, it's Daniel Yarmey, in *Law and Human Behavior*. He's done some interesting research on the accuracy of eyewitness memory. And it's time to start reviewing all the material we've covered so far, because the midterm is fast approaching."

Verraday switched off the projection system and began unplugging the connections on his laptop. As the bottleneck of students filing out of the room began to clear, he got a better look at the person hovering in the hall. It was a woman—in her early thirties, he guessed. She was tall and attractive, with dark hair. A tailored black pantsuit complemented her slim, athletic build.

She wasn't anybody from the psychology department. He knew everyone in the faculty and all the teaching assistants. And he didn't think she was any of the new hires from admin—he wouldn't have forgotten meeting her. She was too young to be one of those helicopter parents coming to complain that he should have given their kid higher marks. She carried herself with an air of authority, he noted. He considered the possibility that she was there from the dean's office to request he bump up a student's mark because the parents were rich and donated to the university. It was a request he always refused.

As the last student exited, the woman slipped into the room and approached him at the lectern. She had intelligent eyes and a thoughtful expression. He really hoped she wasn't here to ask him to pull a favor for an undeserving student.

"Can I help you?" he asked.

"Professor Verraday?"

"That's me."

She held out her badge. "I'm Detective Constance Maclean, Seattle Police Department."

Verraday immediately bristled. This was worse than if she had been a flunkey from the dean's office. Much worse.

"If you're here to try to talk me into dropping the lawsuit, you can forget it," he said.

"I'm not here to talk you out of anything, Professor."

"And if the Seattle Police Department thinks that they can send someone to my place of employment to hang around the halls in front of my students and try to intimidate me, I can assure you and your bosses that is not going to work."

"That is not my intention. I—"

"Good," snapped Verraday, cutting her off, "because I don't appreciate being pepper-sprayed, then having some two-hundred-pound lunkhead throw me facedown onto a sidewalk, crack my ribs, and then wrongfully detain me."

Six months earlier, Verraday had been working on a research project about the psychology of crowd behavior. He had been legally video recording an Occupy Seattle demonstration when a riot cop by the name of Bosko had blindsided him. Bosko had tackled him from behind, knocking Verraday to the pavement, then handcuffing and arresting him. The refusal by the city or the police department to offer any sort of explanation or apology had prompted Verraday to file a suit to get their attention.

Before she could speak, he continued indignantly. "Know what? Maybe I should just call my lawyer right now." He reached into the lower right-hand pocket of his blazer for his cell phone. It wasn't there. Then he checked his left pocket. It wasn't there either, and he was annoyed to realize he couldn't remember where he'd put it.

Flustered, he noticed that she seemed to be suppressing a smile.

"Look," she said, "I know about the Occupy thing, and I can see that you're very upset about it. But I didn't come to get you to drop any lawsuit."

"Then why are you here?"

"Because I need your help."

"You need my help?" he asked incredulously. He raised an eyebrow in disbelief. "Okay, I'm listening."

Maclean glanced out into the hall and noticed a few students lounging on benches nearby.

"Is there somewhere we can talk in private?"

"My office. The department secretary will be just outside the door. But don't worry—she won't hear anything we say . . . unless I call for help, which she'll be able to hear just fine."

CHAPTER 2

His office was small and crowded, just the way Maclean imagined a professor's office would be. It smelled like books. He gestured to a visitor's chair facing his desk.

"Have a seat."

He squeezed past the desk, brushing up against the books and papers that were bursting out of the shelves, and sat down in what she observed was an old-fashioned oak office chair with a padded leather seat and backrest. She also noticed that on the shelf next to him was a brass Buddha. Not a fat, smiling, happy Buddha, but rather one of the serious, spiritual-looking versions, a serene expression on his face, right hand raised to chest level with the thumb and index finger touching to form a circle. People who kept statues of the Buddha near to them, in her experience, fell into one of two categories: those who were so full of loving kindness that they just had to share it with everyone and those who needed to be reminded to exercise loving kindness instead of taking a swing at somebody. She was beginning to get a strong sense of which category Verraday fit into.

He noticed her looking at the statue.

"A gift from my sister. She thinks I need it."

"And do you?"

Verraday smiled faintly. "Probably. So what can I help you with?"

"Can we talk in confidence? Nothing I say can leave this room."

He hesitated. "Fine, but if anything comes up that's related in any way to my case, then we have to stop immediately."

"Fair enough," replied Maclean, leaning forward.

"Two days ago, a young woman's body was found in a cranberry bog down in Buckley."

"I heard about it on the news. A Jane Doe."

"We've ID'd her now. Her name is Rachel Friesen, and she lived in Seattle. We're treating it as a homicide, and I've been assigned as lead investigator. She was beaten and strangled. The MO is extremely similar to another homicide that happened in Seattle six months ago. The Alana Carmichael case."

"I thought you had a suspect in custody for that?"

"The *department* has a suspect in custody."

"But?"

"But I don't think he did it. The lead investigator on that case is a guy named Bob Fowler. I believe you're familiar with him."

"I know who he is," said Verraday. "Some of the Somali refugees I worked with a few years ago said that he planted dope on them when he was on the drug squad, told them he'd get them deported if they didn't give him information about criminals higher up the food chain.

I saw his name in the papers after he was charged with corruption."

"That's him," responded Maclean. "There were four of them named in that case: Fowler, Garson, Babitch, and Perreira. Fowler was the ringleader. The charges against them were conspiracy, assault, extortion, and theft. These drug dealers claimed that Fowler and the other three entered their homes without warrants, beat them up even though they didn't put up any resistance, and then stole their dope, jewelry, and cash. A week before trial, the key witness was found floating by Harbor Island with a couple of nasty exit wounds in the back of his head. Some of the surviving dealers suddenly retracted their statements. The trial went ahead without the key witness, and in the end, Fowler and most of the others were acquitted. Only the junior officer, Perreira, was convicted on a reduced charge and got forty-five days' house arrest. Guess the jury was just glad to hear some drug dealers got slapped around."

"Right," said Verraday, "even if the guys doing the slapping were getting freebie blow out of it and pocketing some cash and jewelry."

"After it was over, Fowler was transferred to homicide," continued Maclean.

Verraday frowned. "I guess they figured he couldn't get into too much trouble dealing with people who were already dead."

"Unfortunately, I think they were wrong," replied Maclean. "Fowler is building a case against the wrong guy in the Carmichael murder. I can't tell if he actually thinks he's got the right suspect in custody and doesn't have the evidence to prove it yet or if he's just too stubborn or afraid to admit that he screwed up."

"From what I've heard about Fowler," replied Verraday, "he's dumb enough and crooked enough for it to be either scenario. But how do I fit into all this?"

"Professor, if I'm right about the similarities between the victims and the way in which they were murdered, that means we're looking at a serial killer. I need your help profiling him if we're going to have any chance of catching him before he kills again."

Verraday sat back for a moment.

"Detective Maclean, I don't like the idea of a serial killer wandering around the streets any more than you do. But I don't see how I can work with the Seattle PD when I have an outstanding lawsuit against the department and one of its officers."

"You wouldn't be working with me or the department in any official capacity," replied Maclean. She paused. "In fact, it would be very important that they never even know you're involved."

"Okay, this is getting weird."

"The department would never authorize it because of your lawsuit. They're just as pissed at you as you are at them."

"Well, the difference is, I have a legitimate grievance. They don't. I'm the injured party here, not them. They can go screw themselves."

"Listen, I understand your anger about the arrest . . . and I'm aware of what happened with your mother and your sister. When you were a kid, I mean."

"How do you know about that?"

"It's in your file."

A flicker of anger flashed across Verraday's face, and Maclean worried that she was about to lose any chance she ever had with him.

"Look, I don't want to compromise your case," she said quickly. "I will do everything humanly possible to make sure that doesn't happen. But you have the sort of expertise we need."

"I'm not following, Detective Maclean. Surely the Seattle PD has its own experts on staff. Why enlist an academic with a grudge?"

"That's exactly the point. Since Fowler beat that rap, he's a hero to a lot of the rank and file, especially the ones who think we're letting bad guys walk by having to cross all those t's and dot the i's. And the ones who don't love Fowler are scared of him now. They think he's untouchable. So I don't know who I can trust in the department on this one. Maybe nobody."

"If they find out that you've gone outside the system, they'll crucify you."

"They won't crucify me as long as I deliver the real killer. And an airtight case. That's all they want. That's all I want."

"I get that. My problem is that I don't have any way of knowing that for sure."

"That's true. Except for what your training and your gut tell you."

"Right now, Detective, my training and my gut are telling me that you seem like a decent person. But I'm wrestling an eight-hundred-pound gorilla in a phone booth. And from past experience, I know that gorilla will do whatever it takes to beat me to a pulp. So with all due respect, I'll have to decline."

Maclean pursed her lips, considering what to say. She drew in a breath and was about to speak, then changed her mind. After a long moment, she simply said, "I understand. Thanks anyway." Maclean stood up, taking a manila envelope from her briefcase and slipping an eight-by-ten glossy onto Verraday's desk.

"Just FYI, this is Rachel Friesen. Or it was."

Verraday looked at the police photographer's head-and-shoulders photo of Rachel Friesen, taken while she was still floating in the bog. Her eyes stared up lifelessly into his. They were red, the capillaries exploded from what he knew, even from a quick glance, had been strangulation executed with savage force. Fragments of leaves and tiny dirt clots clung to her skin. He noted that there was still a hint of baby fat on her high cheekbones. She was barely out of her teens, he guessed. He examined the dark-brown ligature marks on her neck where the killer had choked her. He also noticed that a corner of her upper left incisor was missing and that what appeared to be a rosary had been shoved into her mouth. If the incisor had been chipped by the force of the necklace being slammed into her teeth, thought Verraday, it had to have been done by someone in a frenzy.

He said nothing.

Maclean set her business card down beside the photograph. "If you change your mind, this is where you can reach me."

★   ★   ★

After she had gone, Verraday did an online search for Maclean. He found a picture of her and two of her colleagues in full dress uniform at a Seattle Police Foundation ceremony, receiving something called the Impact Award. He read the official blurb, which stated that it was given out to recognize "a team or unit that, through their collaborative and innovative working style, has had a significant impact on a crime or crime-related problem."

The award had been bestowed on them for their efforts in crisis intervention—official-speak for talking suicidal people down off bridges and ledges. The article also mentioned that Maclean volunteered her time to work with youth at risk as well as with an organization called IslandWood, which was dedicated to connecting urban dwellers with the natural environment.

He looked more closely at Maclean's business card and noticed now that she had an "MSW" after her name for a master's degree in social work. *So she's a saint*, he thought. Snatching the suicidal from the jaws of death and taking underprivileged children off the streets and on canoe trips, keeping them safe from both pimps and grizzlies while exploring the forests and streams so they would love nature and not want to strip-mine it, clear-cut it, or turn it into condos when they grew up. *What the hell is she doing working as a cop?*

Verraday felt guilty about declining the case for a moment, but a saint could get you in just as much trouble as a sinner could. Maybe more. And cops had never been anything but trouble for him.

He took a last glance at the photo that Maclean had left on his desk, then turned it upside down and slid it back into the manila envelope. *Sorry, Rachel Friesen,* he thought. *If you knew me, knew my story, you'd understand.*

CHAPTER 3

That night, Verraday had The Dream. He hated having The Dream. It was a recurring dream that he'd been having in various iterations ever since he was a kid, ever since the accident. He hadn't had it in almost a year now, had told himself that maybe he was over it. But now here it was again.

In it, he gradually came out of a fog, regaining consciousness in dim light, his movement restricted as though someone was holding him down. Then he became aware that he was strapped into the back seat of his family's sedan. It was night. The interior of the car was dark except for headlights from a second vehicle shining across the beige headliner above him. He could smell gasoline vapors wafting up from wet asphalt and became aware that he was in the middle of an intersection.

Then an acrid chemical smell began to overpower all the others: coolant from a smashed radiator leaking onto a hot engine block and evaporating off it in white stinking plumes. But there was an even more disturbing smell. Something metallic, coppery. Blood, he realized.

He could see it splattered on the upholstery, the twisted roof pillars, and the shattered windshield in front of his mother, who was slumped forward in her seat. Barely able to mouth the words, he called to her, but she didn't answer. Behind his mother, on the bench seat to the left of Verraday, his sister Penny lay motionless, moaning, her legs contorted at sickeningly impossible angles under the front seat, forced backward halfway over her.

He heard a door open. Through the tendrils of evaporating antifreeze, he saw the silhouette of someone getting out of the other car and approaching their vehicle. It was a tall, beefy man in a patrolman's uniform. As he approached and leaned in, the headlights of the man's car illuminated him just enough on one side that Verraday could see his watery blue eyes and the gin blossoms on his meaty cheeks. The man seemed uncertain, confused, like he didn't quite know what to do. There was no one else around. The intersection was deserted. This man, Verraday desperately realized, might be their only lifeline. Struggling to make his mouth move, Verraday tried to form the word "help," but was only able to emit a feeble croak. The man came around to Verraday's side of the car. Verraday tried to shout. His tongue felt thick and paralyzed, like it was glued to his palate.

He was barely able to whisper a muted, "Help us, please!"

The man didn't answer. Had he even heard his plea? The stranger scanned the scene inside the sedan, taking it all in. Then he backed away from the car. The last thing Verraday saw was the jowly man in uniform turning on his heels and walking away into the night.

★　　★　　★

Verraday awoke with a start, embarrassed to realize he had actually been bellowing the words "help me" aloud into the darkness of his bedroom. His breathing was rapid and shallow, and his heart pounded like a jackhammer, so hard he could feel it in his ears. He tried to get up but realized he had rolled over onto his left arm in his sleep, cutting off the circulation. He reached over with his right hand and began massaging it, coaxing the feeling back into it. He turned his head and saw from his alarm clock that it was just before three thirty in the morning. *There's a reason the secret police come to arrest people at this time*, thought Verraday. *Your body, your spirit, it's all at its lowest ebb.*

While he waited to regain the feeling in his arm, he took several deep breaths to the count of five, the way his older sister Penny had taught him. Finally his arm recovered, the numbness replaced by an uncomfortable prickling sensation. His heart had slowed down and the pounding in his ears had subsided to a manageable roar. He threw back the covers, put his feet on the floor, and turned on the bedside lamp.

He realized now that the booze he had smelled in his dream was from a glass of brandy that he'd poured for himself and left unfinished before he'd fallen asleep.

He didn't know what it was about him that made him crave alcohol in the evening. He had absolutely zero interest in drinking during the daytime. It was at night, when he was tired, that the urge crept in. He picked up the glass, walked to the bathroom and poured the dregs down the sink. He rinsed the glass twice before filling it with water. He took a deep sip, then another. He set the glass down on the counter and walked down the hall to his den.

Carefully, he picked his way through the shadows until he reached his desk, bent over, and switched on the small halogen lamp that sat atop it. He found Maclean's card where he had left it the previous evening, sliding it into the narrow beam of light so he could make out her office phone number. He lifted the phone receiver off its cradle and keyed it in. He had a moment of apprehension, wondering what he would say if she were still there and answered—how strange it would seem getting a call from him at three thirty in the morning. He was relieved when, after four rings, her voice mail picked up. At the prompt, he said simply, "Detective Maclean, this is James Verraday. I've been thinking it over. If you'd still like my help, I'm in."

CHAPTER 4

Verraday shivered involuntarily. It wasn't the sight of Rachel Friesen's body on the stainless steel table in front of him, though that was disturbing enough. It was the fact that the morgue in the King County Medical Examiner's Office was kept at precisely 36 degrees Fahrenheit, not giving him the chance to shake off the chill of the cool, damp, fog that had rolled in from Puget Sound that morning. As a forensic psychologist, Verraday was more accustomed to coming face to face with murderers than with their victims, and it hadn't occurred to him to wear an extra layer of clothing to keep the relentless iciness of the morgue out of his bones. Verraday appreciated that if Maclean had noticed him shiver, she hadn't commented on it. He also appreciated that if she had noticed the electronic time stamp on the message he'd left on her office voice mail, she hadn't let on either. Nobody ever left messages at that time of night unless they were a shift worker or someone being visited by demons. And Verraday wasn't a shift worker.

"So what do you know about her?" he asked.

"Rachel Friesen was twenty-two years old," replied Maclean. "She attended University of Washington, same campus you're at."

He didn't recognize her. UW Seattle was a large campus. Hundreds of students passed through his lecture hall every year. Even so, he didn't like to think that the halls of academia had become quite as depersonalized and factory-like as the critics claimed.

"She had a double major, English and theater," Maclean continued. "She also took an intro to psychology course."

Verraday's face relaxed slightly. "I've never taught Intro to Psych. So she wouldn't have been one of my students."

"I know. I would have warned you if you had."

"So what makes you think that this murder is linked to the Carmichael case?"

"For starters, the victims' profiles are similar." She led him toward the body. "They were about the same age. Similar look. The tattoos, the piercings."

Verraday now saw that Rachel had a number of tattoos that weren't visible in the photo that Maclean had laid out on his office desk the previous afternoon. One scripted tattoo followed the cleft line beneath her left breast. It read, "If you don't live for something, you'll die for nothing."

On the inside of her left ankle was a Buddhist mandala, a symbol he was familiar with because his sister Penny had a pair of them tattooed defiantly on the feet that she could no longer feel.

Verraday examined a small hole in the skin at the top of her navel. "Was she wearing any jewelry in this piercing when they found her?"

"No."

"If she was wearing a piece there when she was murdered, the killer probably took it as a souvenir. We should find out what she wore there and keep an eye out for it. If the killer took something from Rachel, he would have done the same with Alana Carmichael."

"The way in which the victims were murdered is distinctive," said Maclean. "Take a look at the strangulation marks."

Verraday leaned in close and examined a pattern of bruises as well as an ugly brown line encircling her neck.

"So those two bruises on the throat indicate thumb pressure," he commented.

"That's right," said Maclean. "But according to the medical examiner, death was the result of strangulation with the garrote that left that ligature mark around her neck."

Verraday nodded agreement. "The killer started off choking her with his hands," he said. "He would have gotten more and more aroused. Then when he got really turned on, he switched to the garrote. That's his end game."

Verraday looked at Rachel's chipped upper left incisor.

"According to the examiner," said Maclean. "The killer probably broke Rachel's tooth using her necklace."

Maclean pulled out a transparent evidence bag holding the piece of jewelry, a string of black beads separated by silver links. It was not, as he had first thought, a rosary. The pendant was a hieroglyphic cross with a loop at its head. The cross bar was dented.

"An ankh," said Verraday. "The Ancient Egyptian symbol of eternal life." He knew from seeing students around the campus that it was popular with goths, though he guessed that their concept of eternal life owed more to late-night B horror movies than to pharaohs and sun worship. He balled his hand into a fist and tensed his arm muscles as he played out in his mind the force that must have been necessary to chip that piece off Rachel's tooth and dent the ankh.

"He must have punched her with the beads wrapped around his hand like a set of brass knuckles," said Verraday. "The force necessary to do that implies extreme sexual rage."

"Wait till you see this," said Maclean.

She turned to the medical technician, a large, impassive-looking man who had stood by silently throughout, and instructed him to turn the body over. The technician gently tilted Rachel until her back was exposed, revealing more tattoos. In silhouette, a small flock of black birds took flight in a line that ran from just inside her left shoulder blade diagonally across her spine and upper back to a point just behind her right ear. There were marks on her back and shoulders that appeared to have been made by a belt or a strap. There were large, ugly welts on her buttocks.

"Besides the academic background, what else do you know about her?" Verraday asked.

"Not a lot yet. That she was an only child. Grew up in Phinney Ridge with her biological parents."

Verraday knew Phinney Ridge well. It was a fifteen-minute drive northwest of the campus, just beyond Green Lake. When he needed to clear his head, he would go up to Green Lake and go for a run along the three-mile path around its shoreline. It was a comfortable neighborhood that had gotten its name from Guy C. Phinney, a lumber baron who made a fortune by clear-cutting the virgin forest then shrewdly subdividing the denuded land into housing lots and selling them to middle-class families at a huge profit.

"What about her parents?" he asked. "What do you know about them?"

"Nothing unusual about them," answered Maclean. "The father is a dental equipment salesman. The mother manages a women's clothing store. No criminal records. Not so much as a speeding ticket."

"Were they the ones who reported her missing?"

"No. When the body turned up, I checked the missing persons reports and photos. When I found the match, I discovered that the report had been filed by an ex-boyfriend. There's no record of anything from the parents."

"Nothing from the parents. Got to be a story there," said Verraday.

"There is. Apparently she was living at home up until last May. Couldn't get a job after graduating from university the year before, except for working part-time retail. The parents say she had anxiety issues on and off through childhood and high school. It got worse after she finished university and couldn't get a job. She started self-medicating. Smashed up their car. Things were getting out of control. Her parents asked her to get counseling, but she refused and moved out."

"When did they last hear from her?"

"About a month before her body was found."

"And they weren't concerned when she didn't get in touch with them for a whole month?"

"The father said it wasn't that they weren't worried about her. They just couldn't handle her any more. He said after she moved out and started seeing this new boyfriend, Kyle Davis, the guy who eventually reported her missing, she sounded happier. When they didn't hear from her for a while, they hoped she was working through her issues, getting her life together."

By now, Verraday's fingertips were getting numb. He rubbed them against his palms and folded them under his arms and against his chest to try to warm them up. Maclean noticed his discomfort. She thanked the technician for his time.

★   ★   ★

Verraday was relieved when they stepped out of the morgue and into the relative warmth of the hall. Seeing that they were alone, he turned to Maclean.

"Did you mention the similarities of the cases to Fowler?" he asked in a tone of voice just above a whisper.

"I let him know," replied Maclean. "He didn't have any interest in pursuing it."

"Have you two ever worked together on anything before?"

"No. I just know him from around the department. But he and I don't exactly have a happy history together. He doesn't like the idea of female cops, and he doesn't hide it. Says no woman is worth a detective's salary. At least not standing up."

"Sounds like a real charmer."

"He's not much of an investigator either. Fowler's convinced that he's got the right guy solely because there was semen on Alana Carmichael's clothing that matches his suspect's DNA."

"And what do you think?"

"I think that just because this girl was working in the sex trade and had his semen on her doesn't mean that he's the killer. All it proves is that Cray had sex with her at some point that night. He's in jail awaiting trial now and couldn't have committed this latest homicide, so Fowler will refuse to admit there's any possibility of a link between the two murders. Because if he did, he'd have to admit he was wrong. He's got too much riding on this."

"Tell me about the suspect in the Carmichael killing."

"Guy named Peter Cray. He's been in trouble with the law before. Minor drug convictions. Small-time robberies. Breaking and entering. Sex offenses. Done time for beating up prostitutes. I'll give you his rap sheet with the case files for Alana Carmichael and Rachel Friesen."

"What do you know about Davis, Friesen's ex-boyfriend?"

"Not much yet. After I matched the body together with the missing persons report he filed, I called him and gave him the news."

"How did he take it?"

"He seemed pretty broken up. For real. And there's something else. Rachel Friesen's body was found almost two weeks *after* he filed the report."

"But what if he killed her then reported her missing just to cover it up?"

"The coroner says she had been dead for less than a day when her body turned up in the cranberry bog."

"He's either an innocent man or a criminal genius."

"I'm hoping you'll help me figure out which. I'm interviewing him this evening."

"My class ends at five thirty. Any time after that is good."

"All right. I'll arrange a sit down with him, hear what he has to say. I'll pick you up at your place at six thirty."

CHAPTER 5

Verraday checked his watch and saw that it was 6:29. He looked out the window of his small two-story house just north of the campus and saw the unmarked Ford Interceptor SUV pull up by his front gate. He slipped his Blundstone boots on, grabbed his leather jacket, and stepped out onto his front porch. Despite the early hour, there was only the faintest glow of twilight through a thick layer of gray clouds. The long nights and short days were upon the Pacific Northwest now. The sensors in the garden lights along the pathway had already switched on automatically, having judged that the evening was gloomy enough to qualify as night.

Verraday unlatched his gate, stepped out onto the sidewalk, then closed it carefully to ensure that it shut behind him. Then he climbed into the Interceptor where Maclean was waiting.

"Just so you know," he said, "this is the first time in my entire life that I've ever voluntarily taken a ride in a police vehicle."

Maclean grinned. "I'm honored to be present on such a momentous occasion."

She checked the street behind her and, finding it clear, hit the accelerator and pulled out before Verraday had gotten his seat belt buckled. He wondered if it had been retaliation for his comment and took a sidelong glance at her. But Maclean's sphinxlike expression revealed nothing; she was either concentrating entirely on the road or was damned good at pretending to be.

★   ★   ★

The rush-hour traffic that choked Seattle's streets with tidal regularity had thinned out, and within a few minutes, they were heading west on Fiftieth, passing neat blocks of low-rise apartments. Drizzle had begun to fall, so light that Maclean only had to put her windshield wipers on intermittent. Verraday noted that she didn't reduce her speed, which was consistently over the posted limit—enough that he couldn't help musing to himself that if this wasn't a police cruiser, she would probably be pulled over for speeding. That aggressive driving style was something that Verraday noticed almost all cops did when they were behind the wheel of a cruiser. He found it interesting that although they were tasked with enforcing the law, they didn't feel any need to obey it themselves.

They were skirting the southern edge of Woodland Park when the yellowish-green eyes of a large creature glowed suddenly in the dark, directly ahead of them.

Maclean hit the brakes, and for an instant, the cruiser lost traction and skidded on the slick pavement. Verraday shot a hand out onto the dashboard, bracing for the impact. In a stroboscopic flash of light and shadow, a large coyote raced across their path, just clearing the passenger-side fender.

"Shit!" exclaimed Maclean as she recovered. "What the hell is a coyote doing up here?"

Verraday watched as the creature slipped nimbly through a line of hedges and disappeared, unharmed, into the park.

"At the risk of sounding pedantic," he replied, "the zoology department at UW just finished a study on them. There are two separate packs of them out here."

"How do two packs of coyotes manage to find enough to eat in the suburbs?"

"Woodland Park used to be the dumping ground for the city's unwanted pet rabbits. Every year at Easter, parents would buy bunnies for their kids. And every year about a month or two later, after the novelty of cleaning up rabbit turds had worn off, they'd dump them here. The rabbits bred like what they are and overran the neighborhood. Until the coyotes noticed."

"How did the coyotes even get into this neighborhood to find out that the rabbits were here?"

Verraday shrugged. "That's the psychology of predators. They're always out there. We might not see them. But they see us."

A few minutes later, they pulled up outside the entrance to a low-rise apartment building tucked in between a crowded espresso bar and a harshly lit pho restaurant. Maclean climbed out of the Interceptor. Verraday followed her the few yards to the lobby. She buzzed apartment 205. A moment later the door clicked open.

CHAPTER 6

"Kyle Davis?" asked Maclean.

"That's me," said the young man who opened the door.

"I'm Inspector Maclean, and this is my colleague, Dr. James Verraday. We spoke on the phone. Again, I'm sorry for your loss."

"Thank you," he said quietly. "Come on in," he added, gesturing to the sparse, open-concept apartment.

Kyle Davis appeared to be in his late twenties. He had brown eyes that looked out guilelessly from behind horn-rimmed glasses, his face framed by a neatly trimmed beard and a short-sided pompadour. He wore a plaid shirt and jeans with the cuffs rolled up, exposing a pair of brogues. His home and his workplace appeared to be one and the same. Sitting atop a desk in one corner was a Mac Pro with a large video monitor and a printer, as well as the most expensive laptop that Apple had released that year. Verraday noted a shoji screen at the rear of the flat, behind which was a simple futon and dresser. Whatever money this guy had was going straight into his equipment.

"Have a seat," said Kyle, gesturing toward three mesh office chairs that seemed more intended for client visits than socializing.

As they sat down, Maclean gazed at the array of equipment.

"You've got a lot of gear," she commented. "What do you do for a living?"

"I'm a video editor, and I do a bit of animation work too."

"Sounds interesting. What kind of projects?"

"Ultimately I want to do feature films. But for now, I'm mostly making explainers to pay the bills."

"Explainers?" asked Maclean.

"They're short videos, kind of like owner's manuals, that companies post on their websites and on YouTube to explain how their products or services work. Like how to connect a Bluetooth speaker or do your banking with a mobile app."

"Too bad they don't make them to explain why people are the way they are," said Verraday.

Kyle Davis frowned slightly and sighed. "If they did, I wouldn't be the guy to write one, that's for sure."

He said it like only someone who's had the stuffing knocked out of him can.

"How long did you know Rachel?" asked Maclean.

"Since June second of this year."

"You remember the date?" said Verraday.

"It was my niece Tabitha's birthday," Kyle replied. "But even if it hadn't been, it would have been hard to forget it. Rachel had that effect on people."

Maclean smiled at him gently. "How did you two meet?"

"Actually, it had been a sort of crappy day with a really difficult client. I was on the way to my brother and sister-in-law's place, and I stopped at this toy store to get something for Tabitha's birthday. I was feeling stressed 'cause I'd been so busy that week, I hadn't had a chance to get anything for her. I walked into the store and saw this beautiful girl serving some customers—a boy about six years old and his parents. The boy was comparing these dragons and their different superpowers. The parents looked bored, but the salesgirl was totally into it, having fun with the boy, making him laugh, asking about the superpowers of each dragon, which one was better, and what kind of superpowers he'd pick for himself if he were a dragon."

Verraday leaned forward in his chair and gazed at Kyle empathetically.

"Rachel must have made quite an impression on you."

Kyle looked wistful. "Rachel made an impression on everybody. After the boy and his parents left, she came over and asked me if she could help me. I told her about my niece's birthday, said she was turning five and asked what girls that age like. Because honestly, I wouldn't have had the faintest clue except that I hoped it wouldn't be My Little Pony. She asked me a few questions about Tabitha: what she enjoyed doing, what her personality was like. Then she suggested a few possible gifts in different price ranges. She was so into it. Not in the sense of trying to upsell me, but really into it, like she was taking pleasure from thinking about the effect that the gift would have on the person getting it."

"What did you end up choosing?" asked Verraday.

"Rachel recommended a stuffed tiger that a portion of the price goes to the World Wildlife Fund. I thought it looked a bit ferocious for a five-year-old, but Rachel said to tell my niece that it was a 'watch tiger' designed to watch over little girls and protect them when they slept. So I got it for her."

Verraday smiled slightly. "What did your niece think of it?"

"She loved it. Especially the part that Rachel made up about it being a 'watch tiger' that would look after her. My brother said Tabitha took it to bed with her the very first night and it's been beside her pillow ever since."

"And how did you and Rachel become involved?" asked Verraday.

"As I was paying for the tiger, I spotted these Mega Bloks. You know, those construction toys that are sort of like Lego? I was feeling good by then, a lot better after talking to Rachel, so I made this dumb joke to her asking whether Mega Bloks were anything like mental blocks. Rachel laughed so hard she snorted. And I just thought, wouldn't it be amazing if my life were always this good? To have a beautiful, intuitive girlfriend who laughs at my jokes? I tried to build up the courage to ask her out. But I'm really bad at stuff like that. My mouth went dry and my heart started racing. I mean, I'm confident about my work, but I'm sort of on the shy side when it comes to putting myself in situations where people can reject me."

Verraday nodded agreement. "Risking rejection isn't exactly my strong suit either."

Kyle allowed himself a nostalgic smile as he continued. "My stomach was full of knots, and I hesitated. Then I saw this family walking toward the store. I knew once they came in, I'd miss my chance. So I asked her point blank if she'd go out with me. She said, 'Yes, as long as you don't have any mega mental blocks.'"

Verraday saw a complex mixture of affection and loss in Kyle's expression. "And when did you two go out?"

"The next evening."

"How did the relationship develop after that?" asked Verraday.

"What do you mean?"

"I mean did you see much of each other?"

Kyle looked like he was about to speak, then hesitated, like he was searching for words. "It was a whirlwind. We had sex on our first date. I've never done that before. Ever. But she made me feel so relaxed. And so wanted. After that, we were together pretty much all the time. She basically moved in after our second date."

Verraday raised an eyebrow. "Did that seem a little fast to you?"

Kyle reflexively rubbed his chin like he was pulling something out of his memory. "Dating Rachel was like being hit by a hurricane. She liked to have sex twice a day. She was just so intense, totally present. At first. I felt like maybe she was the one, you know? One night, I was watching her light some candles for a dinner we made together. And I could picture spending the rest of my life with her. Having kids. Grandkids. Having this amazing life together. I would never have imagined it would end like this."

"Did you ever ask her to marry you?"

"It was weird. The same week that I was planning to propose to her, she started to change. She began to have these mood swings for what seemed to be no reason.

Started complaining about her job situation, how she wasn't getting paid enough. She'd criticize me for my work, said I was a pawn of the system. She began to ask questions about how much I earned with my projects, which isn't all that much really, but it was more than what she made at the store. She'd get angry and say it was so unfair that she was paid so much less than everybody else and that her life was degrading."

"Did she want expensive things?" asked Maclean.

"No. It wasn't that she wanted to live like the House-wives of Beverly Hills. Her anger seemed to be more about having low social status. I think if she'd even earned enough to put a decent roof over her head and not be dependent on other people financially, that would've been enough for her. But she had this rage that just kept growing."

"Did you ever fight about it?" asked Verraday.

"Not at first. She had been so upbeat when we first met that I thought it must be something temporary getting her down. She didn't have her career sorted out, but I mean, who does nowadays? You get your degree and all it guarantees you is that you'll be paying down your student loan for the next ten years. I thought she'd work her way through it. So I tried to be patient with her. But over the next few weeks it escalated more and more, blaming me for her problems, blaming me for everything. She was constantly picking fights."

"Was Rachel living at your apartment when she was murdered?" asked Maclean.

"No. Around the same time she began to get angry, she started spending less time here."

"Whose idea was that?"

"Hers. I hoped it was something we could work through and that I would get the old Rachel back. She was worth it. But it became impossible. She stopped wanting to have sex. Like not just 'not in the mood,' but getting upset when I even touched her. Saying I was oppressive, boring. I was still in love with her but I just couldn't figure out what to do to make things work."

"How did it end between you two?" asked Verraday.

"She called me up one night and asked me to meet her in a bar. She sounded happy, like her old self. I was hoping that, you know, maybe Rachel had worked through her feelings and things would be the way they used to be. So even though I was on a deadline, I agreed to go out. But when I got to the bar, she was sitting there at a table with some guy, looking drunk, flirting with him."

"That sounds awkward," said Verraday.

Kyle blew a breath out through his teeth. "Awkward isn't the word for it. I've never had anybody pull anything like that on me before."

"Was there any kind of a confrontation?" asked Maclean.

"With the guy? No. He was as surprised to see me as I was to see him. As soon as he realized I was 'the boyfriend,' he found the first excuse he could and got up and left."

"What did Rachel have to say about it?"

"She told me she'd just started talking to the guy in the bar while she was waiting for me. Said he was gay and was having problems with his boyfriend that she was helping him work through. It was a total bullshit story. She just wanted the attention. So I called her on it."

"And what happened?"

"She laughed at me and started shouting in the middle of the bar that I was a pathetic asshole."

Kyle ran a hand through his hair and tugged on a lock of it. "Everybody in the place was looking around to see what the commotion was. I'd finally had enough. Of all of it, I mean. Her rejections, her insults, her moods. So I got up and walked out. I could still hear her laughing this crazy, maniacal sort of laugh as I left the bar. That was the last time I ever saw her in person."

Verraday leaned forward toward Kyle. "How'd you take it? I know I'd be furious."

"It was degrading. But when I saw that look on her face, heard her screaming, I finally saw past my own shit and realized that this wasn't about me, that whatever was bothering her had to be some kind of psychological issue. So I called her the next day to tell her so. Before I could say anything, she apologized. Profusely. I accepted her apology. But I also told her I would only see her from now on if she got professional counseling and that I'd help her get it."

"And?"

"She went totally ballistic. Screamed at me that I was just like her parents and that I was even more of an asshole than she had thought. Then she hung up."

"What day was that?" asked Maclean.

"It was a Sunday, second week of August, I think."

"But you didn't file the missing persons report until September thirtieth. What happened in between?"

"At first, I just tried to forget about her. Get on with my life. But then she started calling me."

"She called you? You didn't call her?"

"That's right. I hoped that if I backed off, it would make her realize that I was serious about insisting that she got some help. But she refused."

"How did she sound when she called? What did she talk about?"

"She was always upbeat and energetic, but in kind of a forced, artificial way. Like she was high. Or manic. She said she was getting her act together. She told me she had quit her job at the store so she could focus on becoming famous. She said she was going to build an 'online following' and become a web personality."

"Meaning what?" asked Maclean.

"She was always a little short on details, but she told me she had been accepted as a model on an online site called Assassin Girls and that she had a lot of admirers. She was really proud of that."

"Assassin Girls?" said Verraday. "I've never heard of it. What is it?"

"It's an alt-erotica website. Pinup girls with tattoos, piercings, scarification, that sort of thing."

"Can you show it to us?" asked Maclean.

"Yeah, sure."

Kyle moved to his computer and started typing.

"Did you ever look at her profile there?" asked Verraday.

"Just once, when she first told me about it."

"Why only once?"

"You'll know in a second when this page loads."

A moment later, the monitor was filled with images of young, scantily clad girls with tattoos and piercings.

Even now, Kyle only looked at the screen long enough to confirm that the page had loaded, then he looked away.

"I found it depressing that Rachel's sense of self-esteem was dependent on exposing herself to strangers like this. And that whatever I could give her, it wasn't enough."

Maclean nodded sympathetically. "Is her profile still on the site?"

"I don't know," replied Kyle. "Like I said, I only saw it the one time."

"Mind if we check?" said Maclean.

Kyle sighed. "Sure. No problem."

A moment later, Rachel's profile page appeared on the screen. She was identified only by her first name. Verraday noticed that Kyle's face was momentarily frozen in grief at the sight of her. Even in death, she still had a powerful hold on him.

In one of the photos, she was making a flirty, pouting expression and pulling on her necklace, touching the tip of an ankh to her lips seductively. Verraday was certain that whoever had killed Rachel must have seen this portrait and mentally filed it away to devise his own response to it. In another photo, Rachel stood in front of a mirror wearing nothing but a seductive smile, a pair of black over-the-knee boots, and her beaded ankh necklace. She had a lot of tattoos and piercings, the jewelry all rings and studs except for one unusual piece that caught Verraday's eye. It was a tiny version of a Native American dream catcher that hung from a piercing in her navel.

"Did she always wear that dream catcher?" asked Verraday.

"No," replied Kyle. "She got her navel pierced after we split up."

Another photo featured a close-up of the scripted tattoo beneath her left breast. "Rachel got that after we split up too," said Kyle. "I never saw it 'til she was on this site. She said that was her new motto."

Maclean read it off the screen. "'If you don't live for something, you'll die for nothing.'"

"Yeah," said Kyle. "A lot of those piercings are new too. She said she was going to reinvent herself."

Down one side of Rachel's page was a comments section showing the profile pictures of her admirers. The assortment included art school boys, alternative musicians, guys with jail tattoos, gang bangers, and even doughy middle-aged family men who looked like they had written their urgent declarations of passion with the door to their den locked, in between shuttling their broods to and from Chuck E. Cheese's.

Verraday read some of their predictable comments to himself. Seeing Rachel's so-called admirers, and the sorrowful expression on Kyle Davis's face reflected in the monitor, put him in a melancholy frame of mind.

"Thanks," said Maclean gently. "You don't have to show us any more."

Kyle closed the Assassin Girls page. "Like I told you, I only looked once. That was enough for me," he said. "I never looked at her page after that until just now with you."

"You said earlier that after that night in the bar, you never saw her again 'in person.' What exactly did you mean by that?"

"Rachel texted me about a month before she disappeared and asked to have a Skype call."

"And did you agree to it?" asked Maclean.

"Yes. When we connected, I saw that she was in her studio apartment. She looked high. She was acting flirty, leaning forward toward the screen, twisting her hair around her fingers. She said she was starting a new business and she wanted me to be her focus group."

"What was the business?" asked Verraday.

"When Rachel stood up and backed away from her webcam, I saw that she was wearing a black latex dress and high heels. Then I noticed that there was a blonde girl in the background sitting on the edge of Rachel's bed. Rachel put some music on and started dancing. Then she gestured to the other girl to join her. They started close dancing together and making out in front of the camera. Then she said this was going to be her webcam business, putting on shows for her 'fans.' Rachel asked me if I was turned on."

"And were you?" asked Verraday.

Kyle hesitated before answering. "What guy wouldn't be? But I was sort of pissed too, because it was another one of her control things. You know, keeping me hanging on."

"Did it make you feel angry?"

"Yeah, but not at her. At myself. For being such a loser."

"Did you record any of the video call?" asked Maclean gently.

Kyle hesitated again. He bowed his chin slowly and looked at his feet. "Yeah."

"Nobody's judging you," said Maclean. "We're just trying to find her killer. Do you know who the other girl was?"

"No, I don't. Rachel never mentioned her name."

"It could help the investigation if we can identify who she was," said Maclean. "Do you still have the screenshot?"

"Yes," said Kyle, rubbing his cheek. "I can e-mail the file to you."

"Thanks, I know this isn't easy, and we really appreciate it," said Maclean. "Now, can you think of anyone who would want to hurt her?"

"No. We were so caught up in each other at first that we didn't socialize at all. My friends even began to joke that I was turning into a recluse and started asking if this girlfriend of mine even existed." Kyle hesitated. "I just can't figure out why somebody did this to her. It's hard to imagine someone being such a sick fuck."

And Kyle Davis would be shocked to his core, thought Verraday, if he knew just how many sick fucks there actually were out there and how sick they could be.

Maclean looked at Verraday. "Any other questions you want to ask?"

"Just one. Do you remember what superpower the boy said he'd pick if he were a dragon?"

"Yeah," replied Kyle. "He said he wanted to read people's minds."

CHAPTER 7

Maclean was silent and seemed distracted as they headed back to the Interceptor. Verraday was glad for it. He was distracted by memories that had been stirred up by hearing Kyle talk about Rachel. He had had one such relationship. Nikki, his girlfriend for three and a half months when he was working on his doctoral thesis. She was an up-and-coming singer he had met when her band was playing at the campus pub. He was taken by her stage presence and soulful voice. He had met all his previous girlfriends in class or research labs, where introductions occurred naturally and you could generally tell in advance if your overtures would be favorably received.

That was not the case with Nikki. He had taken a chance and introduced himself to her at the bar during a break between sets. He had told her how much he loved her voice. She smiled easily and thanked him. To his surprise, instead of talking about herself, she asked him about his studies. When he told her he was working toward his doctorate in psychology, she raised an eyebrow appraisingly.

"So you think about what other people are thinking?"

"Something along those lines."

"Good luck with that," she had replied with mock skepticism.

But her teasing was playful, the kind of teasing meant to entice someone with the right sort of nerve to take it to the next level. He asked for her number, and she gave it to him. He called her later that week. At her suggestion, their first date was at a disco where the DJ was playing heavy electronic grooves.

"Do you dance?" she had asked.

Verraday didn't. Not well, anyway. But he had quipped, "Sure, when I'm not thinking about what people are thinking."

"Then stop thinking and come dance with me," she had responded, slipping off the barstool, hips rolling seductively to the beat, not giving him a chance to deliberate or even take the lead. She didn't look back until she was in the center of the dance floor. Then she turned around, a Cheshire-cat grin already on her face, knowing he would follow.

They had gone back to his apartment afterward. He had planned to offer her a drink. But the moment he closed the front door behind them, he saw an expectant, feral smile on her face again. So he slipped his arms inside her jacket and pulled her toward him. Her pupils were dilated with desire, but even as he drew her in, she still had that grin on her face, right up until the moment he pressed his lips against hers.

The Cheshire cat became a tigress. They made love twice that first night, and again in the morning, five hours later. He had never had a lover so voracious before. For the next three days, his pelvic bone was bruised and sore. But he savored it as a reminder of that consuming look on her face when she came hard, how instead of closing her eyes, she had locked her gaze with his and urged him on.

Just like Kyle, Verraday ruefully thought, he believed he had found the love of his life. And he had been as wrong as it was possible to be.

Two months after they started dating, Nikki's band was offered a spot as an opening act for the West Coast leg of a Foo Fighters tour. The tour would wrap up with a finale in LA, with all the major record label executives in attendance. It was an incredible break.

He was thrilled for her. And by then he'd fallen so hard that he'd given her a key to his apartment. And it excited him every time he heard that key in the door and a small bundle of immense talent and energy burst in like a force of nature and bounded into his arms.

Then one day, he'd come home and found her lying in bed. Not seductively but listlessly. She was distant and said she was just having an off day. He tried to talk to her, but she told him she just needed to sleep. But she didn't sleep—just lay there until the evening, smoking cigarettes, a habit she said she had kicked for the sake of her voice. He knew this was more than just a down day. But when he tried to discuss it, she made a sarcastic remark about him being a half-baked head-shrinker and to leave her alone. When he came to bed that night and tried to embrace her, she had pushed his hands away.

The next morning she told him she had quit the band. They weren't good enough, she said, and she didn't want to undermine her reputation by having record company execs see her in a band that wasn't up to snuff. He knew there was nothing wrong with the other musicians in her group and that she had bailed because of her own insecurities. He had tried to say as much as gently as he could, and just like Rachel Friesen, she had become furious. Nikki had stormed out of his apartment, cursing him so loudly that his neighbors opened their doors to see what the commotion was.

He was awakened by the sound of her key in the lock around four AM that night. She slipped quietly into the bedroom and, in the dark, stripped down to her panties and slid in under the sheets next to him.

"Make love to me," she whispered in his ear.

He resisted at first. She hadn't apologized, and she reeked of bourbon and cigarettes. Then she pressed her pelvis against his leg.

"Touch me. *Please.*"

He had reached down tentatively and caressed her thigh. She slipped his fingers under her panties. She was wet, but not the way he expected. It was semen. Not his.

"What the fuck?" he had exclaimed, throwing back the sheets as he recoiled from her.

She snorted with amusement, then began laughing maniacally. "You're such an asshole. You think you know what people are thinking with all your psychology crap. But you know fuck all about anything."

He'd had a sudden urge to backhand her, to wipe that crazed smirk off her face. And Nikki knew it.

"Go ahead. Hit me, you piece of shit. I know you want to. You act so superior, so in control, but you're just a fuckup like everybody else. So go ahead, big fucking mind reader, hit me."

Instead, suppressing the violent impulses that he knew she was trying to provoke, he grabbed his pillow and headed for the sofa.

On the way out, he looked over his shoulder and said as calmly as he could, "I want you out of here first thing in the morning."

"Fine," she had replied, smirking. "It'll be a pleasure. Asshole."

He had awakened the next morning feeling exhausted and morally hungover. Nikki on the other hand was already up and dressed, manically energetic despite having slept for four hours at most.

"Give me the key," he had said.

"Gladly," she had responded, flinging it at his feet.

He held the door open and gestured to the hall. "Now get the fuck out of my place and don't ever, ever call me again."

"You can count on it," she said, giving him a mocking version of the Cheshire-cat grin that he had once loved.

She rolled her hips as she strode out, to torture him, to remind him exactly what he would be missing from this day on.

★   ★   ★

Verraday was embarrassed to think he'd ever been as needy as Kyle Davis, and when Maclean finally broke the silence, he was relieved to be extracted from his angst-ridden reverie.

"So? What did you think of Kyle Davis?" she asked.

"He's not your serial killer," replied Verraday. "He doesn't have any of the markers. I'm not hearing much anger from Kyle toward her. Just sadness and frustration with himself. He was head over heels for her, even when she was horribly abusive to him. And did you notice that he didn't have the Assassin Girls page bookmarked? He had to type in the search."

"Just to play devil's advocate for a moment: let's suppose that the Carmichael and Friesen cases aren't connected. Couldn't Kyle still be an angry, jilted boyfriend who became homicidal? You know, an 'If I can't have her, nobody can' kind of guy?"

"No. He doesn't exhibit any jealousy. But he did present a lot of dependency, and if he killed Rachel, he wouldn't ever get to see her again. A guy that dependent would never be able to throw away the object of his fixation."

"And what about her? What's your take?"

"My best guess is that she suffered from some kind of mental illness precipitated by stress. That coupled with some other personality traits could have gotten her into trouble. Sounds like she had a narcissistic streak. Also exhibitionism, anxiety, and a tendency toward risk-taking behavior. She was emotionally needy."

"As needy as Kyle?"

"Yes, although their neediness manifested itself in different ways. That's why their relationship was so intense. 'At first.' Notice how many times Kyle said 'at first'? Everything was amazing 'at first,' and then it suddenly fizzled."

"Well, maybe it fizzled because there was something he did, something about him that she didn't like."

"Correct. What she didn't like about him was that he was an ordinary human being. Rachel's diminishing interest in Kyle wasn't cognitive. It was biochemical."

"In plain English, meaning what?"

"The intensity of the sort of love he describes is common in people with insecure attachment issues. Check into his background, and you'll find a father who was distant or not present at all and a mother who was inconsistent in providing for her children's emotional needs. Someone unpredictable, who blew hot and cold without warning, so he never felt certain of her love. He would have to be insecure to fall that hard for somebody he hardly knows. Rachel was beautiful, intuitive, and passionate. So with that combination, for a while, they both felt like they'd found what they'd always been looking for, a 'soul mate.' No more insecure attachment for him, and for her, the high of being totally adored by another human being. But it couldn't continue at that level of intensity."

"Why not?"

"Chemistry. When we fall in love, our nerve cells release dopamine, a neurochemical transmitter. It makes people feel so good that they want to believe that person really is the love of their life, because they don't want it to ever stop, any more than a crackhead can let go of a rock and a pipe."

"That sounds awfully clinical."

"It is. But that's nature. Touching and orgasms release oxytocin—that's why it's called the love hormone. If you inject oxytocin into a vole, it will fall in love with whatever other vole it's looking at."

"But a vole doesn't have the power to think rationally like a human."

"You think Kyle Davis and Rachel Friesen were thinking rationally when they were living in their little bubble together?"

"Point taken, but if Rachel Friesen and Kyle Davis were so head over heels in love, full of oxytocin and neurotransmitters, why did she suddenly get tired of him but he didn't get tired of her?"

"Rachel had anxiety issues combined with an underlying narcissistic nature. The positive interaction—adulation from the kids and from Kyle—made her feel good and kept her anxiety at bay 'at first.' But like all chemical addictions, over time you need to increase the dose to get the same effect. Rachel had a strong sex drive. All that lovemaking would stimulate those neurotransmitters that kept her anxiety under control. And for Kyle, having a beautiful girlfriend with a powerful sexual appetite like Rachel would have been enough to keep him in oxytocin for months. He was over the moon."

"But he wasn't enough for her?"

"Exactly. He couldn't be. No matter how hard he tried. Rachel's brain chemistry gave her a compelling need for novelty and stimulation to counteract her anxiety and depression."

"So Rachel's body stopped releasing oxytocin sooner than Kyle's did because she needed a new thrill?"

"That's right. In the end it came down to circumstance and biochemistry. Ironically, Kyle's endorphin level would have peaked just around the time Rachel's had already dropped off. Since Rachel Friesen had a much greater need for novelty than Kyle Davis did, then in order for her to continue to feel the endorphin high at the same level that he did after the first few months, she needed new experiences."

"Like going out and flirting with strangers? Or putting her photos up on Assassin Girls?"

"Exactly. But his endorphin would have dropped eventually too. If she'd walked out of his life after two years of working part time in toy stores and bitching about her parents and her student loans, he probably would have been glad to see her go."

"Oxytocin and endorphins aside, don't you think that sometimes people just know they're right for each other? I mean, my father proposed to my mother when they'd only known each other two months."

"And you're going to tell me that they just had their thirty-fifth wedding anniversary?"

"Actually, no. My dad died when I was eleven."

Verraday squirmed inwardly, annoyed at himself now for his flippant remark.

"I'm sorry," he said, feeling awkward and inept. "How did it happen?"

"He was a firefighter. He went out to a call at a warehouse on a three-alarm blaze. Place belonged to a company that wanted to knock it down and turn it into condos. But it was zoned historical, so they couldn't— that is, until it conveniently got torched. My father and two other firefighters were trapped when a floor collapsed. The fire inspectors thought it was arson, but the city quashed their investigation because the developers were major contributors to the mayor's campaign. They collected five million dollars in insurance and were able to build their condos after all."

"That's terrible."

"Well, I guess you know what it feels like."

"That I do," he replied, "It's toxic."

Maclean nodded. "And the worst thing is," she said, "that's when you suddenly discover that your life and the lives of the people you love are just this one tiny, tiny corner of the universe. And even though this terrible injustice has been committed, the world moves on."

Verraday glanced across at Maclean. She never took her gaze off the road, but he saw vulnerability in her eyes. He wasn't sure if they had a slight sheen to them now or if he was imagining it. He felt impolite and invasive gazing at her, so he turned and stared out the window into the night, the storefronts and apartments and people flashing past them like incomplete fragments of a zoetrope sequence that would never be shown again.

"This Assassin Girls site," he said at last. "It seems like it's tailor-made for predators to find victims. You ever hear of it before?"

"It's been around for a couple of years now," said Maclean. "Mostly it's girls looking for attention. But some of them try to work it too. The site pays them sixty dollars per set of nude selfies. They can post up to four sets a month."

"Two hundred and forty dollars a month to post nude pictures of yourself on the Internet? Are you kidding me? That's what, less than three grand a year for giving the world unlimited access to nude photos of yourself. I wonder how much the owners of the site make."

"Probably millions. Welcome to the digital economy."

"Welcome to the race to the bottom."

"Some girls in the sex trade use it like advertising too, to make contacts. They figure they can charge more money and get a better sort of clientele if they build a public image and a fan base."

"Well, my money says that that 'fan base' is exactly where Rachel met her killer. Rachel needed a new high, and she was looking for a bad boy."

"And unfortunately for her, she found one."

"So can we find out who contacted her through the site?"

"Yes, but Assassin Girls is based in the Netherlands. That means we need to go through Interpol. The National Central Bureau in DC will make the request to the Dutch police for us. It'll happen, but it will take a while."

"Meanwhile our killer could be out and killing again."

"That's why we have to find another way to get to him. Time is one thing we don't have."

"I'm curious. What was the Seattle PD doing in the time between when Kyle Davis filed the report and when Rachel's body was found?"

"Nothing. I checked into it. When I was trying to ID the Jane Doe and pulled Rachel Friesen's file, it was the first time it had been opened since the day he reported her missing."

Verraday shook his head, disgusted.

"Listen," said Maclean, "it's not that simple. Rachel dumped Kyle. Usually when a jilted partner reports someone missing, that person doesn't want to be found, at least not by their ex. Particularly in the case of a girl-friend reported missing. The police department doesn't want to be helping an abusive boyfriend stalk his ex. There are twenty thousand missing persons cases in Washington State at any given moment. Do you have any idea of the kind of manpower you'd need to track them all down?"

Verraday frowned. How in hell do twenty thousand people just go missing, even in a place the size of Washington State?

"What about Alana Carmichael?" he asked. "What do you know about her? I mean, besides what's in the official report?"

"I dug around in the social services file. Her parents divorced when she was seven. Father moved to California, and she lived with her mother after that. Mom had a series of boyfriends, finally married one who sexually assaulted Alana when she was twelve. That was the first time she ran away from home. After the fifth time, the authorities finally clued in to what was going on. They were going to place her with her father, but by that time, Dad was in a halfway house and a methadone program, so instead Alana was made a ward of the state and went through a series of foster homes. Alana left as soon as she was old enough, never finished high school, and ended up working as a stripper, doing some webcam stuff on the side."

"Totally different background than Rachel Friesen, but the same outcome," Verraday wearily mused.

Maclean pulled the Interceptor up to the curb in front of Verraday's small two-story clapboard house.

"I'll get Rachel's bank and cell records tomorrow and see what turns up," said Maclean. "Meanwhile, if you can look over the case files for her and Alana Carmichael, and the rap sheet for Fowler's suspect, Peter Cray, I'd be grateful. They were a little tricky for me to get; I had to sneak the originals for the Carmichael case out and get them copied on the sly, so as far as the rest of the world is concerned, you don't have them, okay?"

"Got it."

Verraday caught a glimpse of something in Maclean's expression.

"What?" he asked.

Maclean was hesitant for a moment, then spoke.

"How can a family give up on their own flesh and blood like the Friesens did? I see it all the time, but I just can't wrap my head around that."

"You ever date anyone who was bipolar?" asked Verraday.

There was a long moment of silence between them. Then Maclean handed Verraday two manila envelopes. "These are the case files. There's some pretty unsettling stuff in there. I'll be up for a couple of hours. Call me if you want."

He climbed out of the vehicle and closed the door behind him. She lowered the passenger window.

"Seriously. Call me if you need to."

"Thanks, I'll be okay," said Verraday. "Good night."

She pulled away from the curb, and he watched her until the thrum of the Interceptor's engine faded away and the vehicle rounded the corner and disappeared from view.

Then his attention was drawn to the sound of a creaking hinge. He turned toward his gate and noticed that it was open, swinging slightly in the light breeze. He knew he'd closed it before he went out. That was something he was particular about. He looked both ways down his street and saw that all the other front gates were latched. That pissed him off. An open gate was a form of semiotics that singled one's home out, made it stand out from the others, leaving a subliminal message to possible intruders that this dwelling and its occupants were less carefully guarded than those of his more security-conscious neighbors. Ordinary people might not notice such seemingly minor details, but people with deviant psyches were hyperaware of them. Psychopaths he had interviewed in prisons told him they could pick a suitable victim out of a crowd just by the way he or she walked.

Verraday latched the gate firmly behind him and made his way up the path, spotting a bundle of flyers on his doorstep—immediately beneath the "No Flyers" sign. He picked them up, inwardly cursing the delivery person who had not only disregarded his explicit request but then left his gate open and made him a mark.

Most of the flyers were the usual junk mail standards: vinyl siding installers, window cleaners, chimney rebuilders, and carpet cleaners. One caught his eye however. It was for a burlesque and rockabilly show at a club downtown, near Pike Place Market, featuring a troupe of performers called Sinner Saint. He'd heard about them. There was something clever and arch about their presentation. Their retro outfits were sexy but artistic and left something to the imagination. Their attitude was campy and tongue in cheek, and the dancers gave themselves witty names like Evilyn Sin Claire. He threw all the flyers into the recycle bin—except the one from Sinner Saint, which he slipped inside his briefcase. It looked like a fun night out. And as his sister Penny regularly reminded him, fun was something he didn't have enough of in his life, a fact he considered as he put his key in the front door lock, not looking forward to the task that awaited him.

CHAPTER 8

Verraday entered the foyer, kicked off his boots, and hung his leather jacket up on a large Victorian hall tree. It was the only family heirloom he possessed. His great-grandparents had bought it new just after they made the move west to San Francisco from Toronto in the 1890s. There was something reassuring about this piece of Victoriana. After more than a century of existence, its color had deepened to the warm hue of aged whiskey, and it remained solid, like the people who had crafted it. Unlike the disposable, box store crap that was everywhere today, it had been built to last.

Verraday lived alone and kept the thermostat low when he was out, so the house was cold and made him feel like he hadn't shaken off the chill of the morgue. He slid the thermostat needle up to 74 degrees and heard the furnace rumble to life below him in the basement. He checked his landline and saw from the display that someone had left a voice mail. He punched in the code to play it back. It was Penny.

"Hey James, it's me. Just checking to see if you're still coming over for dinner next week. Also, there's this neat thing happening that you might be interested in. Call me when you get a chance."

He was curious about what the "neat thing" she was talking about might be. Penny was always upbeat and optimistic, and he was tempted to call her. But the day had left him feeling unsettled. All his professional training emphasized that reaching out and sharing his feelings was the recommended way of coping with unpleasant emotions and traumatic experiences. It was one of the most basic pieces of advice that psychologists gave to their patients—and to each other. But he didn't feel up to speaking to anyone now, at least not about himself.

Ironically, talking to criminals didn't bother him anymore. But that was because he shared nothing of himself with the convicts he interviewed. They were always eager to take part in studies. Some thought it might help buy them early parole. Others just liked being interviewed because even an audience of one made them feel important. The psychopaths were the most challenging interview subjects. They came from many different social, economic, cultural, and ethnic backgrounds. But Verraday noted that there were certain characteristics that they all had in common. Chief among them was that they were cocky, self-assured, and always shifted blame for their crimes onto their victims. "She should have known better than to get in the car with a stranger," or "Anybody who keeps that much cash around is just asking for trouble." He had observed that psychopaths contrived to avoid first-person pronouns. They used a distinctive syntax that employed a passive voice and made the victim the subject of the sentence rather than the object so that a statement of fact like "I killed her" or "I beat him and robbed him" became "She lost her life" or "He was beaten and robbed," so that they, the perpetrator, were strangely absent from their accounts of the crimes they had committed.

Their uniquely self-serving manner of speech had irritated him when he had first started going into prisons to interview convicted murderers for his profiling research. But Verraday was now inured to their manipulative behavior, unaffected by their bullshit, their attempts to curry favor and minimize the heinousness of what they had done. What *did* affect him still, and deeply, was the thought of the victims' ordeals, their deaths or life-shattering injuries, and the toxic outcome it had, not only on them, but on their families, spouses, and significant others. He knew what it felt like to be one of those survivors, knew what it had done to his father and his sister.

Verraday strode across the living room into the kitchen and extracted a bottle of red wine from a rack, a big Cabernet from the hot, dry Yakima Valley. He uncorked it and poured himself a large glass. He swirled it around, inhaled its nose of blackberries and leather, and allowed himself the sensual pleasure that momentarily transported him away from the ugliness of the world. He took a sip of the wine and held it in his mouth a moment, savoring it, imagining he could feel the heat of the sun locked within it.

He carried the glass into the living room and, still feeling a chill despite the warm air now rising out of the vents, switched on the gas fireplace. Trying to shake off the leaden emotions that the day had left him with, he selected a book that Penny had given him for Christmas the year before last, *The Dalai Lama's Little Book of Inner Peace.* Penny had told him, in her blunt but affectionate manner, that it might help him with his anger and anxiety issues. His older sister had a particular gift when it came to dealing with the vicissitudes of life.

She had been a star basketball player at her school. Her skill on the court was so extraordinary that at the age of twelve, her school counselors had predicted that she would go to university on a full athletic scholarship. That is, until the night thirty years ago when Verraday, his mother, and his sister were returning from an evening of Christmas shopping and Officer David Robson of the Seattle Police Department ran a red light and broadsided their car. The police cruiser rammed into the driver's side door, killing their mother instantly. Penny had been sitting directly behind her. The force of the impact crumpled the family's sedan in on her, crushing her legs and pelvis and irreparably injuring her spinal cord. She had been paraplegic ever since. It had taken two years of physiotherapy for Penny to have even a semblance of physical independence. But though she managed to accomplish a surprising number of everyday tasks on her own, she had never managed to escape from the wheelchair that the accident had put her in. And barring some medical miracle yet to be devised, she never would. Somehow, despite the fact that the crash had robbed her of a scholarship and the use of her legs, Penny was more stoic and accepting of her situation than her younger brother, who had been sitting farthest from the point of impact and so had received only cuts and bruises.

Verraday was rushed along with his mother and sister to the emergency ward at Harborview. His mother was pronounced dead upon arrival. Verraday was kept overnight for observation and released into his father's care the next day. Penny however, stayed in the hospital to begin the long rehabilitation from her grievous injuries. Though arduous, the rehab regimen had also given her years to talk through her feelings with therapists and work through not only her physical traumas but her emotional ones as well, with the aid of sympathetic and knowledgeable adult ears. But because Verraday didn't have any physical injuries, he never needed to see a doctor again and received no counseling on how to cope with the loss of his mother. His situation was aggravated by the fact that the city, the police department, and their lawyers circled the wagons and did their best to discredit Verraday's memory of the accident, shifting the blame away from their officer and onto his mother, who, being dead, was conveniently unable to speak for herself.

Even as an adult, the memories of the cajoling and bullying by police and their legal counsel in the weeks after the crash were enough to provoke an adrenaline response in Verraday, raising his blood pressure and making his muscles tighten involuntarily. After a police lawyer had repeatedly failed to find a flaw in Verraday's recounting of the events during cross-examination, the counselor had told the judge in a faux-compassionate tone that "a child that age, having been subjected to such a distressing event, can't be expected to recall it accurately.

To place that burden on the boy would be cruel to him and grossly unjust to the accused." The judge agreed. The case was thrown out of court for lack of evidence and Robson was allowed to keep his job on the force.

Verraday sat down in front of the fire with his wine and the Dalai Lama's book. Penny, he knew in his heart, was rational and wise to a degree that he never would or could be. She didn't feel rage about injustices the way he did. She just made her personal corner of the world as uplifting as possible and seemed to accept the rest as an inevitable part of the human condition. Verraday knew that Penny's tribulations far exceeded his and continued to affect every moment of her waking life. Yet here she was, as far as he could tell, full of grace and laughter. He loved and respected his sister enough that normally, he would at least try to take her advice. But not tonight. He skimmed a few paragraphs of the Dalai Lama's book and found it singularly unhelpful.

"Sorry, Penny," he said as he set the book aside.

The only thing that would bring him any inner peace tonight would be to find out who had tortured and killed Rachel Friesen and Alana Carmichael and make sure the son of a bitch never had the chance to do it to anyone else.

He finished his wine and switched off the gas fireplace. The heat dissipated immediately and the chill air began to close in around him once again. Verraday went to the kitchen, poured himself a glass of brandy, and headed for his study, resigned to the darkness that awaited him there.

CHAPTER 9

Verraday set his brandy and the two envelopes down on his desk. He opened his filing cabinet and pulled out the crime scene photo of Rachel Friesen that Maclean had given him the previous day. Then he sat down, reached into the center drawer, and took out the Boeing letter opener that his father, a lifelong machinist with the company, had given him as a graduation present. He slit the seals and laid the contents of the envelopes out in two separate piles, one for Rachel Friesen's case, the other for Alana Carmichael.

He decided to begin with Rachel Friesen's file, rationalizing that since he'd already seen her at the morgue and knew what to expect, it would ease him into the disagreeable task of examining the unfamiliar crime scene photos of Alana Carmichael. At the top of the file were photos of tracks, which, the report noted, appeared to have been made by tires of the sort found on full-size commercial vans. They had been sent to the police lab and identification was pending. The report stated that the owners of the cranberry farm, the Kerkhoff family, owned a heavy International Harvester truck as well as a Dodge Ram pickup but that neither of those vehicles' tires matched the tracks found near the crime scene. There were photos of the bog itself, as well as the forested area around it. One was an aerial view with marks on it showing where the body was found and where the tire tracks were in relation to the cranberry bog. In the overhead shot, he could see that the farm was surrounded on three sides by encroaching new suburbs. Verraday supposed it would be only a decade at most until the farm ceased to exist and was sold off to developers to make cookie-cutter bungalows and townhouses.

At last Verraday had to face the inevitable close-ups of the body. The fact that he had seen Rachel Friesen's corpse in the flesh less than twelve hours earlier didn't make looking at the photos any less disturbing. There were several angles showing Rachel Friesen's body in relation to the flooded bog and the shoreline. And there were several more from the same series Maclean had given him the previous day, but they were far more graphic. Examining the photos, he saw that there were numerous angles of the bruises and welts that covered her shoulders, back, buttocks, and thighs. They were wide and dark, not the type that would be made by most lovers engaged in sadomasochistic play. The blows needed to leave the marks that were on Rachel Friesen could only be the product of someone whose anger was uncontrollable once unleashed.

Verraday took a sip of his brandy. Then he examined the second set of crime scene photos and the reports that

Maclean had copied from Fowler's investigation of the Alana Carmichael murder.

First, Verraday looked at one of the missing persons pictures supplied by Carmichael's mother to the police department when her daughter first disappeared. It was a snapshot that looked like it had been taken in a back garden on a sunny July afternoon. In it, Alana wore a retro, pastel-green summer dress, something that looked like it was from the early 1950s. Her hair was even darker than Rachel's, dyed black probably, thought Verraday, and cut medium-length in a Dita Von Teese, rockabilly style. Like Rachel, she had more piercings than most young women, but unlike the other victim, Alana's were more prominent. She had a stud through her right eyebrow, as well as a nose ring. On her left ear, which was the side visible in the photograph, she had three rings at the bottom, in her lobule, and two more at the top of the ear, along the helix, beside two prominent studs. But what stood out the most was a cupid's arrow. It was stainless steel, about two inches long and ran diagonally across her upper ear. The entry point, from which the arrow's fletchings stuck out, was on the upper front helix. The arrow's head emerged from a point at the back of her ear about three-quarters of an inch lower than the entry point. There was a black-and-red tattoo running down the left side of her throat, curving round her neck. The picture was small, but it appeared to be a cluster of roses. There was a second tattoo on her right arm, stretching from just above her wrist to a few inches above her elbow. This also seemed to be a cluster of roses, but in a more colorful red, yellow, and blue rendering. She held a tray on which there were two glasses and what appeared to be a pitcher of daiquiris. She wore a comically exaggerated expression of cordiality that morphed that "perfect hostess" smile seen so often in midcentury women's magazines into a satirical "mad housewife" effect.

Clearly something in the visual culture of that era appealed to Alana, and a lot of young women like her, yet they felt the compulsion to mock it at the same time. But despite her sardonic mugging, Alana's eyes didn't have the brightness and light of a true smile. There was melancholy behind the vivid colors she surrounded herself with and the wit and style she projected. In another life, thought Verraday, someone with Alana's highly developed aesthetic sense might have become an in-demand art director, costume designer, or set decorator. He wondered what her story might have been had she never been sexually assaulted by a stepfather, had never experienced all those setbacks that put her on a trajectory that would ultimately intersect with that of her killer.

That was Alana Carmichael in life. Now came the inevitability of observing Alana Carmichael in death. With a sense of foreboding, Verraday slid the first crime scene photo out from beneath the missing persons report. It was an overhead view of a dumpster. On top of broken furniture, pizza boxes, discarded flowerpots, and other detritus of everyday life lay the naked body of Alana Carmichael. Her head was slumped to the left, hanging over the side of a garbage bag. On the inside of her upper left thigh was a green tattoo, a forest or jungle of some sort. Upon closer examination, Verraday saw that it was the Garden of Eden, with Eve, an apple, and a serpent lurking within it.

Then he pulled out another photo of the crime scene, this one showing Alana Carmichael's face and neck from the same overhead viewpoint, only in close-up. Like the photos of Rachel Friesen from the cranberry bog, it revealed deep ligature marks around the victim's neck. Whatever the killer had used to strangle Alana Carmichael, it had been pulled so tightly that it had begun to cut into her skin. The blood vessels in her eyes had hemorrhaged from the force of the strangulation, just as Rachel Friesen's had.

The next photo he removed from the pile was another close-up, this time a view of her left side. It revealed the neck tattoo he had seen in the backyard photo. At first glance, it appeared to be what he had observed before, a cluster of roses at a slightly odd angle. For some reason, beyond the fact that they were tattooed onto what was now a young woman murdered in a particularly vicious fashion, the image gave him a strangely uneasy feeling when he viewed it up close. He lifted the photo up and slowly rotated it around its axis. When he viewed it from a point behind the victim's left ear, the now nearly upside-down tattoo suddenly revealed itself to be a cleverly macabre optical illusion. Someone viewing Alana close up and from behind would have been surprised, as Verraday now was, to see the roses artfully morph into a black-and-white skull surrounded by fronds and petals. He noticed something else not visible in the overhead shot: that the Cupid's arrow pin that Alana Carmichael had been wearing in the backyard photograph was missing. He also noted that like Rachel, she had a piercing in her navel, but there was no ring or stud there in any of the crime scene pictures.

Then Verraday pulled out a photo taken at the morgue. It revealed that the victim's back, buttocks, and thighs were heavily bruised and covered in welts, the same way Rachel Friesen's were. According to the coroner's report, the one major difference was that semen had been found on Alana's panties, and it matched that of the accused, Peter Cray. It was an odd discrepancy. There was considerable forethought in the commission of both crimes. Whoever did this had chosen his victims, as well as his means of killing and disposing of them, with great care. Leaving traces of semen behind had been a major gaffe. Or had it?

Verraday set the coroner's report down then pulled out Peter Cray's file, starting with the mug shots. Verraday gazed at the photos and took an immediate dislike to him. Cray was a stocky man in his early thirties, with a neck that seemed bigger in circumference than his head. He had a pugnacious set to his jaw and gazed out from piglike eyes with a look that was simultaneously belligerent and stupid. It was an expression that Verraday had seen scores of times. It was the look of the repeat offender. Verraday's instinctive dislike of Cray only increased when he read his rap sheet, a revolving door of charges and occasional convictions dating back to age fifteen. There were two arrests for beating up prostitutes and another for indecent exposure. Rounding out his record were several thefts, a robbery, a couple of assaults committed while intoxicated, and a few charges of receiving stolen merchandise that were dismissed because of lack of evidence. There was a break-and-entry charge that he'd beaten only because he was so drunk and high on OxyContin that he had fallen asleep behind the wheel of the getaway car while his partner was apprehended inside the victims' home. When police questioned Cray, he claimed that he had no idea his friend was planning a break-in. He insisted that he had thought that the man was getting out to relieve himself, and that Cray had nodded off while waiting for him to return. Cray might not wind up on death row through his own efforts, thought Verraday, but he'd likely spend a lot of his life in prison for crimes not yet committed. Unless by some miracle, he rehabilitated himself, which seemed unlikely. Verraday's eyes were beginning to sting, and his lids felt heavy. He took a sip of his brandy then closed them just for a moment to give them some rest. He wasn't sure how long he'd been sleeping when the motion of his head slumping forward jerked him awake. He pushed his chair away from the desk and headed to his bedroom, where he quickly peeled off his clothes and climbed under the covers before the effects of the natural melatonin could wear off and the misery and bleakness of the photos could creep back into his consciousness.

CHAPTER 10

Verraday entered the Trabant Café and reflexively checked the clock above the cash register by the front door. Ten o'clock sharp, just as they had arranged. Verraday was precise about being punctual and, without even consciously doing so, took one last look to make sure he wasn't late. He didn't demand such a level of fastidiousness from anyone else. It was, he knew, one of his quirks, probably something pounded into him by a grade school teacher whose face he couldn't even visualize any more, but whose quirk had become his quirk.

He glanced around the room and saw that Maclean was already there. She had taken up a position at a table at the very back, in an alcove beneath the stairway to the mezzanine. It was, he noted, a strategic location where she could watch without being watched and speak without being overheard. Maclean had suggested this café. It was just north of the University of Washington campus, near the Neptune Theatre, and was popular with students and artsy types.

Verraday noted that she was already halfway through the mug of coffee sitting on the table in front of her. He'd had an uneasy night. He had awakened twice, haunted by his thoughts and the images from the files, and had had difficulty dozing off again. He noticed that Maclean looked a little weary too, though she managed a smile that seemed genuinely warm.

"How you doing?" she asked. "You sleep okay?"

"Sure, fine," he lied, stifling a yawn. "How about you?"

"Oh, you know . . ." she replied.

"Yeah, me too," he said at last, appreciating her candor.

He felt disheveled and marveled at the way Maclean managed to look well put together despite what seemed to be routine twelve-hour days.

"This is an unusual choice of meeting place for a police officer," said Verraday. "It's pretty bohemian."

"I wasn't always a cop," Maclean replied. "I did my undergrad social work studies at U Dub Seattle. I used to get caffeinated here when I was pulling all-nighters."

"When were you there?"

"From 2002 to 2006."

"I must have just missed you," said Verraday, wondering what it would have been like to meet this attractive but somewhat world-weary woman when she was a fresh-faced and probably very idealistic social work student.

She signaled to the waitress, then they settled down to business.

"So now that you've had some time with the photos and reports, what do you think?" asked Maclean.

"Well, first of all, that your instincts about Fowler's suspect were right. Peter Cray didn't murder Alana Carmichael. I read his rap sheet and the court records on his convictions for rape, aggravated assault, and robbery. They were all committed with about as much forethought as you or I would devote to ordering a pizza. I mean, you wouldn't want Cray to take your favorite granny to a picnic in a secluded spot, or leave him alone with small children or pets. But in my opinion, your assessment is correct. He didn't kill Alana Carmichael."

"What about the semen stain on her underwear? Fowler is pinning his case on it."

"The stain—" he began to reply, then abruptly stopped speaking as, in his peripheral vision, he noticed the waitress coming to take his order. She was in her midtwenties, had a rolling gait, wore heavy kohl eyeliner, and had a Celtic knot tattoo around her left wrist. She looked at him with a flirtatious grin that he would have responded to with more than a polite smile had he not been sitting with another woman and had he not stayed up late the previous evening evaluating crime scene photos of brutally murdered young women who looked very much like this waitress. He ordered a green tea and fell silent until she was out of earshot.

"The semen stain doesn't mean that Cray killed her. It just means he had sex with her at some point in the night and was sloppy. Cray is a habitually disorganized criminal, not the sort of person to mastermind a murder. At least not one that he'd get away with."

Maclean pursed her lips as she considered the point.

"But as Lao Tzu said, 'The journey of a thousand miles begins with a single step.' No?"

"True," replied Verraday. "But if Cray did do this, it would have been an extremely rapid progression in his skill level. Like a chimp suddenly learning how to do your tax return. Not that I'd have any objection to that. Cray plays checkers, not chess. The sex assaults he committed were targets of opportunity, people in vulnerable situations that he thought he could take advantage of. Same with his robberies. No planning or due diligence. Ditto the beatings. They were spontaneous and over trivial things—petty drug deals gone bad, perceived slights from acquaintances and strangers. With him, it's all about impulses. That's why he gets caught so often. Even the sex with Alana Carmichael shows his lack of self-control."

"How so?"

"The fact that semen was found on her underwear and skin, but not in her vagina is a clear indication. He ejaculated so prematurely that he probably never even penetrated her. As the report says, there was a Handi Wipe with his semen on it found in her apartment. She probably used it to clean herself and missed a few spots. Just like Rachel Friesen, she doesn't have any defensive wounds. And Cray didn't have any scratches or cuts on him either. If Cray was stupid enough to leave traces of his semen on someone he was planning to murder, how was he smart enough to manipulate his victim into a bondage situation where she voluntarily gave up her means of defending herself? Plus Alana Carmichael's body was found in a dumpster five miles from Cray's home. But he always commits his crimes within blocks of where he lives. It doesn't add up. He was probably just the last client Alana Carmichael had before she encountered her killer. The Carmichael and Friesen killings were meticulously planned. The perpetrator was an organized offender who didn't leave any clues. In fact, the only clue he allowed to remain behind was a false clue, to pin it on somebody else."

"What's he like, the real killer?"

"Probably white male. He's got that much in common with Cray. Sex killers are usually attracted to members of their own race. It's not written in stone, but it's almost always how it is. This guy's probably not much older than his victims, or he's a somewhat older person who is into alternative culture and hangs out with people who are mostly younger than he is. The killer probably saw Rachel Friesen and Alana Carmichael while he was cruising those websites. Reading the comments from the 'fans,' seeing that other men were turned on by Rachel and Alana, made them more attractive to him as well."

"If he's so attracted to them, then why does he want to kill them?"

"Because they make him feel inadequate. They'd probably reject him if he wasn't paying for them. Something in his past makes him feel he's not good enough. Luring them, taking away their power, makes him feel superior to them. This guy wants to feel cool, but he's deeply insecure."

"What's his temperament?"

"He's filled with rage. Explosive rage. He feels emasculated on some level and sexually inadequate. Serial killers are usually socially stunted. As children, their family situations are unsocial and unstable. Eventually it becomes self-fulfilling. They never learn how to have real relationships, so their lives are mostly fantasy. Fantasies of control over people that they can't have in real life. And when they can't control even themselves any more, they act out those fantasies. He's a fuckup. But that doesn't mean he's stupid. The fact that Cray's DNA was all over Alana Carmichael was a perfect cover for the real killer. I think our perpetrator is highly technical in his approach. For example, he must have had a UV light to check for semen phosphorescence. When he found traces of semen on Alana Carmichael, he left them there so it would throw an investigator, at least a second-rate investigator like Fowler, off the trail."

"But how could he know that she would have semen on her?"

"He couldn't. Not entirely. But it's a reasonable assumption if you're having sex with someone who does it for a living that they might have DNA from other johns on them. From the time of death of both victims—late at night—it wouldn't even surprise me if the killer purposely arranged to be their last customer of the day so there would be a better chance that there would be DNA contamination on them from other people."

"Seems like a long way to go for someone in a rage."

"The rage is what drives him, but he controls it until the last moment. He plans these murders like they're a moon launch. The smart killers always do. The Unabomber collected pubic hairs from public washroom urinals and planted them in his bomb packages to throw off investigators and lead them to other suspects."

"I guess it just goes to show that being smart doesn't mean you can't be crazy too. What else do we know about the killer?"

"The Cupid's arrow that Alana Carmichael wore in the missing persons photo is absent in the postmortem pictures. Plus she had a pierced navel, but there was no jewelry in that location on the body. Same thing with Rachel Friesen. The dream catcher she wore was missing."

"Maybe they just got tired of those pieces and took them out in between when the first photos were taken and when they were murdered."

"It's a possibility. But Alana Carmichael liked to make an impression. She hadn't changed her style of hair, makeup, or clothing, so it's unlikely that she would suddenly stop wearing jewelry, especially something really attention getting like that arrow. Same with Rachel's dream catcher. She had only recently gotten it too, so there was probably still a lot of novelty value in it for her. She wouldn't have wanted to stop wearing it yet. And serial killers almost always take souvenirs from their victim's bodies. Not only would the Cupid's arrow have drawn his attention by being the largest item of jewelry on her, but think about the symbolism. What does it say?"

"It implies that the wearer has some special romantic or sexual power?"

"Exactly. Just the kind of symbol and statement that would antagonize someone who wanted power, wanted to dominate and subjugate another human. So the killer would have gotten particular satisfaction from taking it from his victim, the same way a scalper gets pleasure from taking a bloody prize from an opponent they've defeated in combat. Rachel's dream catcher was eye catching, and like the arrow, it also implied a certain kind of power."

"The power to stop nightmares."

"That's right. If the killer understood its meaning, it would have given him an extra thrill to exert his dominance over it, defying its power and actually becoming the nightmare that Rachel couldn't control."

"What else do the photos tell you?"

Verraday began to pull a couple of photos out of his briefcase then stopped when he noticed the waitress approaching with his green tea. He noticed her noticing him doing it. He knew that she couldn't possibly have overheard him. He had been too careful for that. But he realized she was able to intuit that he was pausing because of her, hiding something from her, and it caused her to visibly cool toward him.

"There you go," she said, placing his tea on the table, her flirty grin now gone. "I'll bring the check whenever you're ready."

"Thanks," Verraday replied awkwardly, marveling at how some people, like this waitress, had invisible social antennae that caused them to read meaning into the smallest gestures, even if they were wrong about it. Hypervigilant, he guessed. Probably the result of an unstable home life with emotionally volatile parents who could explode in anger without warning. Children who grew up in such homes, he had observed, developed amazing abilities to detect nuances of voice and expression, even posture, as survival mechanisms around unpredictable and potentially abusive parents.

With the waitress out of earshot, he handed two of the crime scene photos to Maclean, one from Alana Carmichael, the other from Rachel Friesen.

"Take a look. They have identical marks on their lower backs, right along the spine. That's a no-go zone even for people who like it rough. And there are no defensive wounds on the victims. No cuts on the hands, no scrapes on the knuckles. Not so much as a broken fingernail."

"Indicating they were both willing participants?" asked Maclean.

"Exactly. To a point. BDSM is all about trust, and even in a sex-trade transaction, it's the submissive partner who's controlling the action, saying how far things can go."

"But you lose the ability to enforce those limits once you're tied up," said Maclean. "I'd have to really trust someone to let them make me that vulnerable."

"So would I. It's a social contract between participants. In a sex-trade context though, there's an additional assumption that if all goes well, there will be lots more work like this for the sub, because the dominant party needs to play out the same scenario every time in order to experience arousal. So quite understandably, Alana Carmichael and Rachel Friesen were expecting that the sex play would only go so far."

"A bait-and-switch situation?"

"That's right. The killer was particularly insidious, because judging by the absence of marks on the wrists and ankles, he used something comfortable or even sensual like silk to restrain them. The tactile pleasure of the restraints probably lulled the victims into a false sense of security, into thinking that this guy wasn't a threat, that he was gentler than someone who was into handcuffs, for example. For this guy, it's all part of a buildup."

"Sounds like deception is his foreplay."

"Nicely put, Detective. That's very perceptive of you."

"When you're a woman, you get to know these things. The guy with the wedding band in his wallet or the girlfriend he somehow forgot to mention. Fortunately, not everyone of the male persuasion is like that."

"Or the female persuasion," added Verraday. "But as for our killer, there are very few ways in which he doesn't deceive his victims. This guy is either wealthy enough to hire high-end escorts and dangle out the possibility of a long-term client relationship with them, or he's able to create the illusion that he's got the money. His aura of wealth and status would play on a woman's instinctive desire to find a partner who can provide her with financial security."

"Wait, are you saying that all women are looking for a man to make them financially secure?"

"No, not all women, of course. But our victims were both in situations that made them financially dependent, so it would have exaggerated that innate behavior."

"'Innate behavior?' Look, lots of women earn their own money, and they're not going to throw themselves on some guy just for a little financial security."

"With all due respect, they still do. Have you ever heard of the study done at Syracuse University?" asked Verraday.

"No, what was it?"

"They showed two groups of high-status women—women who had made their own money—pictures of the same man. In one picture he's wearing an expensive suit and a Rolex. In another the same guy is wearing a Burger King uniform. Guess which version of the same man the women rated as more attractive and desirable?"

"Yeah, yeah," retorted Maclean, "and all I have to say is that instead of dressing the guy up in something polyester that smells like a grease trap, maybe he should have worn a UPS summer-issue delivery uniform instead. You know, the one with those little shorts?"

Verraday smiled. "Point taken. But the fact remains that the women consistently chose the photo of the high-status male over the low-status male as potential partner material."

"Yes," Maclean shot back, "because it was a *photo*. The women were only allowed to make their decision based on visual appearances. Let me guess. The person who created the study was a man?"

Verraday nodded.

"Want to know how I knew?" Maclean asked.

"I'd very much like to hear it."

"Because a woman would never create a study of sexual attractiveness based only on visual appearance. Visuals are totally a guy thing. If a woman had made that study, the choices would have been between a man who comes home and asks you what the best and worst parts of your day were, versus some self-absorbed asshole in Armani who flops down on the sofa in front of the game and forgets that you even exist."

"And this guy who asks you about your day—ideally, would he be wearing the UPS summer uniform with the short-shorts?"

"It wouldn't hurt."

"I'm getting the feeling this is an argument that I can't win," said Verraday.

"Well, that's very perceptive of *you*, Professor."

He could tell from Maclean's faint smile that she wasn't genuinely angry, but neither would she ever back down without a fight.

"You're right about men being more visual," said Verraday, "I hadn't considered that. I'll have to rethink that study."

Maclean smiled. "Thank you."

"All I was trying to say about our killer," continued Verraday, "is that he plays on his victims' needs. Even if he doesn't know their backstories, he can sense their wants, their insecurities. And he would play to those needs. And the more it worked for him, the more excited he would become. He would have gotten more and more aroused as he duped his victims into putting themselves in a vulnerable situation where he could then totally dominate them. That sense of fooling them would have continued even as he began to flail them with the belt. The early stages wouldn't have alarmed the victims. They likely even moaned with pleasure, or pretended to, when he was hitting them relatively lightly. That would have aroused him even more, knowing they had no idea what was coming next. Then when it got to be too rough, they would have begun to protest. That's the part that would really get him off. That they'd tell him to stop, but he could ignore them. He would have savored beating them and humiliating them, showing his power over them."

He saw a muscle in Maclean's jaw contract with anger. "This guy's thing is all about power, domination, and control. The beatings were severe, but they were just preamble. He could have beaten the women to death if he'd wanted to, but that's not what gets him off. Strangulation is what turns his crank. The reports suggest that he started by choking them with his hands, then switched to the garrote. That's when his victims would have finally known what his true intention was. They would have realized they weren't getting out of there alive. They would have begged him to stop. He would have taken special pleasure from their desperation as they realized they'd fallen into his trap. That's the moment that excited him most of all: when he wound that cable around their necks and started tightening it. If deception was his foreplay, this was his climax."

Verraday could see the knuckles of Maclean's right hand turning white as she unconsciously balled it into a fist. He saw that her face had turned white too, not from fear but from fury. It was more unconscious semiotics of the human mind. At the most extreme stage of anger, the blood flows away from the body's extremities and into its core, as preparation for physical combat. Verraday knew from Maclean's unconscious display that if the killer had suddenly materialized in the café at this moment, she would have gone after him with her bare hands. He knew what he was about to tell her wouldn't do anything to soothe that instinct.

"If strangulation is the climax, then the disposal—the act of getting away with the crime itself—is the cigarette in bed afterwards. It gives him a feeling of superiority to get attention in the headlines, that the authorities are apparently powerless to stop him. He feels like he's tricked everyone. He feels smart as hell."

"I want to get this son of a bitch," said Maclean. "I want to nail his ass to the wall and put him away forever."

"So do I," said Verraday. "So do I. But this guy's cunning. He's highly organized and, typical for those profiles, his abductions, crimes, and disposals are played out in multiple locations as part of his system."

"So what *is* his system?"

"He lures them. Because of the BDSM context, we know that sex was used openly as the pretext for their association. And since both victims were engaged in the sex trade, using the cover of a transaction to draw them to the kill room would have been easy. He would have done it in a way that left virtually no evidence trail. He probably contacted them in what appeared to be a spontaneous, last-minute way, so there would be less chance that they'd tell friends, coworkers, whatever, where they were going."

"What about the location?"

"The kill room would have to be a place that he had absolute control over, at least during the time that he committed the murders. It would be somewhere that he either built especially for the job, or that just happened to suit it perfectly. Few if any other people would have had access to it. This guy's so concerned with not alarming his victims until it's too late, with how everything looks to his victims, that the kill room is probably stylish and luxurious. The girls would feel like they were somewhere exclusive, pampered even. Then, once he killed them, he would move them to a different location to clean them and remove any traces of himself."

"Not the same location?"

"No. I mean, he's got to persuade a total stranger to strip off her clothes, prostrate herself, and allow herself to be bound by her wrists and ankles. Nobody in their right mind is going to do that in a tiled room with drains in the floors. That would come later."

"Where? Like in a bathroom?"

"Maybe. But this guy kills when all the conditions are right and he feels sure that he can get away with it. So I think he would use a location that allows for a highly efficient cleanup and that would be unlikely to have his DNA in it."

"What are we talking about?"

"Someplace that he'd never use for any of his own personal hygiene. An industrial cleaning basin, for example. He would place the bodies in the basin. Use soap and water to remove all traces of semen or other sources of DNA, except for the ones he wanted us to see to throw us off. He enjoys washing the bodies of his victims almost as much as he enjoys killing them. Psychopathic killers always prolong contact with the bodies as long as they can. So he would take his time and be thorough, not just to destroy evidence, but to savor the experience."

"That's probably when he took the jewelry off them too?"

"Most likely. He probably stores his trophies in some special container that he keeps well hidden and only brings out when he's either fondling the jewelry or taking new prizes off his victims."

"And after that? How does he dispose of their bodies?"

"The fact that he has twice left bodies in publicly accessible locations suggests to me that he feels his property is safe enough to kill on, but not safe enough to dispose of a body on. He has enough time to kill them and clean them, but he can't keep them around because wherever he's doing this, he fears that other people— public or family members—will find out. So he gets rid of them somewhere else."

"What's his process?"

"He would plan that out meticulously too. He uses some sort of vehicle that would be easy to load and unload from, something like a van. It would have some sort of liner, like heavy vapor barrier plastic, that he can remove afterwards and then dispose of in some way that wouldn't attract any attention, like in an incinerator. The loading area is also some place where he feels safe, where he's certain that he can take his time without being observed."

"So either indoors or shielded from view."

"Yes. And the vehicle would be nondescript. Something that wouldn't attract attention."

"What about the choice of dump sites for the bodies?"

"So far we only have the two to go on. Both were fairly secluded places where there was little chance of him being observed. He left Alana Carmichael's body in a dumpster behind a school, not only late at night, but over the Easter long weekend."

"So it's a holiday and there isn't going to be anybody there to see him."

"Exactly. He would have scouted the locations, learned the habits of the people around there. Knew when it was least likely that he'd run into police or anybody else."

"But there was no attempt to hide the bodies in the long term," said Maclean.

"Exactly. Ditto for the cranberry bog. If he did his research—and I guarantee he did—he knew that the bog would be drained once the cranberries were harvested. He's so confident that he can remove any evidence tying him to the bodies that he doesn't need the bodies to disappear forever."

"Just long enough for him to get safely back to wherever he operates from."

"Exactly. And that's something that bothers me about all this. I mean, beyond the fact that young women are being murdered."

"What's that?"

"There's no serial killer who starts out this polished. Pickton, Dahmer, they all made mistakes. They were just lucky enough that the local cops were even more incompetent than they were, otherwise they would have been caught."

"But you said this guy's methodical and intelligent. Couldn't our killer just have done a lot of research? If he's as organized and painstaking as you say he is, maybe he just knew exactly what he was doing from the get-go?"

"That's the part I still haven't sorted out," replied Verraday. "I don't care if you're Stephen Hawking or Usain Bolt. There's a learning curve to everything. Nobody's this flawless right out of the gate. Alana Carmichael was not his first victim."

"So why are we only finding out about him now?"

"He may have lived somewhere else and moved to the Seattle area recently. Or he may have lived in Seattle all his life and is now just getting so confident that he doesn't care about the bodies being found."

"You're saying there are more bodies out there."

"I'd say the chances against it are almost nil. And unless we catch him, there will be more."

CHAPTER 11

Verraday was in the lecture hall preparing for his afternoon class in criminal psychology and behavior when he heard his cell phone buzzing in his briefcase. For a moment, he considered ignoring it. But he rarely received calls on his cell during the day and guessed it was Maclean. Students were still trickling in, and the computer he used for his PowerPoint presentation hadn't quite finished booting up. So he reached in to retrieve it and answer the call.

The soft leather briefcase had been a birthday present from his sister Penny and had a cleverly designed array of internal pockets to keep items separated—perfect for a highly organized person like Penny. Verraday's problem was that he did not share his older sibling's predisposition. He'd forgotten which pocket he'd placed the phone in, and its vibrations were spread out evenly, seeming to come from every part of the case's dark interior at the same time. Verraday fumbled around blindly in pouch after pouch and found nothing. He reached down into one large pocket and, too late, detected the edge of the burlesque house flyer. He'd forgotten to take it out of his briefcase the previous night, and a corner of the sharp, crisply guillotined stock slid in under his index fingernail and gave him a nasty paper cut.

"Fuck!" he exclaimed, managing to keep it down to a stage whisper.

On the fifth ring, he located the cell and finally answered. He could hear the excitement in Maclean's voice as soon as she began speaking.

"We've got a lead. I found a PayPal transfer to Rachel's bank account, which showed that it came from some place called The Victorian Closet. I Googled it. It's a store downtown. I checked the phone number, and it matches one of the numbers in Alana Carmichael's cell records. I got her bank statements and it turns out there's a payment to her there too. There's a solid connection to both victims."

Verraday turned his back to his students so they couldn't see or hear him.

"Good work, Detective."

"I'm heading down there now. Want to come scope the place out with me?"

"Love to, but I'm just about to teach a class. I'll be done in two hours. I can join you then if you can hang on."

"Sorry, can't wait that long. I'll keep you posted."

"Thanks."

Verraday ended the call and shut off the ringer. The last of the stragglers were taking their seats.

"All right. Since everybody seems to be ready now, let's begin. Today we'll be talking about biological theories of criminal behavior."

A hand went up. It was a student named Koller. Verraday remembered Koller's name only because the kid was so annoying, frequently interrupting Verraday's lectures with inane points and irrelevant questions. Worse, he was in both classes that Verraday taught, so Verraday had to see him four times a week.

Verraday ignored him for a moment, then gave in to Koller's persistent eye contact and raised hand.

"Yes, what is it?" he asked, betraying his slight annoyance.

Koller pointed toward Verraday's hand. "You're bleeding, dude."

Verraday looked down. He wasn't sure what surprised him more. To see drops of blood on the lectern or to have a student call him "dude." Koller was irritating even when he was trying to help, thought Verraday.

"Thank you, Mr. Koller," he replied.

He felt inside his blazer for a tissue and realized he didn't have one.

"Um, anybody got a clean tissue or a wipe that I can have?"

The frumpy girl in the baggy jeans and big sweater made her way toward him. Janzen or Jensen or Johansen. He still couldn't remember. She took a small travel-size package of sanitizing wipes from her purse.

"There you go, Professor," she said timidly, hunching her shoulders as she handed it to him.

"Thank you," he replied as he took one from the package. He pressed the alcohol wipe against the cut. It stung but absorbed the blood on his fingertip and staunched the flow.

"And there's a Band-Aid too if you need it," she added, handing him one from her purse.

"You come fully equipped," he said.

She smiled shyly but said nothing.

"Thanks," he replied.

"You're welcome, sir."

Even with her slightly olive-hued skin, he could see that she was blushing. She returned to her seat somewhat self-consciously. She was smart, but not the kind of person who liked being the center of attention, he thought. She'd probably go into the research side of the profession, he mused, become a number cruncher for a polling or marketing company. She had an eye for detail that would serve her well in that role. Verraday cleaned the few drops of blood off the lectern and tossed the wipe into a nearby wastebasket. Then he wrapped the Band-Aid around his finger.

"All right, now that the medical emergency is over, let's carry on, shall we?"

CHAPTER 12

Maclean cruised past Pioneer Square, went a couple more blocks then made a right-hand turn. She pulled the unmarked Interceptor up to the curb a couple of doors short of The Victorian Closet so the vehicle wouldn't draw attention from within the store. She walked back to the cruiser accompanying her and leaned in to speak to the uniformed officer behind the wheel.

"Wait here. I'll call you when I'm ready."

As she surveyed the front window, Maclean tried to look like a casual shopper. Or as casual as you could look surveying a window display that included a female mannequin dressed in a nineteenth-century whalebone corset holding a riding crop with which she was spanking a winged taxidermy monkey that wore a gold-tasseled fez and a salacious grin.

Maclean drew in a deep breath and entered. A small brass bell chimed. She didn't immediately see the proprietor or any other signs of life. The shop was musty-smelling and crowded with the sort of antiques that would appeal only to customers of extremely particular tastes. There were more vintage corsets, Victorian spanking mechanisms, antique paddles, and several cast-iron "Naughty Nellie" boot jacks, their 120-year-old legs spread wide, at the ready to accept a gentleman's heel. There was a nineteenth-century sex swing. Maclean pretended to browse what appeared to be an entire case filled with antique vibrators, creaky-looking, alternating-current affairs to be used at one's peril.

At the end of another aisle, in a place of honor within a glass case, was a phallic-looking carved wooden object. Its handle was decorated with a crudely fashioned diamond pattern. The business end consisted of three long prongs the length of a large human hand, gradually curving inward until the tips almost met. Maclean didn't know what to make of it, but it looked utterly depraved.

"It's probably not what you think it is," said a male voice from behind her. "It's probably worse."

She turned to see a man in his forties, with a thick moustache and deep-set eyes. His hair was long and slicked back, some of it pulled into a topknot. He appeared to be the only other person in the store.

"Would you like to hazard a guess?" he asked.

"I'm thinking a utensil of some sort, but not for anything I do on a regular basis."

The man chuckled and smiled at Maclean lasciviously. "It's a Fijian cannibal fork. It was the personal property of chief Ratu Udre Udre. He was the greatest of the Fijian rulers, the most prolific cannibal in the history of the islands, and the last one to consume human flesh. At least officially. According to the Guinness Book of World Records, he devoured eight hundred and seventy-two men. That's the very fork with which he held the remains of his last victim, a rival chieftain named Lahelahe."

"How much is it?"

"Oh, it's not for sale. But I do bring it out for what you might call 'private ceremonial occasions.' Is there something in particular that you're looking for?"

He leaned in uncomfortably close until she could feel his breath and smell some sort of industrial cleaner or disinfectant on him.

"I'm just browsing, really."

"Well, if you need any help, I'll be at the counter. Just got a new shipment of Peruvian shrunken heads in that I need to sort through. The exporters will try to pass off capuchins as Aguarana tribesmen if you don't keep your eye on them."

He stood close to her a moment longer than necessary, then slipped back behind the counter. There, he perched on a stool and began extracting shrunken heads from a wooden crate.

Maclean spotted a windowless door at the back of the shop. She moved toward it slowly, continuing to peruse the aisles, feigning interest in a rack of Victorian erotic postcards. In one sepia-toned picture, a pair of women were naked except for the horseheads they wore over their own heads and the harnesses around their necks and waists. Another featured a staged variation on an *Upstairs, Downstairs*–type discipline scenario. In it, a stern-faced house steward in a tuxedo was meting out corporal punishment to three contrite-looking maids. They knelt before him, their long skirts pulled up to their waists to bare their impossibly white buttocks, which received the steward's wrath in the form of a spanking with a twig broom. In another postcard, a bare-chested brute in boots, wrestling tights, and a black executioner's hood was strangling a young woman dressed like a pre-Raphaelite water nymph. The nymph's eyes bugged out in alarm and her mouth was open wide like a koi gasping for air. Her petite arms pulled ineffectually at the garrote that was wrapped tightly around her throat by her attacker, his huge, hairy biceps bulging. The photograph had one of those explanatory titles that Victorian pornographers felt a compulsion to use, as if it somehow elevated their prurient wares to the level of high art. *"The Death of Innocence at the Hands of Lust."* Maclean thought about Verraday's description of the killer's climactic moment and the ligature marks on both Rachel Friesen's and Alana Carmichael's necks. Despite the slightly curled edges of the paper and its patina of age, Maclean found the photo extremely disturbing. She wondered what sort of depraved mind would have any interest in it, in this or any other era.

The phone rang. The man with the topknot answered. Maclean saw her chance and crept up toward the handle of the door to the back room, checking over her shoulder to make sure Whitney wasn't watching. She saw that he was now completely engrossed in his phone conversation, which seemed to be about a lost shipment. She opened the door a crack and peered in.

The room was dimly lit, but she could see a loading dock door at the far end. Between her and the dock was an array of antique furniture. It didn't look like it was in storage, but rather that it was arranged to some purpose.

As Maclean's eyes adjusted to the light, she realized it was some sort of erotic dungeon. In its center was a device that looked like a massage table with leather restraining straps and sections cut out of it in places that Maclean supposed corresponded to strategic points of human anatomy. A few feet away from it was another device featuring diagonal wooden crossbars the approximate length of an adult human. It too was heavily padded and had restraints placed at various points around it. In a wooden rack located within easy reach of all these devices was an array of whips, paddles, and floggers. If there was anything that Whitney didn't have in the way of bondage and discipline paraphernalia, Maclean literally would have had no idea what it was. To one side of the room was an area hidden behind crimson velvet drapes that hung like a stage curtain. She took one last look to make sure that Whitney wasn't coming, then stealthily moved across the room. She pushed the heavy drapes aside and felt a surge of adrenaline. There, immediately in front of her, was a six-foot-long stainless steel industrial basin. In the bottom of it was an assortment of unidentifiable bones and skulls, bathing in what smelled like a bleach solution that stung the inside of her nose.

She spotted rubber gloves, scrub brushes, and a hazmat suit hanging up nearby. A pair of industrial grade rubber boots stood on a bench a few feet away. She reached into her jacket, pulled out her handheld radio, and called the uniformed officer waiting outside.

"Move in. We've got our suspect."

CHAPTER 13

Verraday had been distracted throughout his lecture. He was excited by Maclean's news and a bit resentful at having to stay behind while she went out to investigate the suspect. As soon as the last student exited the hall, he called Maclean. Her cell immediately went to voice mail. Verraday left the lecture hall and decided to head home to do some work on the midterm exam while he was waiting to hear back from Maclean.

When he arrived at his house, Verraday checked his messages. Maclean hadn't called his landline, but there was a new message from his sister. He played it back.

"Hey, it's Penny. Still haven't heard back from you about next week. Let me know if we're on for dinner, okay?"

Penny was one of the few people he knew who still relied on actual phone calls instead of e-mail or texting. He dialed her number.

She picked up after the fourth ring.

"Hey James," she answered. "Just a sec, okay?"

She paused for a moment. He could hear rustling in the background on her end of the call. She sounded like she was in the middle of doing something. That was typical of Penny, who was a perpetual-motion machine when she wasn't asleep or meditating. He wondered if her constant activity was because of her physical handicap or in spite of it.

"Okay, I'm back. How you doing?" she asked cheerfully.

"Just calling to confirm dinner next week."

He heard more rustling of paper.

"What's all that noise in the background?" he asked. "Sounds like a giant hamster."

Penny laughed. "Sorry, I was just opening up a package when you called. I'll put it down 'til we're done. I was just kind of curious to see what was in it."

"Now I'm curious to know too," he said. "What kind of stuff?"

"Looks like a pair of welder's goggles and a top hat. But never mind."

"Wait, you can't follow the words 'welder's goggles and a top hat' with 'never mind.' I want to hear about this."

"I'm going to a steampunk convention in Vancouver next weekend. I'm cosplaying Kenneth Branagh's version of Doctor Loveless from *Wild Wild West*. I'm getting my costume together. You should see what I'm doing to my wheelchair. I built a smokestack for it and I've got a little dry ice compartment so it will actually look like steam is coming out of the pipe. I'm going to blow everybody's mind when I roll in."

Penny never disappointed him. She always had something up her sleeve.

"I didn't know you were into steampunk," said Verraday.

"One of my clients turned me on to it. They're a really fun bunch."

"Is this the 'neat thing' you said I might be interested in?"

"Yes. You should come along with me. Some of those steampunk cosplay girls are super cute. Maybe you could meet someone."

"I'd love to, but I can't."

"Now you sound like Dad."

That stopped him in his tracks. *Did* he sound like their father, always backing away from life instead of engaging with it? Ever since the accident that had killed their mother, their father had become withdrawn, even from his own children.

"You're a good-looking guy," Penny continued. "I could picture you in a zeppelin commander's outfit, or maybe more of a secret agent look: you know, Dalton Huxley, Chronomic Regulator."

"Can't say I'm familiar with that Mr. Huxley or with chronomic regulation," said Verraday with a trace of sarcasm.

Penny was undaunted. "Well, it's a Callahan frock coat, some double-row front-button trousers, a gambler hat. And a chronomic regulator."

"Chronomic regulator?"

"Looks sort of like a blunderbuss, except it's brass with vacuum tubes and it fires time-adjustment rays instead of bullets."

"You waited all this time to tell me about time-adjustment rays?"

Penny laughed. "It looks sharp, I'm telling you. Those steampunk girls would go nuts over you."

His first impulse was to dismiss Penny's idea as ridiculous. Then it hit him that that's exactly how their father would have reacted to anything that bore even the remotest suggestion of fun.

"Sounds good, but I've got to work on the midterm exam over the weekend. I don't want to give the students the same old crap the department's been recycling for the last ten years."

"Oh come on, James, have some fun. Twenty years from now, what are you going to care about more? Having created the bitchin'est psychology midterm exam in the history of U Dub, or making some cool friends and maybe meeting a nice girl who looks like Lady Mechanika."

Verraday had no idea who Lady Mechanika was, but whoever she was, she was probably a hell of a lot more fun than working on a midterm exam. Then he thought about Maclean and his promise to help her. He was beginning to regret having said yes.

"Honestly, I'd love to come, but I also promised someone I'd help them with something, and they'll probably need me this weekend."

"Is it really that important?"

"Yes. I'll tell you when I see you, okay?"

"Is she good-looking?"

"Yes, but it's not that kind of thing."

"There's no such thing as not that kind of thing."

"Will you stop?"

"All right. So are we still on for dinner next week? You're not going to bail on me, are you?"

"No. I'm looking forward to it."

"Great. Because I've got a new personal mobility device. I want you to see it."

He was a bit surprised that Penny was so excited about something as mundane as an electric buggy to get around in. But he guessed that if you didn't have the use of your legs, anything that removed a barrier would be exciting. Penny still played wheelchair basketball—aggressively. So instead of expressing his surprise, he just said, "Sure. I'd like to see it."

"Okay. See you then. Six o'clock?"

"Sounds good."

"And if you change your mind about the steampunk convention, let me know."

"I will."

After he hung up, Verraday went to his study, switched on his computer, and Googled the store Maclean had gone to check out. It was kinky and morbid but with a hint of kitsch. There was a lot of fetish gear and nineteenth-century curios that suggested a fixation on the macabre and sadistic. He clicked on the "About Us" link and was taken to an artfully composed, high-contrast photo portrait of the proprietor, one Aldous Whitney. He was half in shadow, half in light. There was a gorilla skull near Whitney's elbow, but the photo had intentionally left the details obscure. An eye socket, a couple of large canine teeth, and the dim outline of a cranial ridge were the only clues as to the identity of the strange object lurking in the dark. In the foreground was a taxidermy "mermaid." Verraday guessed that this "mermaid" was comprised of the head, arms, and chest of a macaque grafted to the silvery body of a carp. It was topped off by a blonde Barbie doll–style wig.

Within a glass counter just in front of Whitney's chest lay an array of disturbing devices that defied their beholder to envision precisely how they might be used. But judging by the various clamps, straps, prongs, nodules, and screws on the devices, he thought it safe to assume they were intended for people of either very sadistic or very masochistic tastes.

These were the accessories with which Whitney chose to associate himself in order to project a visual impression to the rest of the world. Sex and death. That, concluded Verraday, is what drove this man's psyche. Then again, sex and death is what drove most humans' psyches—at least if you believed Freud. Not that Verraday did.

Now Verraday turned his attentions from the props to the man himself. Whitney's facial expression was smug and his slight smile was almost a sneer. Verraday found it distasteful and vaguely provocative. The fact that Whitney enjoyed surrounding himself with the preserved corpses of animals that had first lost their lives and then their dignity through a taxidermist's whims was both morbid and sadistic. Whitney had created a sexual aura around himself because it was good for business. But he no doubt had also chosen this line of work because he enjoyed it and the attention it brought him.

Verraday looked Whitney up on Facebook. It didn't take long to find him. Clearly he was a man who enjoyed a party, particularly if that party was a fetish night. He had upwards of fifteen hundred Facebook friends, presumably too many for him to be on a first-name basis with them all. It appeared to be more of an affinity list. Checking Whitney's "likes" section, he discovered a swingers' club and semiannual fetish wear conventions in Seattle, Portland, San Francisco, and Vancouver. Many of the photos in his album had been taken at these events, where Whitney had a booth and was promoting his store and its wares. In all his photos, he was surrounded by a throng of people in fetish gear, mostly shapely young men and women. Like the ringleader at a circus, Whitney was the central focus in all of them. There were a number of people tagged in his photos, mostly young men. Verraday systematically clicked on the tags so that he was taken to their individual Facebook pages. It soon became apparent that Whitney's love of antiques did not extend to his partners, who were mainly young men with leather fetishes, and who appeared to be about half his age. In one photo, Whitney was locking lips on the dance floor with a man dressed in a kilt. In another photo, on the page of someone named Darryl G., who described his occupation as "model/agent provocateur," Whitney stood in the midst of a cheering crowd. He was posing like a warrior, holding two leashes, at the end of which were two muscular, twenty-something leather-clad men wearing studded collars and harnesses. One of them was "Darryl G." Verraday picked up his phone and keyed in Maclean's number.

CHAPTER 14

In interrogation room number six at the Seattle PD headquarters on Fifth Avenue, Maclean was leaning hard on Whitney. He was a creep, the sort of man who took pleasure in making women feel uncomfortable, and she despised him for it. And she was growing extremely tired of his flippant responses to her questions.

"Mr. Whitney, do you remember sending payments to Rachel Friesen or Alana Carmichael, or having phone calls with either of them?"

He responded in a tone of voice that was both dismissive and evasive, which punched a button inside Maclean that set her on slow boil. "Detective, I purchase vintage and antique curios from many sources for discerning collectors all over the world. I can't possibly remember all of them by name."

"I've got a hunch it's not their names that you'd remember. And neither one of them were old enough to qualify as antiques. But maybe this will jog your memory."

Maclean produced the photo of Alana Carmichael in the garden holding the tray of daiquiris, as well as the picture of Rachel Friesen that Kyle Davis had submitted with the missing persons report.

"I can show you receipts for my transactions with them."

"I'm sure you can. Though I don't think the IRS will take kindly to you writing off sex with hookers as antique purchases. You'll also have a tough time getting either one of them to corroborate your story, since by unhappy coincidence, they're both dead."

She laid the crime scene photos of the two murdered women down on the Formica desktop in front of Whitney and his lawyer.

Whitney's lawyer took a breath and leaned forward like he was about to say something in protest, but the sight of the beaten bodies of the two young women seemed to give him pause. Maclean thought she detected a flicker of revulsion in the lawyer's face. He folded his hands as he considered what to say, squeezing them so tightly that Maclean noticed his tendons were tensed and his knuckles were white.

"And besides the fact that Rachel Friesen and Alana Carmichael were both murdered," continued Maclean, "do you know the one other thing these girls had in common? You."

Maclean felt her phone buzzing. She was going to ignore it but then saw Verraday's name on the call display. She had intended to return his earlier message, but things had been moving along too quickly with the investigation. However, she felt that the crime scene photos of the two murdered women were just the thing to leave Whitney and his lawyer stewing over for a few minutes so decided to take the call.

"I'll be back in two," she said to the uniformed officer. She stepped out into the hall. Gazing through the two-way mirror, she saw a concerned expression on the lawyer's face and the suspect himself looking uncharacteristically flustered. She smiled to herself. She would enjoy making Whitney squirm.

"Hey Verraday. Good news. We've brought the owner of the shop in for questioning. His name is Whitney. He confessed to having made payments to both Alana and Rachel. He seems pretty rattled. I'm letting him and his lawyer chew on the crime scene photos for a couple of minutes. Then I'm moving in for the kill. I'm going to push him for a full confession."

"I don't think that's going to happen," replied Verraday.

"What do you mean? I've got his ass nailed to the wall."

"Whitney's not the killer."

"What are you talking about?"

"I've checked him out. He doesn't fit the profile. I know there's a commercial relationship between them, but there's no way it was ever intimate."

"With all due respect, James, this guy may not fit some academic 'profile' of a killer, but Whitney's walking like a duck and quacking like a duck. It makes my skin crawl just to breathe the same air as him. And there's another connection. He paid the exact same amount to both Alana and Rachel: five hundred dollars. I doubt they were both selling him their grandparents' silverware."

"I agree. He's involved with them, but it's not sexual. Whitney is gay. There are about a zillion pictures of him online with young men, and I'm pretty sure they're not discussing taxidermy. My guess is that he hired Rachel and Alana to have sex, but not with him. Maybe with his clients."

"Listen, James, I appreciate your help. But you didn't see Whitney's face when I laid those photos down on the table in front of him. He looked like he'd seen a ghost."

"Yes, because now he's afraid the Seattle PD will start shaking down his clients. You think of that?"

"No, but that's an excellent idea. I'll remind him of that as soon as I go back into the interrogation room. You know, I respect what you do with your profiling. I really do. But sometimes it's just good old-fashioned police legwork that gets the job done. And this is one of those times. This guy is a total creep. I've got my man."

"I'm sure Fowler thought the same thing."

"I am nothing like Fowler," Maclean shot back. "Listen, I've got to get back to the interrogation room before my interview cools down. Trust me, I've got this under control. I'll be in touch when everything's wrapped up."

"Wait, no—"

Maclean ended the call and reentered the interrogation room, where Whitney and his lawyer were huddling together, whispering something. She felt her cell phone vibrating again.

Jesus, you're stubborn, she thought, then clicked the deny button to send Verraday to voice mail. She strode across to the table and stood over Whitney, taking some private pleasure out of the way her physical proximity seemed to irritate his lawyer.

"Okay, where were we?" she asked.

"Let's see," said Whitney, pantomiming someone earnestly searching their memory. "Oh, yes, I remember now. You were becoming tedious."

She felt the heat rising in her cheeks and fought an urge to slap Whitney hard enough to rattle his fillings. Instead she leaned in just inches from his face, intentionally close enough that he could feel the heat of her breath on his skin, the way he had done it to her in his shop.

"Listen to me, you little turd, if you think I'm tedious now, just wait till we've been here for ten hours and I've asked you the same questions twenty-seven times just because I'm getting paid overtime for this and you're not."

Whitney flinched. It was small pleasures like this that helped make up for the many frustrations of being a detective and dealing with scumbags.

As she was savoring Whitney's discomfort, her phone began vibrating once more. Verraday again. She felt her anger rising hot within her, pissed off now at both Verraday *and* Whitney. She turned her phone off completely. In the five seconds it took Maclean to deal with the distraction of her phone, Whitney's lawyer had recovered enough to mount a counterattack.

"Detective Maclean, you're attempting to intimidate my client. I must ask that you keep your distance."

"It's okay, Frank," said Whitney with easy familiarity. Then he turned to Maclean and gave her a smile that was almost a leer.

"You know, Detective, if you ever want to trade in that frowsy pantsuit for something a little strappier— maybe boots, a corset, and a whip? I could get you eight hundred dollars an hour just for dishing out that attitude . . . and a bit of light punishment. There are some very wealthy and respectable people in Seattle who would just love to take orders for a change instead of giving them. If you want, I can even—"

"Just shut the fuck up," shouted Maclean, annoyed as much by Verraday as by Whitney. "You do not talk unless I ask you a question. Got it, asshole?"

"Oooh," responded Whitney with an exaggerated squeal. "Feisty too. But I don't think I want to answer any more of your questions right now."

"Good," replied Maclean. "Then you're welcome to camp out in the lockup until you're feeling more talkative. We've got some crackheads and Crips that I'm sure would love to meet you. Have a nice night, Mr. Whitney."

CHAPTER 15

Verraday's call went directly to voice mail on the third try. He knew that Maclean had turned off her cell so she could ignore him.

"Damn it, Maclean. I'm telling you, the killer's still out there. And you know what that means. Call me."

Verraday terminated the call and put his phone down. Agitated, he went to the kitchen, took his Seattle World's Fair tumbler out of the dish rack, then grabbed the bottle of brandy from the counter and went back upstairs to his den. He unscrewed the cap and was about to pour it, saw that it was still early, then screwed the cap back on the bottle and put it up on his bookcase where it wouldn't be within immediate reach. *Damn it.* Maclean's comment about good old-fashioned legwork stung him. But maybe there was something to it. He was already certain about the psychology of the victims and the perpetrator or perpetrators. But that wasn't going to bring them any closer to catching the killer. Not yet. There was a missing piece of the puzzle that they had to find first.

He pulled up the screengrab that Kyle Davis had taken of Rachel Friesen dancing with the unidentified blonde girl. She might be able to tell them what Rachel no longer could. He zoomed in on her to look for any identifying marks. She had lots of piercings, including one in her nose, but all the studs and rings were nondescript. Her legs were mercifully free of the tattoos that marred so many otherwise beautiful young women these days. But that would make it harder to identify her. He scanned her chest, arms, and face. Finally, he spotted something distinctive. On her shoulder was a tattoo of the Norse goddess Freya.

Verraday reasoned that since this unknown young woman had been part of Rachel's scheme to work the webcam sex circuit doing girl-on-girl scenes, there was a better-than-even chance that she too might have a web page on Assassin Girls. He went to the site and scanned through hundreds of photos of alt girls: brunettes, blondes, redheads, girls with black hair, and girls whose hair was streaked with pink or maroon or blue. But the blonde woman from the screengrab remained elusive.

He decided to be more direct and typed in a search for "Escorts + Seattle." There were pages and pages of links and scores of girls on each, hundreds even on some of them. He worked methodically through each site. His task of searching for the unknown blonde was made more difficult by the fact that most of the photos were cropped so that they stopped just above the chin, or the faces had been pixilated to protect the identity of the girl posting the ad. There was a mind-boggling assortment of young women offering themselves. Many claimed to be university students. He wondered if it was true, if any of the young women who sat in his lecture hall twice a week had been driven to the sex trade as the only way to finance their education, forced to pay tuition fees that were twice as high as what their parents and most of their clients had had to pay. He felt a pang of depression at that thought, then returned to scanning the photos. He went through another two hundred or so and was about to take a break, when he spotted a blonde whose face, like most of the others, had been intentionally blurred. Her listing identified her as "Destiny." Her hair was longer than that of the blonde in the screengrab and was pulled up into a French twist, with several long strands left hanging down on either side of her obscured face. Her body was wrapped in a black latex dress that clung as tightly to her as a secret, covering the young woman from her wrists up to her neck, and all the way down to midthigh. Although there were no identifying features visible on Destiny, there was something familiar about her. Verraday pulled up Kyle Davis's screengrab.

His pulse began to race. He realized then it wasn't the pixilated girl he had recognized. It was the dress. In her ad on the escort site, the faceless blonde named Destiny was wearing the same dress that Rachel was wearing in Kyle's photo of her and the blonde dancing together. If Verraday's hunch was right, then Destiny and Rachel, like a lot of young female friends who were on tight budgets, had been sharing wardrobes to get the most fashion bang for the buck. Verraday clicked on the link to the young woman's gallery of thumbnail photos. In all of them, her face was pixelated, but the camera explored her body voyeuristically, in ways designed to arouse desire in a potential customer. Verraday scrolled through a dozen of them. Then he spotted it: the Freya tattoo.

This woman was one of the last people to see Rachel alive, and she might provide the clues they needed to catch Rachel's killer. And, Verraday realized, she might be in danger herself. Verraday groped around the site, looking for a contact link. He went back to Destiny's main page and at the bottom, under her description, found a text number. He grabbed his cell and quickly typed, "Hello, Destiny. I would like to hear from you as soon as possible. Please message me anytime." He hit send.

He debated calling Maclean again. Maybe she'd pick up this time. So he gave it a try but got her voice mail again. Frustrated, he grabbed the bottle of brandy off his bookcase, hesitated, then thought, *Fuck it*, and poured himself a double shot.

★   ★   ★

Verraday had forgotten to set his alarm. He had awakened several times during the night, his mind beset by disturbing thoughts and images. He hated that state, that limbo that provided neither the rejuvenation of sleep nor the clarity of wakefulness. He had a slight headache from the brandy, so he took some ibuprofen. As a result of oversleeping, he didn't have time to go to the gym to blow away the cobwebs. He had to content himself with some stretches followed by push-ups, crunches, and free weights. The fog of the brandy and his troubled sleep began to fade away a bit.

What wasn't fading away was his foul mood at being dismissed by Maclean, practically fired. Not that he could be fired. He wasn't getting paid for this. Hadn't even wanted to take this on. It wasn't his job. If he'd told his lawyer he was helping out a homicide cop, he'd have gotten a warning that he was endangering his own case.

Even so, Maclean's lack of faith irked him. Verraday felt certain about the killer still being out there. He checked his phone. Destiny still hadn't texted him back. He tried again in case she was a morning person.

He headed for the foyer to pull on his boots and bomber jacket. Evidently Destiny *was* a morning person, because by the time Verraday had stepped onto his front porch, he heard the beep that alerted him to an incoming text. He took out his phone and saw that it was from her.

"Hey creeper, stop sending me messages or I'll call the cops. Now fuck off and leave me alone."

Verraday felt a sudden twinge of shame from the hostile reaction he had provoked from the sender. His intent was to protect her, but he couldn't deny that his chivalry was tinged with some attraction, and he wondered if somehow she had picked up on that. Between the vestiges of a mild hangover, Maclean's abrupt termination of his involvement in the case, and now this scathing rebuke from a stranger he'd try to help, he had a momentary urge to erase the chastising message and make it go away as if it had never existed. Make all of it go away. But he resisted that impulse in case the message would somehow be useful in the future. He slipped his cell phone into his jacket and locked the door. He checked his watch and saw that he had hurried through his morning ablutions and exercise so effectively that he was actually a few minutes ahead of schedule, so he decided to walk to the campus instead of taking his car.

Verraday made sure his front gate was latched behind him then set off on foot, walking south a few blocks then cutting through Ravenna Park over the Twentieth Avenue pedestrian bridge. As he crossed the gully, he noticed that the leaves of the maple trees were turning color now, the green giving way to yellow and orange at the tips. It would advance slowly but relentlessly over the next few weeks until the life had been choked from the leaves. Then they would disengage, drift down into the ravine below to be returned to the earth. He always felt ambivalent about the fall. The harvest and the autumn colors gave him a sense of comfort and continuity, but there was an unsettling duality to it. It was fleeting. The bounty and brilliant colors were followed by the inevitable months of bleakness. It gave him a vague sense of depression. He mused over the emotions that were stirred up in him every year at this time. Was it some metaphor for life that he hadn't decoded yet? Or was it just that the literal representation of the nature of life itself, no metaphor required, that released darkness into every corner of his consciousness?

It wouldn't be long until the Thanksgiving decorations went up in the drugstores and supermarkets—uncharacteristically jovial Puritans as well as smiling images of their unsuspecting victims, the turkeys, and their equally unsuspecting victims, the Native North Americans. Thanksgiving for Verraday was an early reminder of how his family had been torn apart. The day after Thanksgiving, when those absurd decorations came down, the blandly cheerful Santas and elves and reindeer would go up, and the air in every mall and shop would be filled with insipid versions of Christmas music. Worst of all for him was the dreaded "Deck the Halls," because it had been playing on the car radio when Officer Robson T-boned their family's vehicle and had become frozen in Verraday's mind as the official soundtrack to his mother's death and his sister's lifetime of disablement.

Verraday exited the park, continuing down Twentieth toward the university. Despite the disquieting chain of thoughts set off by seeing the changing color of the big-leaf maples, his blood was beginning to pump, the ibuprofen had kicked in, and by the time he reached the campus, the last unpleasant vestiges of the hangover and his insomnia had nearly faded away.

CHAPTER 16

The class that Verraday was teaching that morning was Introduction to Criminal Psychology. Some of the students who took the course were also in his cognitive psychology class. Some planned to make a career in psychology or criminology. And then there were the ones who enrolled because they had developed a morbid interest in serial killers by watching too many documentaries on TLC or Netflix. There was always one in every class—that is, *if* you were lucky and weren't subjected to two or even several of them.

Verraday was about ten minutes into the lecture when a hand went up in the second row. It was Koller again. It was always Koller. After ignoring him long enough to finish his own point and remind the kid which of them was in charge, Verraday glanced at him.

"Yes, Mr. Koller, you have a question?"

The gangly youth nodded. "Yeah, like, I saw this documentary on Charles Manson. They said he had what they called 'indescribable power' over his family of followers, and they saw him as the modern-day messiah. He had to be pretty smart to manipulate all those people into killing other people for him, don't you think?"

"Yes," replied Verraday, "Charles Manson is so smart that he's spent approximately eighty-seven percent of his adult life in jail. He got caught within three months of ordering people to kill for him and won't be eligible for parole until he's ninety-two. He didn't even get the house address right. He didn't make any significant income off his criminal activities nor did he wield any real power, except over a handful of social misfits and certain areas of the media that benefitted from peddling his story. For the record, his IQ is reportedly one hundred and nine—slightly above average, but not exactly rocket scientist material. I would wager most of the people in this room would score at least that high on an IQ test. Not *everyone*, but most."

There were scattered giggles in the room. The other students were as sick of Koller as Verraday was. But Koller showed no signs of giving up.

"But don't you think he must have had something going for him to persuade people to kill for him?"

"Yes. What he had going for him is that he is a psychopath who, because of his neurology, is incapable of feeling emotional empathy for other people. He used techniques he read in a book by Dale Carnegie called *How to Win Friends and Influence People*. But his shtick didn't work on most well-adjusted human beings. The members of his so-called 'family' were unbalanced and emotionally vulnerable. You don't have to be a genius to influence weak people. You just need to be completely unscrupulous. Gary Ridgway, a.k.a. the Green River Murderer, killed forty-nine women right here in Washington. He had an IQ of eighty-four. That's only five points above what's considered impaired. I wouldn't have trusted him to rotate my tires. Richard Macek was a serial killer from Illinois. Along with raping and killing his victims, he liked to bite them while in a state of sexual frenzy, so not a particularly rational behavior. He bit his victims so hard that he left distinctive wounds all over their bodies. When he finally realized that the marks he left would enable police to identify him, he took the rather extreme precaution of having all his teeth pulled out and replaced with dentures so the bite marks couldn't be matched to him. In my book, yanking out your teeth is a long way to go just to indulge a momentary impulse and definitely not indicative of high intelligence. My point is that it's not superior intellect that gives psychopaths power over other people. What gives psychopaths power is that they don't have feelings for the people they hurt, and they don't play by the same rules as the rest of us."

Koller still wasn't done. "But then doesn't that make them more successful than other people from an evolutionary standpoint?"

"That's a common impression perpetuated by *some* media," said Verraday. "In reality, yes, certain psychopaths do extremely well because they're intelligent enough to make it work for them. But they're not killers. At least not directly. They might run a hedge fund, for example, and buy the rights to a lifesaving drug and jack up the price by twelve hundred percent to increase profits and share value. People who then can't afford the drug might die as a result. But no one will call the hedge fund manager a serial killer. In fact, they'll say he's a genius and give him a two-million-dollar bonus. Or he might be the CEO of a company that closes down manufacturing operations here, throwing thousands of Americans out of work. Then he exports the jobs to China, where people who live under a brutal totalitarian regime are forced to work seventy-hour weeks for two hundred dollars a month. So many workers there kill themselves that they have to put up suicide nets around the factories. But we don't call that guy a serial killer either, do we? No, we give him a multimillion-dollar bonus too. Now *that's* a successful psychopath. Not some loser who has to have his teeth pulled out because he couldn't control his impulse to strangle someone and bite them in the ass."

Verraday saw some skeptical looks from some of the business students who were taking his course as an elective, probably having thought that finding out about serial killers would make a pleasant diversion from calculating gross domestic product and the yields on convertible debentures. They could give him all the skeptical looks they wanted, thought Verraday. But in a few years, most of those business students would be out in the corporate world. And the odds were extremely good that all those people smiling at him dubiously from the back rows would at some point become victims of a psychopath: a coworker who would take credit for their best ideas while simultaneously sabotaging them behind their back; a boss who would make them work twelve hours a day for years, control even their minutest decisions, then when something went wrong, blame them for incompetence and have them escorted out the front door by security. Ideally after screwing them out of a pension.

"I'm serious," Verraday continued. "Psychopaths are believed to represent only one percent of the general population. But some studies suggest that as many as one in ten CEOs are psychopaths. Do the math. *That's* where it's an evolutionary advantage: in a corrupt system that values profits over human welfare. But a serial killer? Sorry, no evolutionary advantage to murdering your fellow human beings then becoming the target of society's retribution. So to get back to your original question, just because someone is a psychopathic killer, it does not mean they're smart like Hannibal Lecter and can talk somebody into biting their own tongue off. It is entirely the invention of fiction writers, though I can certainly understand the appeal. There are times I wish I knew how to talk people into biting their tongues off."

There were titters of laughter in the lecture hall. Verraday felt a pang of guilt over his not-particularly-subtle put-down of Koller but decided it was worth it. A bit of applied psychology and tough love was exactly what this kid needed.

"Now, if we can move along, I've still got a lot of material to cover today. Mr. Koller, if you'd like to discuss this further, you're welcome to come see me in my office during the scheduled time, between nine and ten AM Thursdays."

Koller looked pissed off, but settled in and didn't ask any more questions for the rest of the lecture. Ninety minutes later, Verraday was happy to hear the rustling of backpacks and paper and the tearing of Velcro that indicated the end of today's class.

CHAPTER 17

Verraday's agitated mood began to return when he got home. He was still chafing from Maclean's rejection of his help. But he decided that sharing the information about Destiny with Maclean was the right thing to do anyway, even if she was too damned bullheaded to do anything useful with it. He grabbed his cell and typed in the contact information along with a terse message: "In case you care, the other girl in the photo with Rachel is named Destiny. This is where you can reach her." Then he hit send. That was it. He was done with Maclean and the investigation now. He had fulfilled his obligation, done as much as he could for the cause of justice.

He resolved to get a head start on the midterm exam, on the off chance that he decided he wouldn't feel completely foolish going to the steampunk convention that weekend with Penny. So he poured himself a glass of wine, turned on the gas fireplace, and sat down on the sofa with the coursework and his laptop, determined to write some new questions this year. He spent the next hour wading through various scholarly papers and writing, and, satisfied that he'd now come up with the beginnings of something that was not only fresh but also genuinely useful to his students, he put his work away and retired upstairs to the den to check his e-mail.

Most of the messages were questions about the midterm. Predictably, there was one from Koller, continuing to argue the point about psychopaths being more intelligent than the average person and including a link to a dubious pop psychology website that reinforced his belief.

Then there was an e-mail from Jensen, the mousy, nondescript girl.

"Dear Professor Verraday, I have a question about the course material. I'm still not entirely clear on the difference between modus operandi and signature in serial killers. The material from the FBI suggests that a criminal usually has a 'signature' that identifies them. But couldn't a repeat offender confuse investigators by intentionally changing their signature?"

"That's an interesting question," Verraday replied, "To a logical mind, that seems like the obvious thing to do. But the short answer is, killers with a signature behavior do what they do because it's what gratifies them. A strangler would feel cheated if he had to shoot someone. Interviews with convicted killers have confirmed this. It's analogous to the way certain people always have coffee after dinner, while someone else might prefer tea, and a third person would choose brandy instead. They all eat dinner, but their rituals around it are different. And while they savor their own rituals, they would find each other's rituals unsatisfying. I'm glad that you raised this issue, and I will bring it up in the next class."

When he closed her e-mail, he saw that three junk e-mails had popped up on his screen in the meantime. He was surprised. His spam filter usually caught them, but there were always exceptions. The first one had a subject line indicating that hot Russian MILFS were looking for relationships with him. The second one hinted at some especially repugnant form of kiddie porn. He promptly deleted both without looking at them.

The third one was an announcement of a special photographic exhibition of Bettie Page at the MoMA in New York. It sounded interesting. So he clicked the mouse and opened the e-mail. He didn't notice a date, but there was a vintage photo of Bettie Page, wearing a merry widow, brandishing a whip and her trademark grin. Bettie was campy but sexy. And more to the point, as a twelve-year-old, Verraday had stumbled across postcards of her in a used books and comics store in Pike Place Market. He'd had no idea at the time who Bettie Page was, but the effect on his hormone-flooded adolescent brain was as profound as if some alternate-universe fairy godmother in black had tapped him with her wand. Bettie and her provocative and highly distinctive lingerie had been imprinted on his erotic sensibilities then and there. And as his first sexual icon, she still held considerable sway. Not enough to make him fly to New York City just to see an exhibit of photos that he could probably find anywhere on the Internet, mind you, but he couldn't resist at least checking the web page. He clicked on the link. A moment later, he was gazing at a montage of Bettie photos. In one, a corseted Bettie was being spanked by a woman in stockings and a bra. He'd seen that one dozens of times. Ditto on the next picture, in which Bettie was tied up and gagged. In another one, she was taking part in a clumsily staged catfight with a blonde woman. It was classic Bettie Page—erotic, racy yet somehow slightly goofy in spite of the taboo nature of the acts depicted. It was a great idea for a MoMA exhibit, thought Verraday, but the images were a bit well worn and predictable for a gallery whose collection included some of the most imaginative and sublime works of Frank Gehry, Chagall, and Van Gogh.

Then down the side of the screen, he noticed a few thumbnails, photos of Bettie that he'd never seen before. They teased with shadow and light and were artistic, even highbrow, compared to the workmanlike creations of Bettie's usual photographers, Irving Klaw and Bunny Yeager, which had become famous for their subject matter rather than the quality of their execution.

One was a photo of her torso, breasts shapely and full, restrained within a 1950s-style black bullet bra. Her midriff was bare. The photo was cropped so that it stopped just below her navel. Uncharacteristically, Bettie's face was absent from the picture. Only her chin entered the top of the frame. The second photo was exquisitely shot. It featured Bettie in silhouette, posed like a burlesque version of Picasso's *Blue Nude*, backlit by a soft light, her face obscured by shadow but revealing just enough that Verraday could make out a hint of a seductive smile. Verraday clicked on the next thumbprint. It was a close-up of Bettie's legs wrapped in sheer black stockings, her thighs angled artfully inward in a way that encouraged the viewer's eye to follow the line of the black garters up her skin. Then it toyed with the viewer by stopping the barest fraction of an inch short of where the lines of her inner thighs would have converged. Verraday clicked on this thumbnail too so that it went full screen. It was beautifully shot. He admired not only the erotic quality of the photo but the aesthetic way in which it had been lit and framed, carefully designed to arouse the viewer and suggest unseen destinations withheld from the eye, but not from the imagination. Verraday couldn't recall ever having come across this photo of Bettie before. His heart was beating fast, so that when his cell phone beside him unexpectedly rang, he started, something he almost never did.

It was late now. He hoped it wasn't a student. He had been explicit about not being called at night, but to his annoyance, the university directory had published cell numbers for the professors, so it was always a possibility. The display read "Private Caller."

He waited a couple of rings so that he wouldn't sound breathless from the surprise.

"Hello," he answered.

"It's Maclean. Sorry to call so late. I hope I'm not interrupting anything."

"Just answering student e-mails," Verraday lied. "What's up?"

Maclean's voice was tense. "Can you meet me in about twenty minutes?"

"I guess so. At the café?"

"No. I'm off duty, and I could use a drink. I'll give you the address."

CHAPTER 18

The Bellingham was Maclean's suggestion. Verraday had never been there before, but the pub had a warm, low-key ambience that immediately made him feel relaxed and at home. The bar was stained walnut. It stretched half the length of the room and matched the wainscoting as well as the booths on the opposite wall. Frosted-glass pendant lamps hung from the ceiling above the aisle, bathing the room in soft, indirect light. The music was turned up loud enough to ensure that they couldn't be overheard, but not so much that they'd have to raise their voices above a normal conversational level.

As usual, Maclean was already there. Verraday was grateful to see that she'd taken up a position in one of two wingback chairs by the fireplace, in an alcove that would give them some privacy. She wore a close-fitting gray sweater, a denim skirt hemmed just above her knees, and black boots. Her hair was down. It was longer than he'd imagined it to be. He experienced a pang of regret. He was sorry that their trust in each other had hit such a

big bump. He didn't want to be angry with her. He liked
this woman, didn't want to feel estranged from her. But
regardless, as he greeted her and sat down in the wing-
chair, he couldn't help feeling some distance between
them, on his own side if not from hers.

The waiter, a bearded young man with an affable
manner and an easy smile, came by. Maclean ordered a
vodka and soda. Verraday asked for a recommendation
on a dark ale and chose what the waiter suggested, a
local brew from the Willamette Valley. After the waiter
left, Verraday sank back into his comfortable wingback
chair. He loved the light and warmth from the fireplace
and, under other circumstances, could have dozed off.
But the situation he found himself in was far from con-
ducive to sleep.

"What's up?" he asked.

Maclean checked to make sure that no one had come
within earshot, then leaned forward in her wingback chair.

"There's been another murder."

Verraday felt a leaden anticipation in his chest.
"Who is it?"

Maclean pursed her lips. "The girl from the screengrab. Destiny. The one you sent me the message about."

"Oh fuck."

"A construction worker found her body this afternoon in a vacant lot behind a demolition site."

"How was she killed?"

"The MO is the same as with Alana Carmichael and
Rachel Friesen. Heavy beating with a leather belt, then
strangulation, first with hand pressure, then with a garrote. Not a single defensive wound anywhere."

Verraday felt a crushing sense of failure. "I tried to warn her. I texted her twice. First last night, then again this morning. She finally responded with a message telling me to fuck off."

"I don't think you—or anyone—could have saved her. According to the coroner, she'd been dead for about twenty-four hours."

Maclean saw the dejection on Verraday's face. "There's nothing you could have done," she said decisively. "It was probably the killer who texted you, trying to buy himself some time."

Verraday felt revolted to realize he had unwittingly been trading text messages with a murderer. A murderer who could now potentially identify him from his phone number.

"I can't believe I got sucked in," said Verraday.

"James, you had no way of knowing. He fooled all of us. So far. But we *will* get him. I can find out where the text originated by having Destiny's phone signal triangulated, but my guess is that it won't be from the kill site or the dump site."

"No," agreed Verraday. "This guy's much too clever to do that. Wouldn't surprise me if he purposely sent it from near her home address, if he knew it."

"We haven't found her purse, phone, or any ID for that matter," said Maclean. "He probably knew where she lived from her driver's license."

"How did you know who she was?"

"The screenshots you sent over."

They stopped speaking for a moment as the waiter returned with the drinks. Verraday noticed that like the waitress at the Trabant, this waiter seemed to be aware that his arrival at their table caused a lull in the conversation. But unlike the young woman at the Trabant, their waiter just gave them a friendly, confident smile and told them to enjoy their drinks. Then he returned to the bar to polish the pint glasses with a cloth, humming contentedly. Why did some people react so differently to identical stimuli, wondered Verraday? How much was nature and how much was nurture? It was the eternal question that vexed psychologists. It certainly vexed him.

He took a sip of his dark ale. It was deep and rich, with just enough bitterness from the hops to balance the sweetness of the malt. He savored it and felt himself relaxing slightly. Maclean took a healthy sip of her vodka and soda.

"Are you willing to come back to the case?" she asked.

"I'm here, aren't I?" responded Verraday. He was still smarting though. "But are you going to trust me from now on?"

Maclean took another sip of her drink before replying.

"I wouldn't be here if I didn't," she said, shifting slightly in the wingback chair.

Verraday was surprised by how uncomfortable Maclean suddenly looked. It was the first time he'd seen anything other than self-assurance in her manner. He hadn't intended to rake her over the coals for being wrong about Whitney. It wouldn't serve either of them, so he moved the conversation back to the case.

"Was there any escalation in the level of violence?"

Maclean nodded her head slowly. "Yes."

She toyed with the ice in her glass for a moment before looking up.

"This son of a bitch really went to town on her. She's got marks on her back that might be burns. Take a look."

Maclean took a folder out of her briefcase and handed it across to Verraday. He slipped the eight-by-ten crime scene photo out and held it so that the fireplace light allowed him to get a better view of it.

"Christ almighty."

Verraday had seen a lot in the course of his work, but the pairs of dotted burn marks down the spine and up the inner thighs of the girl known only as "Destiny" were new to him. It was a level of sadism he'd only read about from political death squads or inquisitional torturers. The pain must have been prolonged and excruciating.

"I haven't seen anything like this before," said Maclean. "We're waiting for forensics, but I'm guessing it was done with a cattle prod."

"What about Whitney? What did you find out?" asked Verraday.

"You were right about him. At least it looks like it so far. He claims he only hired Alana Carmichael and Rachel Friesen as booth bunnies for The Victorian Closet at fetish nights where he was promoting the store."

"Strange that neither one of them appear in any of his Facebook albums."

"He says he was afraid it would be bad for his business if it got out that two of his models had been murdered. So he deleted every image of them from the store's site and his personal page before the press could get hold of them. I'm still having forensics check out his shop and backroom, but he's got an airtight alibi on this latest murder: he was in a holding cell down at the station when it happened."

"Do you have any idea who Destiny really is?"

"Not yet. There are no recent missing persons reports that match. That cell phone you texted was prepaid and unregistered. Whoever Destiny really is, she was probably afraid of being stalked. For good reason. So she made sure her phone was untraceable. As for the body, our killer didn't miss a beat there either. The coroner says the corpse had been washed with great care. No trace of anything on it, not even soap residue."

"So what's our next move?"

"We caught one break. That escort service site you found her on is based in Seattle. I'll pay a visit to their office tomorrow morning. You want to come along?"

"Yeah."

Verraday still had more than half a pint of ale left in his glass, and Maclean had slowed down on her vodka and soda too. He began to wonder why she had asked him out for a drink instead of just giving him the information when she had called him. She gazed down contemplatively, then turned to look directly at him.

"Listen, there's something else."

"Yes?"

"That cop that you say ran the red light and hit your family's car when you were a kid."

"Robson, yeah."

"I overheard two of the old timers talking today. Uniform cops from the traffic division. He's dead."

Verraday felt like he'd been hit in the chest with a hammer. "Dead? How?"

"The story is that he had an accident cleaning his revolver."

Verraday sat stunned for a moment. He barely knew where to start.

"What else do you know about him?" Verraday asked.

"He retired from the Seattle PD eight years ago. Lived alone in a four-season cottage not far from Everett."

"When did it happen?"

"A week ago. I looked into it a little for you. They did a blood test on Robson. He had a blood alcohol level of point-one-one. That's well over the line for legally impaired. You probably won't find that surprising."

Verraday nodded agreement.

"Apparently he had Ativan in his system too," said Maclean.

"That part does surprise me," said Verraday. "Robson never struck me as the type who'd suffer from anxiety disorders. More the kind of person who would cause them."

"Robson's doctor never prescribed Ativan to him, but obviously anyone who drinks that heavily is doing a lot of self-medicating."

Verraday had a momentary flash of self-consciousness, wondering what Maclean would think if she'd had any idea of his own daily alcohol intake. And he'd only recently tossed out his stock of Ativan after his pharmacist, a soft-spoken young woman from Hong Kong, warned him in her mild and diplomatic way that many doctors were unaware that the drug was highly addictive and that if he had anxiety issues, there were safer ways of dealing with it.

"He probably bought his Ativan online without a prescription," Maclean continued. "In any case, the coroner in Everett has ruled it an accidental death. End of story. But I thought you'd want to know."

Verraday nodded. "Thanks."

Neither of them spoke for a long moment. Verraday distractedly ran a hand through his hair.

"I almost can't believe this has happened," he said at last. "I always thought I'd feel thrilled when I heard that he'd died."

"And now?"

"And now I feel sort of cheated."

"How so?" asked Maclean.

Verraday no longer felt distant from Maclean. He liked this woman, had an urge to share secrets with her, and for a moment, considered telling her the truth: that he felt cheated because he wasn't the one who had gotten to pull the trigger. But he decided it might be impolitic to tell an officer of the law that he had homicidal impulses toward someone who had just blown his brains out under mysterious circumstances.

So instead he answered, "Because now there's no chance that he will ever be brought to justice."

"Maybe it's karma catching up to him," replied Maclean.

"My sister believes in that kind of stuff. Do you?" asked Verraday.

"Unfortunately, after eight years as a cop, I haven't seen anything to convince me of its existence. I just said it because I saw that Buddha in your office. Thought maybe that's what you believed. But I hope there is such a thing. Because I see way too many people getting away with hurting other people. That's the part of this job that bothers me the most." Maclean took another sip of her drink. Then she leaned toward Verraday and spoke softly. "Can I ask you something? About the car crash?"

"Sure," replied Verraday. "I'm not precious about it. Been over it way too many times for that."

"Are you one hundred percent certain that it happened the way you said it did in your police file? That Robson was at fault?"

"I'm positive," replied Verraday. "Penny remembered it the same way as me, right up to when Robson hit us. Then she blacked out. I was in the rear seat on the passenger's side, farthest from the point of impact, so I got the least of it. I was conscious the whole time. And I remember everything like it was this morning."

"You remember it through personal experience. But that can be subjective, can't it? Speaking as a psychologist, how do you *know* that's what happened?"

"Science. It's called flashbulb memory. And it has been tested and proven. It's a moment in time that's so vivid, so emotionally arousing that the episode part of your memory takes a snapshot of it, and you remember key details vividly and forever. The cops that interviewed me afterward tried to get me to change my story to say my mother ran the red light. That's how false memory syndrome happens. But not in my case. I knew she hadn't. And I still know that. Because I can still picture the green traffic light in front of our car in the intersection. 'Deck the Halls' was playing on the radio. I remember the peppermint smell of the candy cane that my sister Penny had in her mouth. I might have only been eight, but unlike Robson, I wasn't drunk. I remember him coming to the window and shining a flashlight in on us. I could smell the booze on his breath. Whiskey. I knew what it was because I used to smell the same thing on my old man's breath once in a while, like at New Year's and Christmas Eve, when he was giving me a goodnight kiss and tucking me into bed. My dad wasn't much of a drinker though. At least not before the accident."

"You really remember all that?"

"Let me ask you something. What were you doing when you first found out about the 9/11 attacks?"

Maclean gazed off into the middle distance, then turned back to Verraday.

"I was in my senior year of high school. It was a quarter after seven in the morning. I'd just gotten up. I had this biology assignment with a question about pathogens that I was having trouble with. Since my mom's a nurse, I knew she'd know that answer, so I was planning to ask her about it. But when I came out of my room, I looked down the hall and saw that her eyes were shiny, like she'd been crying. She was watching CNN, which I remember thinking was unusual, because my mother never watched television in the morning. When she saw me, she said, 'Somebody flew two jets into the World Trade Center. And one of the towers just came down.' She was wearing her green scrubs, getting ready to start her shift at the hospital. She told me that we should both go to the Red Cross later that day and donate blood because they were going to need it. I remember seeing the second tower coming down. I'll never forget that feeling."

"See? That's what I'm talking about," said Verraday. "An event like that is so momentous that our mind freezes everything in time around it. Just like you remember that your mom was wearing her green scrubs and that you had a biology assignment. That's how I know I saw what I saw when my mom died. Especially because the police pressured me so hard to change my story. Even at that age, it struck me as strange that they kept badgering me, so it kind of made me work it through in my mind."

"Is that when you became interested in memory?"

"I never thought about it before. But I guess so. Memory and the truth. And fairness. Or all of it. I mean, it's not like I had any idea what a psychologist was when I was eight. But I do know that it was the first time in my life that I'd felt outrage about being treated unfairly and being browbeaten. Up until then, I was like most boys. I idolized cops. They were the heroes from movies and TV shows, keeping us safe and putting all the 'bad guys' in jail, right? Even after Robson hit our car, I didn't think of it at first as anything but a tragic accident. Not until he ran away and left us there to die, even when I called after him to help. Is that mentioned anywhere in the official files? That I called to him for help and that he ignored me?"

"No. Not exactly, at least. In the internal affairs report, he stated that he left the scene because he was in shock. He lived just a few blocks from the intersection. He said he ran home in a state of mental confusion.

Claimed that it was only after he got to his house that it started to sink in what had happened. He said he poured himself a few stiff shots of whiskey to steady his nerves. Then he called nine-one-one to report the accident."

"What do you believe?"

"I believe that Robson's description of his own actions after the collision fits the pattern of one of the oldest DUI dodges in the book. Leaving the scene of an accident because you're confused and in shock isn't nearly as serious as impaired driving causing death. That one gets you jail time. So if there's nobody around to stop them, a drunk driver can flee the scene, go home, say they had nothing before the accident and half a dozen when they got home. It means that any Breathalyzer test we give them is worthless in court. People do it all the time when they think they can get away with it."

"So you believe me?"

"Look, I was two years old when it happened. But from what I could find out, he didn't exactly have a stellar history on the force even before that night. Whatever anybody told you at the time, the truth is that after the accident, the department took him off the street, out of cars, and transferred him to a desk job until he retired. It's not an admission of guilt, but let me tell you, the Seattle PD doesn't take somebody off the street for no reason. Anyway, I'm sorry for what happened to you. It's a terrible thing to lose a parent. And to have it covered up."

"Well, you know how it feels."

"That I do," said Maclean.

The waiter glanced over in their direction. Maclean picked up on his cue.

"Want to stay for another?" she asked.

"Sure," said Verraday, "That'd be good."

Maclean signaled for another round of drinks. Verraday absent-mindedly tapped the rim of his glass.

"Out of curiosity, do you know Bosko?" he asked.

"Not really," Maclean replied. "Uniform cop. Passed him a couple of times in the station. Never spoken to him. I don't think he'll ever make detective or sergeant. Not after what happened with you. Even if the department won't admit it. Plus he doesn't have the smarts to be a senior officer. But whatever his faults, he's brave, I'll give him that."

"What makes you say that?"

"He saved a kid who fell into a storm sewer during a flood last spring. Went in after him without any backup or equipment. It was an extremely dangerous situation. He got a commendation for it."

"I can never understand that about cops," said Verraday. "I mean, *some* cops."

"What?"

"The fact that they seem to like kids so much. But only until they grow up. What's that about?"

"I can't speak for Bosko. But cops have a protective nature. Kids are easy to protect, philosophically speaking. They're pure and innocent. Unfortunately, by the time people grow up, you can't be as certain of their motives any more. That's why most of us get into this line of work. We want to be the people you once idolized, keeping everybody safe and putting all the 'bad guys' in jail, you know?"

"Right. Superheroes in blue."

"I suppose." Maclean grinned wryly. "Hey, speaking of superheroes, there's something else I've been wondering. Why did you ask Kyle Davis what the special power was that the kid said he'd like to have?"

Just then, the waiter came by with their drinks. Again, it caused a lull in their conversation, and again, unlike the waitress at the Trabant, the waiter just took it in stride that he'd arrived at a private moment.

"There you go, folks," he said with a smile, then quickly slipped away.

When the waiter had left, Verraday answered, "Partly it was a test to see if Davis actually had an answer or if he was just making it up, bullshitting us," replied Verraday. "And partly because I'm just curious about what kind of superpowers kids are into these days."

"Why? Did you ever wish for any superpowers when you were a kid?"

"Sure."

"What kind?" asked Maclean.

Verraday suddenly felt embarrassed. This was the second time tonight that it would have been more convenient to lie to Maclean. But he didn't want to lie to her. He wanted to tell her the truth. So he did.

"At first I wanted to have X-ray vision so I could peek through walls like Superman and see what was beneath women's clothes."

Maclean burst out laughing. "You were a naughty boy."

"I guess I was," said Verraday, annoyed to feel his cheeks getting warm.

"You're blushing," she said.

"What can I say?" he responded with a shrug.

"So you said, 'at first.' Does that mean you wanted a different superpower later on?"

Now Verraday really did feel like lying, just so he wouldn't add a depressing note to their conversation. But he was starting to like Maclean too much to be deceitful. So instead he told the truth.

"But then, after the accident, I wished I had a power ray that could stop a speeding car. I used to imagine myself shooting it out and redirecting Robson's car away from ours, so I could save my mom and my sister."

He paused.

"Sorry, I didn't mean to be a downer."

"Hey, I was the one who asked," said Maclean.

"So what about you?" asked Verraday. "Did you ever wish for a superpower?"

"Yeah. I wanted to be able to control time."

"What, like Doctor Who?"

"No, though a TARDIS would have been cool. I just wanted to go back in time so I could keep my dad from going to work the night that he died. Then I imagined myself staking out the warehouse and catching whoever started the fire, then turning him over to the police."

"And is that when you decided to become a cop?"

"That is *exactly* when I decided to become a cop. Now I have another question for you."

"Shoot."

"When you asked me the other night if I'd ever dated someone who was bipolar. Why did you want to know?"

"I wondered if you'd had that experience. It changes you."

"Who was it?"

"Somebody I met when I was in graduate school."

"A psychologist?"

"No, a singer in an alternative band."

"You dated a singer in an alt band?" she asked, teasing him a little.

"What?" said Verraday. He could feel the heat rising to his cheeks again. "What's so weird about that?"

"Nothing. Nothing weird at all," she said. "I'm just thinking that you are full of surprises. Picturing you in your wild years. What was her name?"

"Nikki."

"Was she beautiful?"

Verraday suddenly realized that he was feeling shy about discussing his love life with Maclean, and especially telling her about another woman's looks.

"She was attractive, sure," said Verraday, carefully omitting the word "beautiful."

"So how did you find out she was bipolar?"

"Mood swings were the first indication. Erratic behavior. But I ignored all the signs in the beginning. Just like Kyle Davis."

"When did it become obvious?"

Verraday smiled archly. "As an expert in human behavior, I'd have to say the big clue was the time she waltzed into my apartment at three in the morning with this crazed smirk on her face, stinking of cigarettes and bourbon after having sex with some guy she'd met four hours earlier."

"Ow. Sorry."

"It's okay. The only part that bothers me anymore is that I put up with her crap for weeks before it got to that point. It's too embarrassing to think I was ever that unassertive."

"You were young. None of us know anything at that age. And you're an idealistic and compassionate person. I can tell that just from spending this much time with you. That makes you vulnerable in one way, but in another way, it makes you stronger because you experience and understand life in ways that other people never come to terms with."

"That's a very generous assessment. So now that we've discussed my horror story, what was your worst experience with the opposite sex?"

Maclean suddenly looked serious. "It's way worse than yours, trust me," she said.

Maclean turned toward the waiter and signaled to him to bring the check.

"Hey," said Verraday. "You can't bail on me now."

By now the waiter was busy getting pints of Guinness for two happy-looking couples who had just come in together. Verraday marveled at how, with nothing but a smile, a nod of acknowledgement, and an eye movement, the waiter managed to convey that he'd be right with Maclean as soon as he'd finished.

Maclean turned back toward Verraday. "Seriously. I doubt if you really want to hear this story."

"Well seriously, yes. I do want to know," said Verraday.

Maclean took a sip of her vodka and soda. "Okay, here's the straight-up version. I used to be married. Fowler is the reason I'm divorced. He sexually assaulted me."

Verraday sat in silence, not knowing how to respond. His impulse was to offer some comforting words, but he knew from training and experience that he'd be more help to Maclean if he just invited her to talk, then let her.

"How did it happen?"

"I had been married nearly four years. My ex is in the Coast Guard. He was away for a couple of days on patrol duty. I was working robberies at the time. It was a Friday evening at the end of a busy week. I went out with the people from my squad to have some drinks and let off a little steam. We all got a bit tipsy but not out of control. A couple of hours later, Fowler and a few of his crew showed up. Fowler went to the bar and bought a round for everyone. About half an hour later, I started to feel tired, and I decided to head home. I was too drunk to drive, so I left my car in the lot. I said I was going to get a cab. Fowler played the chivalry card. He told me it wasn't a good idea for me to be out alone that late at night and that he was going to wait 'til I got a cab. It was raining like hell, so there was nobody on the street and no taxis anywhere. Fowler told me that since he'd only had two drinks, he'd give me a ride home. When we got to my place, he insisted on walking me to the door to make sure I got in safely. I tripped going up the steps and fell. I thought I'd broken my kneecap, it hurt so bad. I was surprised and a little embarrassed. I mean, I'd definitely had more than just a few, but I didn't think I was that sloppy and out of control. Fowler put his arm around me to help me up. I took my front door keys out of my purse, but I dropped them. I bent over to pick them up and started to get the spins. He laughed and reached for the keys, got them and opened the door to let me in. He told me I should go straight to bed. I said I could handle it from there.

"And that's the last thing I remember clearly until the next day. I blacked out. I didn't wake up until the next afternoon, when my husband came home and found me in bed. I had the worst hangover I've ever had in my life and the bedsheets were everywhere. I had this vague memory of Fowler on top of me and me trying to fight him off. But I couldn't remember the specifics."

"It's called anterograde amnesia," said Verraday. "Fowler probably roofied your drink and had it all planned out."

"And I was too stupid to see it."

"It's not your fault. We all have this social contract. That's what people like Gary Ridgway and Ted Bundy play on."

"Yes, but I'm supposed to be smart enough to see through that kind of bullshit."

"Fowler's a colleague, a fellow cop," said Verraday. "He's expected to uphold the law, not break it. There's no reason you would have anticipated him doing what he did."

"But everything about it played into my own carelessness. That's what bothers me the most. I charged him with sexual assault. I had bruises on my arms from where he pinned me down. But because I also had bruises on my knees and legs from when I tripped, Fowler's attorney argued that it all happened when I landed on the steps. And the judge believed him. I felt like an idiot."

"What about semen?"

"Fowler used a condom. And get this: the judge interpreted that as further evidence that it was consensual sex since Fowler 'cared enough to use a condom.' In the end, the sexual assault charge didn't make it past the probable cause hearing. Fowler's lawyer argued that I was just trying to cover up my infidelity because I got caught cheating on my husband. That asshole Fowler actually went up to my ex outside the courtroom and told him he was sorry, that he really thought I'd wanted it. Can you fucking believe it?"

"With Fowler? Yeah, I can believe it. So what about your husband? What happened there?"

"I don't think he knew what to believe. But I've seen enough of this as an investigator to know that a lot of marriages don't survive a sexual assault, particularly if there's any doubt about the victim and her relationship to the accused. My ex stuck around for a few weeks, but it started eating away at him. Then one day I came home from work and he wasn't there. But there *was* a letter from a lawyer initiating divorce proceedings."

"I'm sorry," said Verraday. "But you'll get through this. You've got survivor instincts."

The waiter had finished up with the other customers and brought the check. "There you go, folks," he said, again with that genuine smile.

Verraday pulled out his wallet but Maclean waved it away.

"Your money's no good here, Professor. I'm getting paid for all this. I mean, not overtime. Those days are long gone. But I do get paid my regular hours, and I appreciate what a time suck this is for you."

"Well, your company is a lot more agreeable than most of the time sucks I get sucked into."

"Thanks, but just the same, this one's on me."

"Okay, but only if I get the next one," said Verraday.

"Deal," said Maclean as she threw down a couple of twenty-dollar bills to cover it and then stood up to leave.

Verraday glanced down and saw that she had left a 20 percent tip. Generous, but not so generous as to indicate an emergency exit from the conversation.

"Thanks folks," the waiter called after them. "Enjoy your evening."

When they reached the front door, Verraday held it open for Maclean, then followed behind her to the sidewalk.

"So at the risk of sounding creepy and Fowler-esque, can I walk you to your car?" he asked.

Maclean turned to face him. She smiled. "Trust me, you couldn't possibly sound creepy and Fowler-esque. And I appreciate the offer. But I'm trained in Muay Thai and I've got a box cutter and a Glock nine millimeter in my purse. So barring a zombie apocalypse, I'll be okay. But I'll be happy to escort you to *your* ride."

"I always admire self-confidence," said Verraday. "I can't say I'm packing anything more than attitude, but I *did* make it as far as blue belt in karate, so I think I can handle myself." He pointed to his car. "Plus I'm parked two doors down. I only have about eight or nine seconds to get into trouble, so I should be all right."

Maclean arched an eyebrow at him. "In my experience, Professor, eight or nine seconds is more than enough time to get into all kinds of trouble. But don't worry, I'll keep an eye out for you until you make it to your car. Good night."

She lifted her right hand and made a slight waving gesture at Verraday. It struck him as almost childlike. He was charmed by it. He had no doubt that if anyone could fend off a zombie apocalypse, it was her. But at the same time, he felt compassion and admiration for this woman who had lost her natural male protector at such a formative stage, had fought every inch of the way to get where she was, and had even survived a sexual assault from a senior colleague. Despite all that, she remained open hearted enough to insist on playing the shepherd with him now and was still able to give him such an unselfconscious wave.

"Good night to you, Detective," said Verraday, smiling, with a slight bow that was only partially ironic.

She watched as he walked the few paces to his car door then clicked his remote. She smiled then turned away, giving him one last glance over her shoulder as she crossed the street. He climbed into his car and went to start the engine but felt a protective impulse of his own. He hesitated, lingering while Maclean got into her vehicle, a Jeep of some sort, which was parked under a streetlight. Only after she pulled away from the curb and turned down a side street did Verraday start his own vehicle and leave.

On the drive home, Verraday's head was swimming with the news about Robson. He knew he'd have to tell Penny, but wasn't sure what the best way would be. It was late now, and he was too tired to call her. It would be a long conversation and not the kind he wanted to have on the phone anyway. He was seeing her for dinner next week. But the news was too important to wait until then. He clumsily texted, "Hey sis. Something's come up. Wondering if we could get together for dinner tomorrow instead of next week?"

To his surprise, she texted back almost immediately to confirm. She was better at this than he was. Verraday slipped his cell into his jacket, stepped onto the sidewalk, and was relieved to see that the gate was closed and latched this time. He walked up his path to the front steps, fumbled for his keys only slightly, and then entered the foyer. Inside, he kicked off his boots and hung his jacket up on the hall tree. He went straight to the kitchen, took his Seattle World's Fair tumbler from the dish rack and reached for the bottle of brandy at the back of the counter.

Then he changed his mind. It was late. Almost midnight now. The dark ale and the shared conversation with Maclean had been satisfying. He really didn't need anything else. It was just habit, he told himself. So instead, he poured some water into his glass, took a sip, and headed upstairs with it to bed.

CHAPTER 19

The next morning, Maclean and Verraday pulled up in front of a two-story building in Belltown. They walked up a narrow set of stairs and on the second floor, found a door with a small sign beside it reading "Erotes Hosting."

"This is the place," she said. "They administer four different sites for male, female, and transsexual escorts in the Seattle area, plus an alternative dating site."

They entered. There was no receptionist. In the back, through a glass door, was a tomb-like machine room where the servers stood on a raised floor in the perpetual chill of air-conditioning. At the back of the office, a bespectacled young woman dressed in emo style sat at a desktop computer. She wore heavy eyeliner, a purple streak in her hair, and striped arm warmers pulled down to her knuckles to ward off the cold. She didn't hear Verraday and Maclean over the roar of the fans at first. From their side of the counter, Verraday and Maclean could see that the young woman seemed to be putting together a webpage.

"Excuse me," called Maclean.

In her peripheral vision, the emo girl spotted them. Without taking her gaze off the screen as she dropped some text into a blank box, she said in a welcoming tone of voice that surprised them both, "Hey, what can I do for you?"

Maclean held up her badge. "I'm Detective Maclean. Seattle PD. I'm investigating a homicide."

"Holy shit!" exclaimed the girl, now turning in her swivel chair to look directly at her. "Are you serious?"

The girl had a guileless face under her plastic-rimmed glasses, so wide-eyed and sincerely surprised that under other circumstances Maclean would have had to suppress a laugh.

"Yes, I'm afraid so," she said instead. "Can I speak to whoever is in charge here?"

"Yeah, sure," replied the girl.

She leaned into the back office and called out, "Hey Marty, there's a police detective here. It's about a homicide." Then she turned politely back toward Maclean and Verraday. "He'll be right out. Can I get you guys some coffee or water?"

"No, but thank you," said Maclean.

The young woman went back to work, and Verraday noticed her carefully using a computer paintbrush tool to obscure the face of the girl whose escort page she was putting together. It was pixelated the same way Destiny's was.

"Do you do that to all of them?" Maclean asked. "Obscure the faces, I mean?"

"Yes, all of them," said the young woman. "Unless they specifically request not to have their faces pixelated or blanked out. But almost everybody wants their identity concealed. The men as well as the women. A lot of them are doing this on the side, paying for college, so they don't want their families or the general public to be able to recognize them."

Verraday wondered how many of his students might be on this site to pay for their skyrocketing tuition. And how many of them might end up like Alana Carmichael, Rachel Friesen, or the girl they knew only as Destiny. He didn't want to think about it.

A few moments later, a man in his late twenties emerged from the back office. He did not share the guileless features of the emo girl, nor her fashion sense. He was stocky and wore chinos with a coral-colored polo shirt. His eyes were close set, creating the impression of a suspicious, overstuffed ferret. The young woman halfheartedly went back to her work, her attention more focused on the drama unfolding before her.

"Are you Marty?" asked Maclean.

"Yeah. Can I help you?"

Maclean held up her badge again. "I hope so. Detective Maclean, Seattle PD. A girl listed on one of your websites has been murdered."

"That's very unfortunate," said Marty. "We've never had that happen before."

"I'm looking for the file of a girl called Destiny."

"Do you have a warrant?"

"No, but I can get one by two o'clock this afternoon, by which time our leads will have gone colder, and I will be very, very pissed off. Pissed off enough to bring the vice squad in here to go over your operation and your computer files with a fine-toothed comb. How's that sound?"

"Whoa, I think we're getting off on the wrong foot here," said Marty. "Let's just take a step back, okay?"

"As long as you can help me out with this girl."

"So this person's really dead? You're not doing some kind of sting operation or something, looking for something else under a false pretext? Because if you did, that would be entrapment, you know."

"Trust me, my colleague and I have seen her body at the morgue. Not a pretty sight, thanks to some shit heel who probably found her on your web page."

"Look, people post here voluntarily. We can't control who they go out with. Do you have her last name?"

"No, that's one of the things we're trying to find out."

"A lot of people who post ads here are named Destiny," said the emo girl. "It's a common alias. But I can bring up every file with that username in it. Then you'd just have to cross reference it with the pictures, and we can work backward from there."

She started typing. Marty seemed to have decided that cooperation would be wiser than obstruction.

"Everybody who lists their services on our site has to give us a real first and last name and a matching credit card," he said. "That way we know they're real and not some jealous ex posting nudes of whoever dumped them, or some creep looking to hurt people or pull an Ashley Madison and extort from them, you know? It happens."

"There are twenty-seven people in our system with that name. Shouldn't take too long. Wanna come look?" the emo girl asked.

"Thanks," said Maclean.

Marty lifted the gate in the counter and motioned them in.

Verraday and Maclean watched over the girl's shoulder as she pulled up the files one by one. There was a mind-boggling array of Destinys, of every iteration, more than either of them could have imagined. There was an African American Destiny dressed as Cleopatra. A red-haired Destiny in a thong. There was even a baby-faced young man named Destiny, dressed in the uniform of the Seattle Seahawks' cheerleading squad, the SeaGals. It consisted of a blue-and-white crop top, belt, and short-shorts, plus white go-go boots.

Verraday had the sudden sense that he would never, ever fully understand the human condition.

"Oh, I remember him," said the girl, her lip curling into a grin.

"He'd be hard to forget," offered Maclean.

"Yeah, even around here," agreed the girl.

On the seventeenth Destiny, Verraday spotted the blonde hair and Freya tattoo of Seattle's latest homicide victim.

"Stop. That's her," he said.

"What's her name?" asked Maclean.

The young woman leaned into the screen to check the listing information. "Helen Dale," she responded.

"I'll need her home address," said Maclean.

"I'll print it off," said the girl.

"Do the customers contact the escorts through the site?"

"No," said Marty defensively. "We don't get into any of that stuff at all. The escorts arrange their own means of contact. Usually text. There's no messaging, either incoming or outgoing on our sites, so we have no way of knowing who any of their clients are."

"But you could figure out the IP addresses of the people who had checked her out."

"Good luck with that," said Marty. "You wouldn't believe how many visitors we get."

The emo girl nodded her head in agreement and said, "That guy in the cheerleader outfit?"

She tapped a key and put her finger on a number on the screen. "Twenty-six-thousand three hundred and seventy-one hits since he joined us six months ago. Oh, wait, make that seventy-two. He just had another one."

"If he got hired anywhere near as often as he got gawked at," added Marty, "he wouldn't have to prance around in a SeaGals outfit to make a living. He'd own the whole damned stadium."

"Okay. One last thing," said Maclean. "Are there any more pictures in Helen Dale's file other than what's on the public web page?"

"Could be," replied the girl. "A lot of people like to rotate their photos from time to time, change it up so they appeal to new types of clients, plus give their repeat customers something new to look at."

The girl dragged the cursor over a box and clicked. A number of photos of Helen appeared, designed to appeal to as broad a public as possible. In some, she was nude, in others, she was wearing just panties or lingerie. In still others, she wore fetish gear. And in one photo, she was wearing a flight attendant's uniform and standing in the cockpit of an empty passenger plane. She held a glass of champagne in one hand.

"How old are these?" asked Maclean.

"They've been in her file awhile now. More than a month. Except that flight attendant one. It was uploaded two days ago."

"Can we see it full screen?"

"Sure."

A moment later, the large monitor was filled with the image of Helen Dale, a.k.a. Destiny. She stood in the cockpit, grinning seductively, one arm extended to take a selfie. The flight attendant's uniform that she wore appeared to be vintage and from an airline that neither of them recognized. It was dark outside the plane, as though the photo had been taken at nighttime or in a hangar. In one window, Maclean could make out the reflection of a man's face.

"Send me an electronic copy of that photo, would you?" said Maclean.

"Sure thing," said the girl.

Maclean handed the girl her business card. "Thanks, you've both been a lot of help."

As they headed down the stairs toward the street, Maclean turned to Verraday. "I'm sending a forensics team to Helen Dale's apartment. I'd love to have you come along, but it would attract too much attention."

"I understand," said Verraday. "Let me know if you find anything unusual. Anything at all."

"We need to find out where that flight attendant's uniform comes from. Could give us a clue about who that man is inside the cockpit with her. He might know something."

"I'll check the UW staff directory," said Verraday. "There might be somebody there who can tell us something about the uniform or the plane. The university has a big aerospace faculty because of the work they do with

Boeing. Odds are good that one of the professors is an aviation history geek and might be able to recognize the plane and the uniform. I'll ask around."

"Sounds good. I'll e-mail the photo to you. By the way, did you tell your sister about Robson yet?"

"No, I'm meeting her this evening. Figured it's better to talk about it in person."

"That makes sense. Hope it goes okay. Good luck."

CHAPTER 20

At six o'clock that evening, Verraday pulled up in front of his sister Penny's house. It was a Frank Lloyd Wright style stone-and-cedar bungalow in Ballard, on a hill overlooking Shilshole Bay. There had been a break in the relentless October cloud cover, and the entire hillside and the bay below were bathed in golden-hour light from a sun that for once wasn't obscured by cloud cover. Verraday started up the walkway, then paused and turned toward the setting sun. He luxuriated in the sight of Bainbridge Island and the Olympic Mountains backlit, the sky deep indigo above him, and to the west, a bank of clouds tinged pink and red. He closed his eyes, breathed in the sea air, and savored the warmth and light on his skin.

When he had absorbed as much of it as he could, he reluctantly let go of the moment and continued up the path to Penny's house. He passed her Zen garden with its neatly trimmed junipers and gravel artfully raked to create the sense of water flowing down a riverbed. Penny was the more financially successful of the two of them by a considerable margin. Like her brother, she was a doctor of psychology. But she had chosen to specialize in clinical work rather than the research branch to which Verraday had been drawn. Academia didn't interest her in the least. She had her own private practice specializing in cognitive behavioral therapy. Her clients were either wealthy or covered by insurance, which brought her an income that dwarfed her brother's. She had also made some very shrewd investments in Seattle IT startups that had paid off spectacularly.

Her house had originally been built for an executive at Boeing in the 1950s, and Penny had had it renovated to be fully wheelchair accessible. A ramp led to Penny's front door, with a narrow set of stairs beside it. Verraday reached out to ring the bell, but before he could touch it, the door swung open, revealing Penny in her wheelchair, smiling.

"Fantastic sunset, isn't it?"

"Were you watching me?"

"Not watching. Observing. I observe everything. I'm very, very good at it. Don't ever forget that, little brother," she said in a mock-menacing tone.

Verraday smiled. "You *must* be pretty good at it to be able to afford this place."

"I like to think so. And I observe that you've got something on your mind."

"How can you tell?"

"Sorry, trade secret. Come on in."

Penny wheeled herself easily through the wide foyer into the open-concept main floor. There was a spacious living room with a large fireplace and a low bar area that separated it from the kitchen beyond. In one corner of the living room was a small shrine with a stone Buddha, a hand-painted Tibetan prayer on parchment, and beneath it, a photo of the Dalai Lama. In another corner, water splashed across beach stones in a fountain, bathing the room in gentle white noise. Penny's home was an oasis of calm and sanity. Verraday knew his house would never be like this.

"Do you still meditate?" he asked.

"Every day. Would you like to try it with me?"

"Sure. We could do that sometime, I guess."

"Did you ever listen to that meditation link I sent you?"

"Not yet. But I will."

Penny smiled knowingly. She could always read him, and he knew it. "You look like you need a glass of wine. I've got a Walla Walla Cab or a Willamette Pinot Noir."

"You going to have some?"

"No, but be my guest."

"I'll have the Cab, please,"

She rolled over to the mostly empty wine rack, where she kept a couple of bottles on hand for the benefit of her guests. She pulled out the Cabernet and handed it to her brother.

"I'll let you do the honors. There's a corkscrew in the cutlery drawer."

Verraday examined the label. "Wow. 2008 Leonetti Cellars. This is a spectacular bottle of wine. Not cheap, either. You sure it's okay if I open it?"

"I'm never going to drink it, so knock yourself out. I've got one of those Coravin argon gas gizmos that will preserve whatever you don't drink—and I won't let you drink it all, since you're driving."

He uncorked the wine and poured some into one of the large crystal wine glasses. He swirled it around, savoring the deep garnet color and the earthy, fruity notes on the nose. It was so full of sensual nuances that revealed themselves only gradually that he closed his eyes and inhaled it without actually bringing the wine to his lips. At last, he took a sip.

"My God, that's unbelievable," he said. "Are you sure you don't want some?"

"Positive. There's a bottle of elderflower pressé in the fridge. You can pour me one of those with some ice while I check on the dinner."

"Whatever floats your boat."

"It's delicious. You should try it instead of the wine."

"I'll take your word for it," he replied.

Over dinner, as she always did, Penny gently probed his affairs like the protective older sister that she was.

Finally, she said, "So listen, I'm curious. If you didn't have a hot date lined up for our usual dinner night, why did you ask to see me now instead of next week? I know you. Something's up."

Verraday nodded. His expression became serious. "Yeah. You're right. Something's up."

Penny looked alarmed. "What? It's not something with your health, is it?"

"No, no, I'm fine. It's about Robson."

Penny's face tightened. "Robson? What about him?" The words came out of her like they'd been stuck in her throat.

Verraday looked his sister straight in the eye. "He's dead."

Penny didn't say anything at first. Just took a long breath.

"Dead. You sure?"

"Yeah."

"Son of a bitch."

"The coroner says it was a gun-cleaning accident."

"I wonder if it really was an *accident*."

"No idea. I found out through a contact of mine in the Seattle PD."

"Whoa, back up. You have a contact in the Seattle PD? Someone you're actually on speaking terms with?"

"Long story for another time. Anyway, my contact didn't know Robson. Just heard about it through one of the older guys who had worked with Robson back in the day."

"I never figured him for the suicide type," Penny said.

"Me neither. Seemed like too much of a self-absorbed asshole from what I can remember. But that was thirty years ago."

"There are lots of reasons why even narcissistic people commit suicide. Maybe his health was failing and he couldn't take it anymore."

"I fucking hope so," said Verraday.

Verraday was a little surprised when Penny let his comment go and didn't gently chide him with some compassionate quote from the Dalai Lama or Thich Nhat Hanh.

"I used to fantasize about killing Robson," said Penny. "But being in a wheelchair limited the possibilities. Sometimes I would imagine hiring a hit man, but they have a bad habit of testifying against their former employers when they need to cop a plea bargain. And it also took away the pleasure of the hunt. So I always imagined stalking him with my car, waiting for him to step off a curb, cross a street, then bam, run the bastard down and blame it on faulty hand controls."

"How come you never told me that?"

"I try to save that kind of shit for my counsellors. And I was sort of ashamed of having that amount of hate in my heart. When I discovered Buddhism, the monks told me that the only way I would ever be free of my pain is if I forgave Robson. So I tried. I did loving kindness meditations for him, you know, envisioning his pain and whatever made him the way he was, and wishing happiness for him."

"And?"

"It never worked. Every time I pictured his face, I felt like I was going to puke. What about you?"

"I always had it in my mind that someday, when I figured out how to kill him without getting caught, I really would go murder the son of a bitch. I didn't want you to know, because then you'd either have to rat me out or be an accessory after the fact."

She nodded, then looked at him with sudden curiosity. "*Did* you do it? You could tell me, you know. I'd be cool with it. It'd be our secret."

Verraday shook his head. "No. Though part of me wishes I had. I feel like the old bastard cheated me out of the opportunity."

"Did you tell Dad about Robson yet?"

"No. I don't even know how to tell him. I'm not sure how to process this myself," said Verraday.

Penny paused to consider it. "I have an idea."

"What?"

"We should go visit Robson's grave."

Verraday looked at her incredulously. "Are you fucking kidding me? Why would we visit his grave?"

"Ritual is how humans mark significant life events. And *this* is a significant life event. Problematic people, people who have caused us grief and suffering, are in some ways the most difficult for us to let go of in death. Robson's never going to pick up the phone and tell us he's sorry. He will never take responsibility for what he did now."

"And I'll never have a chance to kill him myself."

"That too. Seeing his grave, being present at it, will help us let it go. Do you know where he lived?"

"My source says Everett."

"There can't be too many cemeteries in Everett. And there's bound to be an obituary online in one of the papers that will give us the details."

Penny rolled over to her desk, picked up her tablet, and tapped in a search.

"Bull's-eye," she said. "There it is. The funeral was two days ago. 'Donations may be made to Saint John the Baptist Church. Visitation to be held at Cypress Lawn Memorial Park.'"

"You seriously want to do this?" Verraday asked.

"Yes. Right now. I just need to use the bathroom before we go. It'll take a while to get there even this late in the evening."

★   ★   ★

Verraday waited on the driveway for Penny as she set the alarm system, then emerged from the doorway. She rolled herself toward him.

Verraday clicked his remote and the lights of his car flashed.

"Actually, I'd rather we not take your car," said Penny.

"Why? I've only had two glasses of wine," protested Verraday. "That's nothing. I'm not even a third of the way to the legal limit."

"I know. But remember I told you I've got that new personal mobility device? I want you to try it out with me."

Verraday cocked his head and looked at her quizzically. "We're going to drive to Everett in an electric buggy?"

"Did I say it was an electric buggy?"

Penny reached into her purse, pulled out a remote and clicked it. The garage door began to creak. As it swung upward, the ceiling light activated automatically, revealing a carmine-red Porsche Boxster GTS with a blue handicap parking tag in the window.

"Well? What do you think?" asked Penny.

"I'd say it beats hell out of those buggies at Walmart."

"They make high-performance hand controls for these nowadays. Comes from racing paddle technology. It's actually faster than using your feet."

"Who knew?"

"Not the kid in the Mustang who wanted to drag race me on the way back from getting the groceries this afternoon. You should have seen the look on his face when I left him behind at the lights like he was standing still."

"And what do the Tibetan monks say about your new ride?"

"They say that attachment to material objects causes us to remain wandering in samsara, bound to birth and rebirth. But that the color suits me."

★   ★   ★

With Penny at the controls, the Boxster made it up the coast to Everett in considerably less than the thirty-four minutes that Google maps recommended budgeting for the trip. With the aid of her GPS, they were soon at Cypress Lawn Memorial Park, cruising the lanes that ran past the headstones. At last they spotted a mound of freshly dug earth. Verraday got out and checked the headstone, then nodded to Penny and waved her over.

"It's him," he called quietly.

Penny turned the car off then deftly pulled her wheelchair out from behind the seat and set it up beside her on the pavement. In one neat motion, she slid out of the driver's seat of the Porsche and into the chair. Then she wheeled herself up to the grave beside Verraday.

For a long moment, neither one spoke. They just stared at the gravesite and tombstone. Then Penny broke the silence.

"David Robson, because of you I will never get to see my beautiful, sweet mother laugh ever again, or hold her close and tell her that I love her. I have not been able to do so for the last thirty years. Because of you, I will never get to see my parents' golden anniversary. You took away my freedom and my childhood. You caused me to suffer terrible physical and emotional pain. You put me in this wheelchair. You wounded my father to his core. He was never the same after you took my mother's life. And now you've taken your own life. You acknowledged none of the terrible things you've done. I want to forgive you. But I can't. And you've done that to me too."

She closed her eyes. The night was still, and in the darkness, Verraday could hear her breathing in the formalized way she'd learned through meditation: in through her nose to a count of five, holding it for a couple of seconds, then releasing it through her mouth to a count of five.

Verraday checked to make sure Penny's eyes really were shut. Then he turned his back to her slightly and undid his fly. Penny's eyes snapped open as she heard a tinkling sound on the freshly turned earth, like a sudden shower on a summer afternoon.

"Jamie, what are you doing?"

"Do you disapprove?" he asked.

"No," she said thoughtfully. "Not if it helps give you closure."

In another ten seconds, he was done. He zipped up his fly, then looked around at Penny.

"Okay, I've done what I've come here to do. We can leave."

"Well, good for you. But I'm not done yet," said Penny. "There's one last thing on my agenda."

Penny reached into her purse and took out a small, delicate vial with Japanese lettering on it. She began sprinkling the contents on Robson's grave.

"What is that?"

"It's a Japanese Kobyo vase. It's said to hold the nectar of compassion for Kannon, the god of forgiveness."

"Kannon? That's an ironic name for a god of forgiveness. So what's that liquid? Some kind of Buddhist holy water?"

"No," replied Penny, sprinkling out the last of the liquid. "It's urine. Mine. I told you I needed to use the bathroom before we came here."

Verraday thought he'd heard wrong until Penny began to laugh. It was a laugh that built in momentum from somewhere deep inside her until her ribs shook.

Verraday began to laugh along with her now too, almost uncontrollably, a conspiratorial kind of laugh they hadn't shared since they were children keeping a mischievous secret together. Their laughter echoed off the tombstones and through the graveyard, and it subsided only when they finally had to catch their breath. Even in the dim light, Verraday could see tears glistening on Penny's face, running down toward her broad, toothy smile. He tasted a salty tear on his own lip and felt another one rolling down his cheek. He wiped it away, still laughing.

CHAPTER 21

By the time Verraday had gotten home from his outing
with Penny, he was too tired to do any work on the midterm or any reading for his next paper. He checked his
e-mails and saw from the addresses that it was mostly the
usual stuff: half a dozen or so from his students, which
he decided to put off reading until the morning.

One e-mail caught his eye, however. The subject line
promised that new preview material had been added on
the Bettie Page MoMA exhibit website. Verraday opened
it and saw a color picture of Bettie wearing a leopard-
print bikini, striking a claws-out cat pose. It was pure
kitsch, not the sort of thing that excited him. Just like
the serial killers, he realized, he had a specific range of
things that turned him on and things that did not. This
did not. However, there were three new thumbnail photos of Bettie.

Like the shots in the previous e-mail, the thumbnails
were ones he had never seen before and were taken with
much greater artistry than the standard Bettie photos. He
clicked on the first one, which showed Bettie from the

midriff down, wearing knee-high, black leather boots, seamed stockings, and a cinched corset that peeked into frame. The next shot was of Bettie's chin and teeth, smiling seductively as she bit into a leather whip. The final photo was a view of Bettie from behind, lying on a bed, wearing nothing but a black bustier, fishnet tights, and stiletto heels.

He remembered when he had felt passionate enough about a woman to create photographs like these. With Nikki. He had taken the time to learn about exposure, depth of field, and lighting. He'd even made his own prints so that no eyes other than his own would ever see the erotic images he created of her. He'd kept them despite his conflicted feelings. The photos of Nikki were the most artistic thing he had ever created, technically accomplished and, he had to admit, extremely erotic. But he could never look at them without being reminded of his own naiveté, his misplaced belief back when he'd clicked the shutter that he'd found the love of his life.

That last thumbnail on the web page of the MoMA exhibit had triggered a memory of one of those photos. He knew he shouldn't take out the images of Nikki to check, but his curiosity got the better of him. The last time he'd looked at the photos of her was four years earlier, when he'd bought this house and was packing up his apartment. At the time, he had thrown them into the garbage as part of the past that he was casting off. Then at the last minute, he had retrieved them, not quite able to break the connection. He took a key out of his desk now, went over to his filing cabinet, and unlocked it. He pulled the drawer out and at the very back, filed behind mortgage information and tax records, he found the folder containing the photos of Nikki.

He took one of them out. It was black and white, Verraday's favored photographic medium. In it, Nikki was lying on her belly atop a duvet on Verraday's sleigh bed, grinning that seductive Cheshire-cat grin at him. One of her long legs was stretched out behind her on the bed. The other was chambered above her, a stiletto pump dangling seductively off the end of her toes. His memory had been correct. The outfit Nikki was wearing was virtually identical to the costume that Bettie Page was modeling in the last thumbnail photo. He supposed that he had seen that picture of Bettie years earlier, had forgotten it on a conscious level, yet unwittingly recreated it when he had bought the lingerie for Nikki that she was wearing in the photo that he now held in his hand.

Gazing at it now, he grudgingly understood how Kyle Davis had been so unable to resist Rachel Friesen. He had an impulse to toss this photo and all the other Nikki photos into the wastebasket but then felt a pang of regret and placed them back in his filing cabinet. He still had more in common with Kyle Davis than he cared to admit.

CHAPTER 22

As Verraday and Maclean walked through the Science Quadrangle past the Drumheller Fountain, he noticed that the first dead leaves of the season had fallen into the water. He watched them swirling about on the surface, some caught in eddies, moving together, others alone, traveling in erratic trajectories. He wondered whether, if you tracked it all long enough, a pattern would emerge, some master Newtonian clockwork, or if it was all just chaos, the random influences of a fickle universe.

"So we didn't find anything interesting in Helen Dale's apartment," said Maclean. "Not yet at least. There were no signs of any struggle, no blood, no disturbance, not even a magazine out of place. And no cell phone or datebook."

"Which is exactly what I'd expect from our killer," said Verraday. "He won't leave a trace of himself any place that he's not able to control."

A strand of Maclean's long hair had come loose, and as they passed the fountain into the open area of the rotunda, a gust of wind caught it, carried it up for a moment, then draped it across the lapel of her short Burberry trench coat. He wondered if he should tell her. Then he decided against it. It wasn't like having a low-flying zipper or spinach stuck between your teeth. He liked the way it looked. Seeing her now, with the wind playing through her hair, looking so natural, he imagined she would be in her element in the woods, taking her inner city kids on wilderness treks. She turned to him.

"What are you smiling at?"

"Oh, nothing," said Verraday. "I hadn't even realized I was smiling."

Maclean followed as Verraday now turned down a walkway toward an attractive brick building with a Gothic arched window in the center.

"Here we are," he said. "This is the Kirsten Wind Tunnel."

"This isn't how I pictured a wind tunnel," said Maclean.

"That's because it was built in the 1930s, when there was Guggenheim money and no one had yet come up with the bright idea of making campus buildings look like Soviet mental hospitals. After you."

He held the door open for her.

Entering, they heard a low hum. They followed the sound a short distance down the hall until they spotted a white-haired man in his midsixties wearing a Hawaiian shirt and gazing intently through a heavy blast window. On the other side of the shatterproof glass, in the wind tunnel, two helmeted men on locked-down racing bikes were pedaling furiously.

"Professor Lowenstein?" called Verraday.

"That's me," replied the man, turning and smiling. He had long, thinning white hair, prominent features, and light-blue eyes that gazed out thoughtfully from behind a pair of wire-rimmed glasses, giving him the demeanor of an overgrown Hobbit.

"We spoke yesterday on the phone. I'm Professor Verraday, and this is Detective Maclean."

"Right. Let me just have a quick word with these gentlemen."

Professor Lowenstein pushed a large red button, and the whine and roar from within the tunnel subsided. He switched on a talk-back microphone.

"Take five, fellas," he told the men riding the bicycles.

"I wasn't expecting to see bicycles in a wind tunnel," said Maclean.

"Well, we gotta pay our way here. They're determining how to reduce drag on racing bike helmets. That's our specialty here—figuring out how to get through life with the least amount of resistance. But I know you're not here to talk about that."

Verraday was already wishing he did have all afternoon to listen to Lowenstein. It would no doubt have been more pleasant than tracking a killer.

"As I said on the phone, Professor," began Verraday, "I understand your hobby is local commercial aviation history. Detective Maclean is working on a criminal case that might have a related angle to it. Could be nothing, but you never know."

"The case is ongoing and none of the details can be public yet," added Maclean.

Lowenstein smiled. "For the last four decades, both the Russians and the Chinese have been trying to play footsie with me, hoping to persuade me to reveal the knowledge we've unlocked here. And in all that time, the only information they've gotten out of me is that it's a bad idea to urinate into high-velocity air masses. So my lips are sealed. Now how can I help?"

Maclean took out the photo and handed it to him. "We're trying to find out what airline the plane and the flight attendant uniform are from. Might be a clue."

Professor Lowenstein studied the photograph for a moment. "I've seen this uniform before. But not in ages. I would guess it's twenty-five or thirty years old. But the cockpit is from a much more recent plane. The instrument panel is from a Cessna Citation M2 executive jet. They didn't go into production until 2013."

"So the uniform and the plane don't go together?"

Lowenstein shook his head. "Not a chance. But that logo on the flight attendant's lapel pin rings a bell. Just a sec."

Professor Lowenstein reached into an equipment cabinet and pulled out a magnifying glass. He held it over the photo and studied it closely. Then his eyes lit up and he smiled.

"Yep, now I remember where I know this from." He put his finger on the photo. "See that 'G' in the center of those wings on the young lady's pin? That was the crest of Griffinair."

"Never heard of it," said Maclean.

"It was a legendary regional airline. Before your time. They started up when *I* was a kid and pterodactyls ruled the skies. At their peak, in the 1970s, Griffinair had about half a dozen war surplus cargo aircraft and three small commuter planes that flew out of Seattle to Spokane, Portland, and Walla Walla. They also had a floatplane charter service. It was founded by a guy named Dick Griffin, a real character. He was a World War II combat veteran who ran the company until he died at ninety-five. Stubborn as hell. He was a trailblazer in the beginning. But as the years went by, he fell out of touch with the industry. He passed away about ten years ago, and by then he'd just about run the company into the ground, from what I hear. But that uniform is Griffinair, for sure. That any use to you, Detective?"

"Thanks, Professor," replied Maclean. "You've been extremely helpful."

CHAPTER 23

"Got time to come pay a visit to Griffinair with me?" asked Maclean as they left the Kirsten building.

"Love to. I've got a class to teach at two o'clock. Can you get me back here by then?"

"I might have to embarrass you by putting the siren and flashers on, but sure, I think that can be arranged," said Maclean. "Now I'd like to do a web search on the company before we talk to them."

"Want to use the computer in my office?"

"We can check it out on my iPad on the way there, if you don't mind doing the honors. It'll save us some time, help make sure I get you back here on schedule."

Within ten minutes, they were headed down Interstate 5, and Verraday had read Maclean a Wikipedia entry on the history of Griffinair as well as several articles about the company in aviation magazines. All of them conveyed the same story that Professor Lowenstein had told them. One community paper contained a paid obituary notice for Fred Griffin, son of the founder. It was written by Fred's son, Jason. It did not reveal the cause of death, but suggested that donations could be directed toward a local mental health organization.

By the time they had exhausted the Google entries for Griffinair, they were cruising along Perimeter Road at King County International Airport, still referred to by the locals as Boeing Field. Built in the 1920s, it had since been eclipsed by the larger and newer Sea-Tac Airport and nowadays was used mainly for cargo operations, maintenance, and flight-testing.

Maclean spotted a hangar with a Griffinair logo on it, which had been updated from the midcentury crest on the uniform pin to a sleek, stylized emblem. Maclean pulled the Interceptor up beside it. The hangar door was open just enough for Maclean and Verraday to step through into the cavernous interior. As their eyes adjusted to the murky light, they saw a twin-engine commuter plane and a small executive jet parked inside. The door of the commuter plane was open, and an access panel under the crew compartment had been removed. From somewhere inside the plane, they heard the whine of an impact wrench.

At the back of the hangar, a door was ajar, allowing a single shaft of light to escape into the gloom. It appeared to be an office area. Verraday now noticed that there was a vintage car parked at the back of the hangar. As he got closer, he recognized the lines as belonging to a 1968 Dodge Charger, highly coveted by collectors. The hood was open, revealing a hulking engine that Verraday could identify because of the unusual way that the spark plug wires came up through the valve covers.

Verraday whistled low under his breath. "Wow, a vintage Dodge Charger with a Hemi. That's one expensive piece of machinery," he commented to Maclean.

She smiled to see him genuinely awestruck. Just then a man stuck his head out of the office. He was partially silhouetted by the office light and was difficult to make out, but they could see that he was muscular and appeared to be in his late twenties.

"Can I help you?" he asked, his tone solicitous.

"Let me take this for a sec," Verraday whispered to Maclean.

"Just admiring your Charger," said Verraday. "I'm guessing by the grille it's a '68?"

"Sure is," said the young man proudly as he approached them. "First year of production for that body type."

"Looks like a 426 Hemi," said Verraday.

The man seemed surprised but pleased that a stranger recognized it. "That's exactly what it is. Four hundred and twenty-five horsepower, straight out of the factory. Zero to sixty in four-point-seven seconds. Fifty years old, and it'll still blow the doors off a Ferrari."

"That's true," agreed Verraday. "A Charger with a 426 Hemi can take just about anything, even off the showroom floor."

"You seem to know your Mopars," said the man.

"My dad had a 1967 Belvedere. Same platform. Except his had a 318. He couldn't afford the Hemi."

"There aren't many of them around, that's for sure. So what can I do for you folks?"

"I'm looking for Jason Griffin," said Maclean.

"Well, you're looking at him," replied the young man confidently.

A loud servo whine now joined the clatter of the impact wrench, drowning out every other sound in the hangar.

Jason grimaced in mock agony. "Why don't you come into my office so we don't have to shout," he shouted, gesturing toward the open door.

Maclean and Verraday followed him toward the office at the back of the hangar.

"Watch your step, folks. I've got the lights off because we're only doing inside work on that one plane right now. This place sucks up electricity like Las Vegas when the overheads are on."

Verraday and Maclean traded a look as they passed a machine shop area where a six-by-eight-foot industrial bath stood. He noticed them looking.

"That's where we repair and manufacture replacement parts. We've got lathes and drill presses to make any mechanical part we could need."

It was evidently a well-practiced sales pitch, and despite having to almost bellow over the racket coming from the commuter plane, the young man was clearly proud of his operation.

"That tank you see is for flushing out and testing radiators. Most of the smaller cargo and commuter operations still run prop planes. Overheating is the number one cause of engine failure. And without an engine, you're not going to stay up there for very long," he said, jerking his thumb skyward. "So you've got to take good care of the cooling systems."

When they reached the office, he stood aside and with a courtly gesture, motioned for them to enter. He followed them in and closed the heavy door behind them. Instantly, the machinery noise became virtually inaudible. He saw the look of surprise on their faces.

"That's better, eh?" he said, smiling. "I spend sixty or seventy hours a week running this place, and believe me, it gets tiring listening to all that racket. That's why the office is professionally soundproofed, so I don't lose my hearing and my marbles by the end of the week."

In contrast to the cavernous maintenance area, the office was well-lit, stylish, and comfortable. Several expensively framed aviation photos hung on the walls. Verraday noticed that in two of them, which were black and white and seemed to date from the 1940s, the same man was looking out the cockpit window of two different airplanes.

"Great pictures," said Verraday. "World War II?"

"Yes," replied Jason. "That's my grandfather, Dick Griffin. He founded this company. He flew a B-17 Flying Fortress with the Eighth Air Force, based in England. That's it in the picture on the left. He did his tour of duty—twenty-five bombing missions over Germany—flying through flak and fighters and anything else the Nazis could throw at him. Then instead of going home, he transferred to Air Transport Command and flew the plane in that other picture."

"Looks like a C-47," said Verraday.

"That's exactly what it is," said Jason. "So you know about planes as well as cars."

"Just a little bit," said Verraday. "My dad was a machinist at Boeing up until he retired."

Verraday noticed another framed image, this one of Jason Griffin, fairly recently, standing on the pontoon of a small floatplane with a Griffinair logo on it. In another frame was a section front from the *Seattle Times*, showing a chubby adolescent boy behind the controls of a plane and a woman in her thirties sitting in the seat beside him.

"Who's that?" asked Verraday.

"That's me when I was twelve," replied Jason. "And my mom."

Verraday leaned in to read the text under the photo. "You set the world's record for youngest solo flight in a twin-engine plane?"

"That's correct," said Jason, smiling. "It was a Beechcraft Super 18."

He motioned them toward a couple of leather and stainless steel Wassily chairs. "Please, have a seat." He took his own place in a black leather captain's chair behind a large desk made from a single slab of mahogany. "What can I do for you?"

"I'm Detective Constance Maclean from the Seattle Police Department. This is James Verraday. He's a forensic psychologist working with me on a case."

"Cool. If I can make a shameless plug for myself, my grandfather taught me some of his combat flying techniques for evading Zeros and Messerschmitts. I know how to stay out of sight, so moving ground targets like speeders or drug boats wouldn't even know I was there. Then when you're ready to pounce, boom! I'd be right on 'em. So if it's aerial surveillance you need, I'm your man, okay? I'll beat anybody else's price, and I'll outfly 'em too. Guaranteed."

"Thank you," said Maclean, fighting to suppress a laugh and hide her befuddlement over this man-child, who obviously had a lot of technical skill but seemed arrested in early adolescence. "I'll keep it in mind, but today we're actually here to discuss something else."

"Not sure how I can help, but I'll try," said Jason affably.

"We can start here," said Maclean.

She pulled out a photo of Helen Dale that had been cropped to omit the reflection of the man in the window as well as the details of the cockpit controls.

"This young woman is wearing what I understand is a Griffinair flight attendant's uniform. Can you tell us who she is?"

"Sorry, no idea."

"She's not a flight attendant here?"

"No," said Jason, "it's been ages since we've had flight attendants. Like literally not since I was a kid. I was only about twelve when the last flight attendants worked here, so I wouldn't remember any of them. That's got to be a really old photo."

"Actually, it was taken two days ago. The woman's name is Helen Dale. Any idea why she's wearing one of your airline's uniforms?"

"I can't speak for her, but it's common knowledge in the aviation industry that flight attendant uniforms are a hot item in the vintage clothing business and the black market. Not to be crude about it, but there are entire Japanese porn sites devoted to stewardess erotica.

Japan Airlines actually had to put serial numbers and tracking chips in their stewardess uniforms because so many of them were getting 'lost' and turning up in hard-core movies and upscale brothels. A lot of girls get really turned on by wearing them, and a lot of guys get turned on by seeing girls in them."

"I guess so," said Maclean, "because this guy looks pretty turned on. Any idea who he is?"

Maclean held out the uncropped version of the photograph, showing not only the aircraft cockpit but also the reflection of the man's face in the window.

"Wow, that's pretty hard to make out. I'm not sure."

Verraday watched Jason closely. Maclean glanced at Verraday, caught an almost imperceptible flicker of something on his face, then leaned forward toward Jason.

"Mr. Griffin, that's the cockpit of a Cessna Citation executive jet in this photo. I'm no aviation expert, but I see that you've got an executive jet parked out there too. If I go out there into your hangar and climb aboard that plane and see that the cockpit is the same, that will put me in a very suspicious frame of mind. And if I take this out to your shop and the rest of the airport and start asking people if they recognize this man, and he's in any way connected with you, I will be very unhappy. Unless you tell me who he is right now."

"Okay. I hear you. It's hard to tell because of the lighting. But it could be Cody North. He's an employee of mine."

"Any idea why he's with that girl in that plane?"

"Well, it looks to me like they were partying. I mean, if there's one thing that turns people on more than flight attendant uniforms, it's getting it on in airplanes. Otherwise there wouldn't be such a thing as a Mile High Club, right?" Jason laughed easily. "If they were at twenty-thousand feet going four-hundred miles an hour, it would be an issue. But there's no rule against partying in the cockpit when the plane's parked in a hangar, so there's no law being broken in this photo."

"That's true," said Maclean. "There was no law being broken in this photo. But there *was* a law broken not long after it was taken."

"Sorry, I don't understand."

"This young woman's name was Helen Dale. She worked as a call girl under the alias of Destiny. And she was murdered just a few hours after she took this selfie."

Jason leaned forward to take a closer look. "That's terrible. She's a nice-looking girl."

"*Was*," emphasized Maclean. "*Was*. She doesn't look like this anymore. Her killer did a real number on her. Now, Helen was a close friend of this girl."

She held out a photo of Rachel Friesen from the Assassin Girls website.

Jason examined the photo then shrugged blankly. "Never seen her before."

"Her name is Rachel Friesen, and besides being a close associate of Helen Dale, she was also recently murdered," said Maclean. "Now, since your employee was one of the last people to see Helen alive, we'd like to talk to him. And I'd also like to know why you lied to us about the woman in the photo."

Jason dropped his facade. "I'm sorry. I lied because I hired her to work a party that I threw here for potential clients. I'm shifting the focus of the company toward executive jet charters. There are a lot of manufacturers here considering moving their operations to the Maquiladora region."

"The Maquiladora?" asked Maclean.

"The Mexican free-trade zone, along the border. You wouldn't believe how many companies are moving their manufacturing operations to Mexico. Hell, they're even making all the Oreo cookies there now. The labor cost south of the border is ten cents on the dollar compared to here. My plan is to fly the CEOs down to Mexico, show them around, give them the magic carpet treatment. I do all the exploratory flights, and once they set up their businesses, I'll provide an on-call shuttle service. I'll be working all the time."

"Good idea for a business," said Verraday. "Too bad a lot of Americans will lose their jobs in the process."

"Possibly, but it'll save jobs right here. The jobs you're talking about are gone whether I fly CEOs down to Mexico or somebody else does. Those people will have to learn to adapt, just like I'm adapting. That's life. This company's been on the ropes a few times. I'm the one pulling it out of the fire. But those senior executives won't be too happy with me if they come to my party and the next thing you know, there are homicide detectives wanting to interview them about a prostitute being murdered."

"Well, Mr. Griffin," said Maclean. "Perhaps you could enlighten me as to why you hired a prostitute to work at your promotional party in the first place."

"Like I said, a lot of these guys get super turned on by seeing a woman in a stewardess outfit. It's a huge fantasy. I didn't specifically hire her to sleep with any-one, but I wanted someone who would be cool wearing the uniform and wasn't going to freak out if somebody got a little fresh with her. In fact, I paid her to flirt with them."

"Just flirt?"

"I didn't get into any details. I assumed that she knew her business."

"When did she leave?"

"Around midnight."

"Can you verify that?"

"Yes. I arranged a car to take her home afterwards."

"Do you have a record of that?"

"Yes. It's right here in the recent calls list of my phone." Jason held out the phone, showing the number display. "See? Emerald City Limousines. I paid with Visa on the company card. I always keep the receipts. It's in the filing cabinet right here, see?"

He slid the drawer open and, within a moment, pro-duced the record. Maclean examined it. It appeared to be legitimate.

"Thank you, Mr. Griffin, I'll check this later. Now walk me through what happened next."

"The guests left shortly after that, then it was just Cody and me. I was pretty drunk by then, and so was Cody. So we left my car and the van here and I called a taxi. I dropped Cody off at his place on the way."

"Can you prove it?"

"Yes, got the receipt for that too."

Jason reached into the filing cabinet and showed the taxi receipt to Maclean.

"All right. Thank you, Mr. Griffin. Now I'd like to speak to Cody North."

"Sure. I'll go get him. That's him working on the Dash 8 out there."

"Do you have a PA system?" asked Maclean.

"Yes."

"Then page him, please. I'd prefer if you don't speak with him alone until after I've finished talking to him. And I'd like a list of all the guests who were here the night that Helen Dale was murdered."

"There were a lot of people here," said Jason. "And I think a lot of them will be upset if a detective shows up at their office, know what I mean?"

"You've got 'til nine o'clock tomorrow morning," said Maclean. "Or you'll be dealing with the vice squad as well as homicide. Now call Cody and then wait outside."

★   ★   ★

Cody North sauntered into the office, looking pleased with himself as he wiped his sweaty brow with a rag before stuffing it into the hip pocket of his coveralls. He was short. About five foot eight, thought Verraday. But he had tried to compensate for it. He had bones tattooed onto the back of his hands, as well as the words "shock" and "awe" on the right and left palms respectively. Even in his mechanic's uniform, it was apparent that he had a disproportionately well-developed upper body. His shoulders were bulked up, and his biceps pressed against his sleeves. Steroid user, thought Verraday.

Cody North paused when he saw Maclean and cocked his head slightly, appraising her. His leering gaze alighted momentarily on her eyes, then trolled down to her feet before scanning back up to her shoulders, assessing the loose strand of hair that Verraday had noticed by the fountain. Cody North took one last glance at Maclean's breasts before meeting her eyes again.

"Cody North?" she asked.

"Yeah."

She pointed to a chair in the middle of the room. "Have a seat."

North hesitated just long enough to show that he didn't take her seriously, then complied.

"I'm Detective Maclean. Seattle PD. This is Dr. James Verraday. He's a forensic psychologist working with me on this case."

Cody looked at Verraday just long enough to give him a derisive smirk. "Headshrinker, huh? I don't believe in any of that stuff. It's all bull if you ask me." Cody then returned his gaze to Maclean as if Verraday had ceased to exist.

"Well, I *didn't* ask you," said Maclean.

Cody North just shrugged. Verraday didn't find the mechanic's dismissive attitude toward him annoying. The fact that he treated Verraday like he was invisible was helpful, gave him a chance to study his subject more closely. North's stray glances at Maclean's anatomy were almost involuntary, some form of compulsion, thought Verraday. But they also seemed to be a kind of dominance display. Behind the greasy coveralls was an even greasier personality, someone who couldn't help gawking and didn't seem to care.

Maclean leaned down toward her briefcase to retrieve the photo of Helen Dale. She glanced up and saw Cody stealing a peek down her blouse. Verraday, whose karate technique was rusty but still effective, had a sudden impulse to backhand the mechanic and rattle his eyeballs into a more respectful line of sight.

Maclean adjusted her blouse in a covering gesture. Verraday wondered if it was a reflexive or conscious move. Verraday noticed that it had provoked another tiny smirk from Cody North. He seemed like the type who enjoyed intimidating and dominating women. But Maclean was unfazed.

She held up the uncropped version of Helen Dale's cockpit selfie. "Is that your reflection in the window?"

"Yeah, that's me. So what?"

"So what can you tell me about the deceased?"

"What do you mean, 'the deceased'?"

"The young woman. Do you know what her name was?"

"Yeah. She said her name was Destiny."

"Well, Mr. North, we have a big problem. Because you're in this picture with her. And a few hours after it was taken, this young lady was murdered."

"Shouldn't I have a lawyer?" asked Cody.

"You're not under arrest," said Maclean. "At this point, we're interviewing you as a witness. That means you're not entitled to a lawyer. Unless you'd prefer that I take you into custody, which is what I'll do in about ten seconds if you don't stop gawking and start talking. Got it, shitbird?"

Verraday saw a flash of fury in Cody North's eyes. Steroid rage for sure, he thought. Cody's jaw muscles tensed and his hands curled into fists. He looked like he might leap straight at Maclean. Verraday shifted forward, calculating the mechanic's likely trajectory and deciding that if North raised his ass out of the chair so much as an inch in Maclean's direction, he'd take him down with a roundhouse. Then North seemed to regain his composure. Either that or the fight had gone out of him. Cody North stared at his knees for a long moment, and when he finally looked back up, he didn't undress Maclean with his eyes. He just frowned sourly.

"So what do you want?"

"Tell me what you know about the murder victim."

"Not a lot. She was hired to entertain guests at a bash that Jason threw to butter up potential clients for his executive jet service."

"And what exactly did this 'buttering up' entail?"

"Well, she mostly just moved through the crowd, greasing the wheels, you know? It was all men. Big-deal senior executive types. She chatted them up, flirted. Touched them a lot. Danced for them."

"What kind of dancing?"

"Well, sort of burlesque, I guess you'd call it. Jason invited the guests into that executive jet out there, pumped music through the sound system. She came through the plane dressed in that stewardess outfit and did lap dances on the guys who wanted it. There was no shortage of takers."

"Did you have a lap dance with her?"

"Yes."

"Any other kind of relations?"

"Why?"

"I'm asking the questions here, Mr. North, not you."

"Okay, yeah."

"What?"

"Right after she took that picture, she closed the cockpit door and started grinding away on my lap. Then she undid my fly, reached in, and, you know."

"No, I don't know," said Maclean. "Would you care to elaborate?"

"Sure, she jerked me off. Said it was orders from the flight deck. I didn't hear any complaints from her, that's for sure. That broad liked the attention. Just ate it up."

"And when did she leave?"

"The party ended pretty early—for a party, that is—because we had a plane to service first thing in the morning. She left around midnight, just before the guests started to go home."

"And what mode of transportation did she use?"

"Jason got her a car. It came right up to the hangar door."

"Did you see her get in?"

"Yeah. Everybody saw her get in and leave. Her exit would have been pretty hard to miss. She flashed her tits out the window just as the car was pulling away."

"Was there anybody else in the car with her?"

"Other than the driver, no. Didn't look like it."

"What kind of a car was it?"

"A Lincoln Town Car. White."

"When did you leave?"

"Not long after that."

"Did you drive home?"

"No. Jason and I were both pretty wasted, so he called a cab. We left together, and he dropped me off at my place on the way back to his condo."

"Mr. North, have you ever been convicted of sexual assault?"

"No."

"Charged?"

"No."

"Any other criminal convictions?"

"No."

Cody was now shifting uneasily in his seat. He was beginning to perspire and Verraday could see that his breathing was shallow. Maclean was getting to him.

"All right. That's it for now. But don't go anywhere. I'm going to check your story out. I mean go over it with a fine-tooth comb. Depending on what I find out, I may want to bring you down to the station tomorrow morning for a longer interview."

Cody North nodded. His eyes no longer wandered up Maclean's calves and thighs, or probed the gaps in her blouse. They had nowhere to look but down.

★   ★   ★

"He's hiding something. I'm sure of it," said Verraday as they drove north on the I-5 back toward the campus.

"I think so too," said Maclean. "I just don't know what yet."

"I also think he's on steroids. Plus he's got a lot of the classic behaviors of a sex offender. He couldn't stop eyeing you up. It was almost involuntary. Partly sexual, partly dominance. He only stopped after you put him in his place. And if he acts like that with an authority figure who's looking for a murder suspect, imagine what he's like with a woman who's in a vulnerable position."

Maclean nodded. "First thing I'll do after I drop you back at the university is to take a visit to that limo company, see if Jason and Cody's story checks out and whether Helen Dale actually made it home. Then I'm going to run both their names. Find out whether they're hiding anything."

Verraday checked his watch and saw that it was getting perilously close to two PM. Maclean noticed him checking the time. She stepped on the accelerator and pulled into the fast lane, suddenly going fifteen miles an hour over the posted limit. Verraday gave her a sidelong glance.

"What? I promised I'd get you to your class on time, didn't I?"

A few minutes later, she pulled the Interceptor up in front of Guthrie Hall. Verraday checked his watch again and saw that it was not quite two o'clock. She had managed to do it. He saw some of his students heading for the doorway. There was Koller, who would no doubt have something inane and annoying to say during class. Behind Koller was Jensen, wearing her usual frumpy sweater and baggy jeans. She spotted Verraday, smiled shyly at him then entered the building.

"Those are my students," said Verraday. "I'd better roll."

"I won't keep you then. Okay if I call you at home later on with some updates?"

"Please do," he said. "I'm going to the gym after class, but I should be finished with my workout and back home by six thirty."

CHAPTER 24

After his class and the gym, Verraday didn't feel like cooking, so on the way home, he stopped in at an unpretentious Middle Eastern café with travel posters of Lebanon on the walls. It was a habit he had acquired in university, when pita bread, hummus, baba ghanoush, and tabouleh had stretched his scant food budget while offering something more exotic and nourishing than the Kraft dinners or ramen noodles favored by most of his classmates. Verraday chose a beef shawarma to go, mentally scrolling through his modest wine collection to select a cheap but decent Sicilian Nero d'Avola that he'd have with it when he got home.

As he approached his house, Verraday saw that someone had once again opened his front gate while he was out and had left it unlatched. Annoyed, he walked up the path toward the front door. By the dim light of the street lamps, Verraday saw now that there was something on his doorstep. From halfway down the path, he could tell it was too irregularly shaped to be another bundle of unsolicited flyers. He pressed the button on his key fob that switched on a small LED and shone it on his doorstep. The narrow beam picked out a furry, slate-gray shape. He knelt to get a closer look and saw that it was a dead rat, face down. He retrieved his garden trowel from under the front steps and used it to turn the rat over.

He expected to find it gutted. He had seen that once before, the outcome of a turf war in the small hours of the night between an alley rat and a neighborhood raccoon. The shrieks of the combatants had formed a hellish and prolonged cacophony, though their skirmish had been completely invisible, cloaked in the darkness of the hour. The struggle between the raccoon and its opponent had ended suddenly with a hideous vocal duet. By grotesque coincidence, the raccoon's growl had formed a discordant lower fourth note against the other animal's shriek, a frenzied trill that was terrifying to hear, shooting up a neural pathway to some ancient part of Verraday's brain that instantly recognized it as a death cry. Verraday had only discovered the outcome the next morning when he took his trash into the alley. The rat had come out the loser and lay dead in a small pool of coagulated blood. The raccoon had ripped the rat open from its crotch to its neck, disemboweling it without eating a single bite, preferring the garbage in the nearby bins to the flesh of its victim.

Verraday now ran the keychain LED beam over the rat on his doorstep and saw that unlike its vanquished predecessor, this one's belly was intact. Its throat, however, had been slit from ear to ear with one single, neat incision, so deep that the ridges of the severed esophagus were visible. He also could feel when he'd turned

it over that rigor mortis had already set in. Verraday
checked the area around the rat with his LED beam
and noted that there was no blood on the steps, the
walkway, or on the gravel around the hedges. Whoever
or whatever had done this had killed it somewhere else
and brought the corpse to his doorstep only after it had
bled out. But why? Could an animal have made a cut
that clean? That seemed unlikely.

He didn't know that much about bodies, but he
understood minds, and his instincts told him this was
the work of a human. Perhaps it was a random act of idi-
ocy, a prank committed by somebody who didn't know
a thing about the person on whose doorstep they had
laid it. Or had he been deliberately targeted?

Verraday considered the most likely candidates. At
the top of his list was Bosko. Or perhaps it was Detective
Fowler. If Fowler had somehow gotten wind that Verraday was working with Maclean, this crude yet sadistic
signal seemed like the sort of thing he'd do to psych
him out, his way of telling him to back off. Then he
wondered if it was possible that a disgruntled student
had done it. Verraday was normally pretty popular with
his students. But there were always some who didn't like
you no matter what. They were the ones who skulked
around the Internet like cowardly assassins, using sites
like RateMyProfessor.com, the bane of academics, to
leave a one out of five rating and comments like "Boring," "useless," or "know-it-all jerk" without ever having to reveal their own identities. He wondered about
Koller. Verraday had gone a little heavy with the public
mockery of him in the last class. Not that Koller didn't

deserve it. But had it been enough to flip Koller's switch to the "crazy" setting, he wondered?

Verraday took his briefcase and his beef shawarma inside. He went to the kitchen, found a plastic bag, and took it out to the front steps. He dropped the rat's body into the bag and placed it in the freezer. If this were anything more than a prank, he would need to preserve the evidence. Even though he had never actually touched the rat directly, he had an urge to wash his hands with soap and water. He retrieved his shawarma, noticing now that it was roughly the same size and proportions as the rat. He felt a wave of revulsion. He put the shawarma in the refrigerator in case his appetite came back later, but suspected it would never happen.

Then he poured himself a brandy. Though the bottle was a deep, almost opaque brown, he could tell by the weight of it that it was nearly empty. He held the bottle up to the overhead kitchen light and confirmed that it only had a few ounces left in it. Verraday had lots of wine in his rack, as well as a nearly full bottle of vodka, and another of gin. But the brandy was a specific part of his nightly winding-down ritual. He made a mental note to stop at the liquor store and get another bottle tomorrow before he came home. He was just heading upstairs to shower off from his workout when he noticed the message light flashing on his phone. It was from Maclean.

"James, I need to speak to you as soon as possible. Doesn't matter how late it is. Call me, okay?"

He immediately punched the callback button. She answered on the first ring.

"What's up?" he asked.

"I paid a visit to the limo company. The story that Jason and Cody told us checks out. The dispatcher said they picked up a fare at the hangar around midnight. The address they took her to was Helen's apartment. They called the driver in. I interviewed him. He said that Helen was the only passenger, and he took her straight to the door of her apartment building. Because it was late, and she was alone, he waited 'til he saw her go through the controlled entrance and into the elevator before he drove away."

"Can the driver account for his time after that?"

"Yes. It occurred to me that a guy with a limousine would be in a position to meet a lot of call girls. And sure enough, he has. Looks like he was busy all night, shuttling them around to and from hotels. But he can answer for every minute of his time right up to the beginning of his shift the next evening. He's got witnesses, including his kids and his wife. She vouches that he slept all day until late afternoon when he went to pick his kids up at school."

"How about Jason and Cody. What did you find out?"

"That's the interesting part. I ran both of them through the computer just to see what came up. Jason doesn't have a record."

"But Cody?"

"Pants on fire. In more ways than one. He's got quite the rap sheet. And Jason Griffin knew it. Because Cody North is registered with a felon employment program that showed Griffinair as his employer and Jason Griffin as the contact. I was wondering if I brought the files by, would you have time to look at his rap sheet and give me your opinion on him?"

"Sure. I could do that. I just got back from the gym though. I need to shower and get cleaned up. Give me an hour?"

"All right. Have you eaten yet?"

"No. Long story."

"Then how about dinner courtesy of the SPD?"

"Sounds good."

"I'll pick something up. You like pizza?"

"Definitely."

"You want pepperoni or Italian sausage on it?"

"No meat for me, thanks."

"You're vegetarian?"

"Not normally. Just tonight. I'll explain when you get here. Actually, I'll explain after we eat."

"Duly noted. Do you like sun-dried tomatoes and black olives?"

"Yes."

"Goat cheese?"

"No."

"Good. Me neither. See you in an hour."

CHAPTER 25

By the time Maclean knocked on the door, Verraday was showered and dried off, and the endorphins from the workout had kicked in. He felt limbered up and refreshed, if still creeped out from the discovery of the dead rat.

"Nice place," she said as she entered carrying the pizza box.

"Thanks. You haven't seen the horrible upstairs carpeting yet though. Been meaning to rip it out since I got the place, but you know how it is."

"I don't have that problem. I'm back in a rental apartment since I got divorced."

"What can I get you?" he asked. "Want some wine?"

"Yes. But officially I'm on duty, so no, thanks. I'll just take some water."

He prepared a glass with ice and a lemon wedge for Maclean. He was about to uncork the Sicilian wine, which he'd been craving since he got the shawarma. Then he decided against it; he didn't feel right about enjoying it while Maclean was deprived of the pleasure. So he made a second ice water with lemon for himself.

He led Maclean to the small dining room table at the back of the main floor where he had the place settings waiting. Maclean set the pizza down on the table and Verraday noticed happily that it came from his favorite place in the University District rather than from one of the big chains. He liked Maclean's taste.

Over dinner they reviewed Cody's rap sheet together.

"Born twenty-six years ago in Stockton, California," said Maclean. "Parents were only eighteen years old themselves. Both had drug addiction problems. Been in and out of rehab. Father's done time for fraud and theft. Mother's been busted for prostitution."

The financial collapse of 2008 had hit Stockton hard. It became the largest city in US history to file for bankruptcy protection until Detroit eclipsed it five years later. It was a better place to leave than to be born.

"Everything about Cody North's life is in contrast to Jason Griffin's upbringing," said Verraday. "No swashbuckling grandparent, nobody taking the time to teach a twelve-year-old to fly a plane and take over a family business."

"A tale of two cities," said Maclean. "Cody's run-ins with the law began around the same time Jason was setting a world record for the youngest solo flight."

"We always come back to that nature-versus-nurture argument," replied Verraday. "It's a conundrum that we can never settle because most of the time, it's the people who provided the DNA who are doing the nurturing, or lack thereof. And professional ethics don't allow us to go around splitting up twins just to see what would happen if one had all the breaks and the other one got the Manson clan as parents. But it's something that as psychologists, we still don't understand. I'm not sure if we ever will."

"Right," said Maclean. "What makes one kid get his name into the Guinness Book of World Records, while another kid gets no further than being written up in a police case book? Cody's early arrests and convictions were for relatively minor things. A lot of it was that 'acting out' kind of stuff that you expect to see in unhappy kids: shoplifting, vandalism, trespassing, joyriding. Things began to get more serious in his later teens. He had arrests for breaking and entering, stripping cars, and narcotics."

"I see that he killed a drug dealer. How old was he?"

"Nineteen. He claimed that he was attacked when a deal went bad. There were no witnesses. It was ruled justifiable homicide, so he walked."

The pizza that Maclean had brought was delicious, and it occurred to Verraday that if the line of conversation hadn't been so unpleasant, he would have very much enjoyed having her company here. And he would have liked for the two of them to share that bottle of Nero d'Avola.

Verraday looked more closely at the rap sheet. "He's got a bunch of animal cruelty charges here. Three resulting in death. This concerns me more than the gang offenses. It's classic serial killer escalation. Jeffrey Dahmer stuck a dog's head on a stick and stripped animal carcasses before shifting his attention to boys. Edmund Kemper chopped the heads off cats before graduating to killing his mother and seven other women, and the

Boston Strangler did his apprenticeship firing arrows at cats and dogs that he'd trapped in boxes."

"I'm glad now that we didn't opt for the Italian sausage," said Maclean.

"You don't know the half of it," replied Verraday. "Now, these alleged sexual assaults on girls who were unlucky enough to be partying with Cody and his pals are also concerning."

"He would have been convicted each of those times," said Maclean, "except that the girls were high when it happened. He had his friends with him, who testified that it was just a house party gone wild. Plus he always wore a condom, so he never left any evidence behind. Their word against his."

"There's another killing here."

"Yes. A prostitute. They were engaged in hypoxyphilia. She died while he was choking her."

"How the hell did he beat that one?"

"The coroner ruled it was a heart attack brought about by cardiovascular disease that just happened to be triggered by the strangulation. The prostitute was a heavy cocaine user and had a weakened heart. Cody claimed it was just sex play. The defense looked into her background and found out that hypoxyphilia was one of her specialties. She charged a premium for catering to clients who had fantasies around strangling women."

"And then he landed in San Quentin."

"Killed another prostitute. He claimed that she stabbed him and robbed him and that it was self-defense. Said he hadn't meant to kill her, just protect himself. He got a manslaughter conviction."

"Well, it might not be a smoking gun, but it's damned close," said Verraday. "Psychologically speaking, I'd say Cody North is capable of making the leap to the level of violence that we saw in the Carmichael, Friesen, and Dale cases."

"I'm going to bring him in for questioning," said Maclean. "Now, before I go, you were going to tell me something about why you didn't want meat on your pizza tonight."

"You all finished? Sure you don't want anything else?"

"I'm good, thanks," Maclean replied.

"Then come on into the kitchen."

★   ★   ★

Maclean stood by Verraday's kitchen counter, examining the corpse of the rat, which he had laid on top of some plastic wrap. In the light, and with Maclean standing by, the rat seemed smaller and less ominous than when he had discovered it earlier that evening.

"So it was just lying on your front steps when you came home?" asked Maclean.

"Yes. I went to the gym and got something to eat, and when I got back, it was here."

"And rigor mortis had already set in?"

"It was stiff as a brick."

"That means it was killed earlier and dumped here. Did you find any blood anywhere on the steps or on the path?"

"No, I checked everywhere."

Maclean took a package of tongue depressors from her shoulder bag and pulled one out. With the depressor, she flipped the rat over on its back and pushed the fur away from the wound.

"That wound wasn't caused by another animal. That's man-made. I used to help my dad dress the geese and deer he had shot. I'd say this cut was made by a hunting knife."

"I've worked with plenty of rats in labs," said Verraday. "If this thing is anywhere near as bright as its cousins, there's nothing in the world that could get it to hold still while someone slit its throat."

"It was already dead when this cut was made. Poisoned," said Maclean. "See how there's blood around its nose? That's from an anticoagulant. Somebody poisoned this rat and slit its throat after it died."

Verraday sucked in a breath. "Nice."

"You ever had anything like this happen before? Any harassment in the past?"

"No, never. But there are definitely people who have an axe to grind with me. Top of the list is Bosko. He'd be able to figure out where I live. Can you send the rat to a lab for analysis? Maybe whoever did this was careless enough to leave some clues."

Maclean looked at him sympathetically, but with finality. "Theoretically the lab could look for human DNA or threads from clothing or carpet. But this is basically a nuisance case. It's pretty minor even as vandalism goes. Wild rats aren't protected under the Animal Welfare Act, so there's no law being broken on that side. As creepy as this is, the city would view it as less serious and destructive than tagging. On top of that, you haven't received any verbal or written threat."

"So the answer is no?"

"Sorry."

"But somebody's been leaving my gate open. Seems like an odd coincidence."

Maclean gazed at the rat again, then turned to Verraday. "You ever own a cat?"

"No," he replied.

"Well, I did, when I was a kid. It used to catch mice and chipmunks and leave them on our doorstep."

"Gross."

"It's just an instinctive feline behavior. A form of intimacy. The cat is not only sharing its kill with what it perceives as its family, it's encouraging its partner or offspring to join in the hunt. Do you have an alarm system?"

"No. Statistically this neighborhood has one of the lowest burglary rates in Seattle."

"Well, statistics or not, my advice is to get one."

"I don't really like having strangers in my house."

"James, that's *why* people get alarms installed. Promise me you'll do it?"

"Okay."

"Now, I'm going to swing by Cody's, bring him in for questioning."

"Don't you ever sleep?"

"Not when I'm this close."

"Can I ride along?"

"Love to have you there, James, but it could get dangerous."

"That's why I want to come along."

"I'm not going in alone. I'll bring two uniformed officers. They'd want to know who you are, and it would raise questions. But if we crack this case, they'll be kissing your ass down at city hall, lawsuit or not. So don't worry. You'll get your chance."

"All right, but only because you say so."

"I insist so."

Maclean donned her Burberry coat, and Verraday held the door open for her.

"Good luck," he said. "Let me know what happens as soon as you can."

"I will," she replied, touching him lightly on the shoulder as she crossed the threshold onto the front porch. "And thanks for your help."

The solar garden lamps were dim as usual, so he turned on the porch light to help guide her down the path. He stood in the doorway, watching as she got into the Interceptor. She leaned over to the passenger's side and, in silhouette, waved to him. He returned her gesture, then watched as she pulled away from the curb and, in typical fashion, quickly accelerated to what he guessed was several miles an hour over the speed limit. He watched her until she turned the corner at the end of the block. Only then did he close the door and turn off the porch light.

★　　★　　★

Verraday was about halfway through the bottle of Sicilian wine when his cell rang. It was Maclean.

"What's up?" he asked.

"I checked out the address that Cody's felon employment program showed as his residence."

"You have backup with you?" Verraday asked, trying not to betray the concern in his voice but not quite pulling it off.

"I've already left the address. But yes, I had two patrolmen with me and I still do. The only thing missing was the suspect. The place was empty. Literally. It's a ground-floor apartment with nothing in it. Not a stick of furniture. I called Jason Griffin twice but didn't get an answer. We're outside his condo now. The lights are off. I've been knocking on the door for the last five minutes. I sent a unit out to the airport to check on the Griffinair hangar. There was nobody there either. I'm putting out an APB on Cody North."

CHAPTER 26

Maclean and Verraday pulled up in front of the Griffinair hangar ten minutes before its official opening time
of eight AM. They got out and Maclean tried the front
door, but it was locked, and there was no response from
within. There were bars over the windows and blackout
blinds, so it was impossible to see inside the building.

Just then the whine of approaching jet engines
caught their attention. They looked around the corner
of the hangar and saw an executive jet taxiing toward
them from the tarmac. As the plane drew nearer,
Maclean and Verraday could see Jason Griffin at the
controls. The howl of the engine began to subside as
he powered the plane down. Maclean waved through
the chain link fence to catch his attention. He waved
back, acknowledging her, and held up his index finger
to indicate he'd be just a minute. They watched as the
passenger compartment door opened and a small set of
stairs flipped down. Jason stepped quickly out of the
plane and jogged double-time toward them, opening
the gate with his keycard.

"Good morning, Detective Maclean, Doctor. What can I do for you?"

Maclean was in his face the moment he stepped through the gate. "Why didn't you tell me you knew that Cody North was a felon?"

"Because I'm sure that he had nothing to do with killing that girl. He's reformed."

"Really? Are you aware of exactly what this man has done to people in the past? To women?"

"Yes. The people from the program told me everything about him. But they also told me he was a good bet for going straight. And I believe in giving people a second chance. I've had a lot of privileges. So I felt like paying it forward was the right thing to do."

"That's awfully altruistic of you, Mr. Griffin."

"I've worked hard in life. But I've also realized that with my success comes a responsibility to give breaks to guys that didn't get them."

"Well, I'm sure that speech will get you a warm round of applause and a stringy chicken dinner at the Rotary Club," said Maclean, "but right now, my bullshit meter is going right off the scale. You'd better start telling me the truth or I will personally visit every one of your CEO party pals at their head offices and ask them if they are aware that prostitution is illegal in this jurisdiction. Then I will send a press release to every media outlet in the city letting them know that your company hired a hooker to give hand jobs to the movers and shakers of Seattle, and now she's dead. How does that sound, Mr. Griffin?"

Jason sighed anxiously. "Look, I'm almost broke. That's the truth. My dad left this company in really bad shape. By the time he died, we were two months away from bankruptcy. The company would have gone straight down the toilet if I hadn't laid off most of the regular mechanics and changed the business model toward executive charters. You may not approve of that party I threw, but I've got three confirmed charters out of it so far, and seven more likely prospects. And it hasn't even been a week. As for Cody, I get federal and state assistance with his salary to upgrade his skills and a tax credit. He's basically free labor. I wanted to tell you the truth about him, but I really didn't think he did it—still don't—and I can't afford to lose him. He's the last employee I've got, and until I get the cash flow from those flights to Mexico, I'm screwed. I can't afford to pay anybody else to take over from him."

"Well, then I think you've got a problem. Because when I ran a check on him last night, along with finding out about his extensive criminal record, I also got his address. And I went by there to question him. But guess what I found? An empty apartment."

"There's nothing to worry about. He moved to a new place at the beginning of October. His new address won't be in the records until my bookkeeper processes the next cycle of paychecks, which is next Friday. His new address is in my office. Everything's cool."

"No everything is not cool, Mr. Griffin. Because Cody North is supposed to be here and he isn't."

"He's always been super reliable. This is literally the first time he's ever been late. Why don't we go inside; I'll call him and find out what's going on and we'll sort this out."

"Okay, let's go," said Maclean.

Jason unlocked the front door, turned off the alarm, and flicked the lights on.

"Cody? You here, man? Cody, yo!"

There was no answer.

"Does Cody often lurk around in here with the lights off?" asked Maclean, betraying more than a little sarcasm.

"No," replied Jason patiently, "but once in a while if he's working late and starting early, he sleeps here in one of the planes or in the back of the van."

"Does he own a vehicle?"

"No. I'm not able to pay him much 'til I get this place back on its feet. He can't afford a car of his own, so I let him use the company vehicle after hours."

"You trust him with your own property. How magnanimous," said Maclean. "But I didn't see your van parked outside. And I don't see it anywhere in the hangar either. This makes me very concerned, Mr. Griffin."

"Look, I know Cody's done some pretty bad things. But when they showed me his criminal file, and I found out his background, it seemed a lot of it was because of circumstance and lousy breaks. I mean, you read his life history and you think, 'There but for the grace of God go I,' you know?"

"There but for the grace of God go you indeed. Because if Cody North turns out to be the murderer and you helped him get away because you concealed his criminal past from me, I will charge you with being an accessory to homicide. And the fact that Cody North is not here when he's supposed to be gives me great cause for alarm."

"Look, I'm calling him right now. You'll see that everything's fine."

Jason took out his cell phone and hit the speed dial. He listened impatiently as the phone rang through to voice mail. "Hey Cody, it's me. Where are you, man? I'm at the hangar. You're supposed to be here. Call me as soon as you get this, okay? It's urgent."

"I'm getting a very bad feeling about this," said Maclean. "I would like Cody's new address right now."

"Yeah, sure. 345 Tamarack Way, Apartment 202. Maybe he slept in or something. Like I said, he's super dependable, but he does like to party, and he does like the ladies."

"Yeah, right," said Maclean. "He likes the ladies so much he may have killed two and sexually assaulted several more. That we know of."

"Look, I'm sure if you go to his apartment, this will all be sorted out."

"Assuming he's not halfway to Mexico by now. What's the make and plate number of the company van?"

"It's a 2010 Ford Econoline. 954TDZ."

Maclean called her dispatcher. "This is Detective Maclean. I've got a follow-up on that APB on a Cody North. He may be driving a 2010 Ford Econoline, license nine five four Tango Delta Zulu. He's a person of interest in a homicide and may be trying to flee the area in that vehicle."

Verraday looked into the darkness of the hangar and noticed that the Dodge Charger was gone.

"What happened to your Charger?" he asked.

"He didn't drive away in it, if that's what you're worried about. It's not running. I had it towed to an upholstery shop yesterday. It's got some interior panels that are rotted and need to be replaced. I'm planning to sell it as soon as I get it fixed up so I can use the cash for the business."

"By the way, are its numbers matching?" asked Verraday.

"Why?"

Verraday gazed at him for a moment before replying. "Just curiosity. Most of the 1968 Chargers were sold with 318 V-8s, like the one in my dad's Belvedere. The 426 Hemi was an expensive option. There were fewer than five hundred sold that first year. And if it's the original engine that came with the car, that makes yours worth a lot more than one that had a 426 dropped in from some other donor car. Be good for your cash flow."

"Oh, right."

Maclean listened as the dispatcher came back on the line. She sighed. "Okay. Put in a request that they don't move anything until I get there." Maclean clicked the end call button.

"What's wrong?" asked Jason, his brow furrowed with concern.

"Cody's dead."

"What?" exclaimed Jason, disbelieving. "How?"

"His body was just found at the bottom of a canyon below a hiking trail in Issaquah. The Griffinair company van was found nearby."

"Ah, shit," said Jason. He looked stunned for a moment, just stood there with his mouth hanging open. "Ah, shit," he said again. "How could he do this? I believed him. And he lied to me."

"What do you mean?" asked Maclean.

"He told me he'd never go back to prison. Ever. I thought that meant that he'd gone straight, that he'd never do anything to make anybody put him back in there. I didn't think it meant he'd kill himself."

"No one said he committed suicide," replied Maclean. Jason looked ashen.

"When did you last see him?" asked Maclean.

"When we closed up last night. He told me he was going home. He took the van."

"And what about you?"

"I stuck around to flight test the Citation. I flew it up to Port Angeles."

"Did you file a flight plan?"

"Yes, of course. You can check."

"And what time did you get back?"

"Just now. I was near Port Angeles when I started getting some gremlins in the instruments. False readings. It was dark and there was low cloud cover moving in. I didn't want to risk flying on instruments alone, so I put down there for the night."

"Where did you stay in Port Angeles?"

"At the Red Lion Hotel."

"Can you prove it?"

"Sure. I always put everything on the company credit card."

Jason showed Maclean the hotel invoice and the Visa receipt.

"How did you get from the airport to the Red Lion?"

"I rented a car. Got a last-minute deal that was way cheaper than the price of a taxi to and from the airport."

Jason retrieved the rental contract from his brief-case and presented it to Maclean. The odometer reading showed that he had put less than twenty miles on it.

"I called you several times last night. Why didn't you answer your phone?" she asked.

"I was exhausted. I turned my phone off. I just didn't want to talk to anybody. I ordered a bottle of wine, poured a big glass of it, and just sat on the shore in front of the hotel, watching the ocean. I've been pretty stressed over the financial situation around here and tired from getting that Citation ready to fly to Mexico, and now this thing with that poor girl being murdered."

"All right, Mr. Griffin. I'll leave you to get on with your day," said Maclean. "You'll be needing to find yourself a new mechanic. Also, I don't know when you have those flights to Mexico planned, but I'd prefer if you stick around town for the next day or two until this is wrapped up. I may want to speak with you again."

CHAPTER 27

Issaquah was less than an hour from downtown Seattle but was rugged enough to have trails that were challenging even for seasoned hikers. Maclean and Verraday spotted the Ford Econoline near a guardrail with a King County Sheriff's department patrol car parked nearby it. A solitary deputy was at the scene. He waved to them as he spotted their vehicle approaching.

Maclean spoke quietly to Verraday as they pulled up. "The good news is that this is under the jurisdiction of the King County Sheriff's department. They're not particularly tight with the Seattle PD, so having you along won't raise any red flags. Even so, it will be best if you leave the questions to me."

The Deputy led them down a steep trail toward where the body lay. It had taken a beating during the fall and was crumpled like a rag doll at the bottom of the rocky canyon, one hundred feet below the trail. But there was no doubt about the identity. The battered face was that of Cody North.

"I didn't touch the body except to remove the wallet for identification purposes," said the deputy. "It was in the pocket of his down-filled vest. The registration for the van was in there too. So was a set of keys. He's got a cell phone on him too. I heard it ringing just after eight o'clock, but I didn't want to touch it in case whoever was trying to reach him could be part of an investigation."

"Good call, Deputy. Did you examine the van?"

"Just a cursory inspection. It was locked, but one of the keys that the deceased had on him fit the vehicle. I had a look inside. Not much to see though. Just the usual stuff: junk-food wrappers, empty coffee cups."

"Mind if we take a look?"

"Be my guest."

After climbing up out of the steep ravine, Verraday and Maclean walked over to the Econoline. They donned latex gloves and leaned in through the open side doors to inspect it. As the deputy had described, there was nothing much visible except food wrappers and empty coffee cups. Then Verraday looked up toward the ceiling at the same moment as Maclean.

"You see what I see?" he asked.

"Oh yeah," she replied.

Tucked into the driver's sun visor was a dream catcher. The same small dream catcher that Rachel Friesen had worn as a navel ring in her Assassin Girls page. Maclean turned to the King County officer.

"Deputy, this site is now part of a homicide investigation."

★　　★　　★

"I'll need to have a Seattle PD forensics team go through Cody Walker's apartment," said Maclean as she and Verraday headed back to Seattle in her Interceptor. "I'd love to have you there to have a look, see what it tells you about Cody, but it would raise a lot of questions. Sorry."

"No worries," said Verraday. "I have several days' worth of e-mails from students to read when I get home. That ought to keep me busy and in a bad mood."

"Well, hopefully I'll have something to cheer you up with after we've finished the search. I'll be in touch again as soon as we're done there."

CHAPTER 28

While one forensics team examined the van, Maclean led another to the address that Jason Griffin had given her for Cody North's new apartment. It was in a dumpy low-rise building in Yessler, not far from the original Skid Row that had lent its name to Skid Rows all over the world. They were let in by the superintendent, a thin man with grayish skin and a ragged smoker's cough.

The white paper masks and coveralls that Maclean and the other members of her team wore prevented them from accidentally contaminating the site. But those measures wouldn't stop the site from contaminating them.

Maclean recoiled slightly as she took her first breath of the apartment. The air was pungent and close. It smelled of stale tobacco, stale beer, and stale takeout food. Maclean caught a faint whiff of mold too. Dirty laundry spilled out of a vinyl hamper onto the floor, adding to the gamy cocktail they were forced to inhale.

Darnell Rivers, a young civilian forensic tech with a high fade and an expression of perpetual surprise, was next in after Maclean. He whistled in amazement at the claustrophobically small bachelor apartment.

"Holy crap, I didn't know they made 'em this tiny. Place is like the Munchkin Manor."

"He spent the last four years at San Quentin," said Maclean. "The occupancy rate there is one hundred and thirty-seven percent. I guess this looks like the Trump Tower by comparison."

The parquet floor was bare. The varnish was worn down to the wood by the entranceway and the bathroom, where the ill-fitting door brushed against it enough to have scraped a track. Three empty beer cans and the remains of a recently consumed pepperoni pizza in a greasy box sat on the coffee table. Beside the unmade bed, there were copies of *Maxim* and *Hustler*, as well as a magazine that Maclean had never seen before, something called *Duty Bound*. On the cover was a girl in a suggestive version of a policewoman's uniform, breasts exposed, short skirt torn and riding up her thighs. She was gagged and handcuffed, an alarmed expression on her face as she gazed wide-eyed at something out of frame.

"Okay, listen up," said Maclean. "The individual who lived here is dead. His body turned up in Issaquah this morning. We believe it was suicide. He is a suspected serial killer who liked to torture his victims first, and he liked taking souvenirs. If this is our man, he saved the justice system a lot of time and money by offing himself. But that doesn't mean our work is done, because the victims' families and significant others need closure. We have no idea how many people our perp may have killed.

So it's very important that we find every possible clue that could identify a victim. Is that clear?"

The team members nodded. Even Rivers looked serious.

"All right then. Let's close this case right here and now."

Maclean's team eagerly set to work. Rivers pulled back the clammy bed sheets and raised an eyebrow with an exaggerated expression of distaste that was only partly mugging. He waved a hand in front of his face as though waving away a bad smell.

"Baby, you need a hazmat suit to go down to this funky town."

"I'll be sure to write you up for a bravery commendation," said Maclean. "Keep looking."

Maclean began taking notes on her iPad, taking her own photos and listing every object that caught her eye, any detail that could be a clue. Rivers felt around in the sheets, working his way down to the foot of the bed where the top sheet was tucked in tightly.

"Something wedged down here," he said.

He gave a gentle tug. Then grinning, he pulled back the sheets and triumphantly held up his prize, a pair of women's black lace panties.

"Unless this guy was a Frederick's of Hollywood model, I'd say we've got some evidence here, boss."

"Bag it up, Rivers," said Maclean. "And get it UV tested to see if there are traces of semen on it."

"I don't need a UV light to give you the answer to that one." He furrowed his brow into another look of distaste. "I'd say these were somebody's playmate of the month. Only question is whose."

"Let me get a shot of them," said Vasquez, a slim young woman who was the team photographer.

Vasquez snapped photos from every angle before moving on to the hall closet. She reached into the closet with a small flashlight and probed the recesses.

"There's something here that you should see, Detective."

Vasquez pointed to a long two-pronged object, partly hidden behind a mop and broom.

"You know what that is?" she asked.

"Yeah," replied Maclean. "It's a cattle prod. That's evidence. Get some photos."

Rivers looked over.

"Judging by this place, that cattle prod got a lot more use than that mop or broom."

"Keep digging, people" said Maclean. "I want everything."

CHAPTER 29

By the time Verraday's cell phone rang that evening, he had already had a couple of large glasses of red wine. Between that, the gas flames from the fireplace, and the patter of rain on the windows, he had been lulled into a pleasant state of drowsiness. Maclean's call changed all that.

"North's apartment is a fucking gold mine, James," said Maclean. He could hear the excitement in her voice.

"What have you got?"

"Panties that match Rachel Friesen's in the Assassin Girls photos. We'll have to check them for her DNA as well as North's to confirm. But it looks like a positive. There was a cattle prod that could have been used on Helen Dale. The dress that they both wore is here. It's got blonde hair in the zipper. Could be Helen's. Found two small tins, one with a locket of dark-brown hair, the other blonde. I'm sending it all to the lab for identification."

"How about Alana Carmichael? Anything of hers there? That Cupid's arrow maybe?"

"No. Nothing's turned up yet. But we're not done looking. When I get off the phone, I'll e-mail my notes to you along with the photos of everything we've got so far."

"Good. I'll take a look as soon as I get them."

"Okay. Let's talk in the morning. And thanks."

Verraday watched as the inbox of his laptop began to fill up with the files Maclean was sending him. He was excited, but also apprehensive. He was relieved that the killer might have been stopped in his tracks once and for all, but he also felt trepidation at having to examine the evidence. The intimate articles of clothing and jewelry that the young women had worn, both to please themselves and their clients, had instead become the perverse trophies of a psychopathic killer. It would be a disturbing process to examine all the evidence piece by piece, but it was necessary in order to conclude the case and provide closure to the survivors.

Verraday steeled himself for the task at hand by going to the kitchen to pour himself a large brandy. He took his Seattle World's Fair tumbler from the dish rack then grabbed the bottle. It felt very light, and as he poured the last of the contents into his glass, he saw that there was less than half an ounce in it. He was annoyed at himself, couldn't believe he'd forgotten to pick up a fresh bottle after making a mental note the previous evening. He didn't feel up to viewing the evidence photos from Cody North's apartment without the numbing effects of the brandy and resigned himself to going out to buy some more. Verraday put his jacket and boots on, grabbed the umbrella off the hall tree, and stepped onto the front porch.

The showers had grown heavier throughout the evening, and now the wind had begun to blow in hard from Puget Sound, whipping the rain diagonally toward the ground. Verraday opened his umbrella. A sudden gust nearly pulled it out of his hands and began to turn it inside out. As Verraday angled the umbrella into the wind to keep the metal frame from snapping, he heard his front gate bang. He saw it swinging freely, rattling against the latch. He knew that he'd pulled it shut behind him when Maclean dropped him off. All the other gates on his street were closed. He bent down to see if there was something faulty with the latch, but it was fine. He stepped out onto the sidewalk and made sure the gate was now properly secured. He had planned on walking the four blocks to the liquor store, but the rain was so heavy that even if his umbrella survived the trip, which was uncertain, he knew he'd be sopping wet by the time he got there and back. He felt vaguely guilty about driving his car for such a short journey but decided it was the lesser of two evils.

When he arrived at the liquor store, the parking lot was deserted. So was the store, and he was in and out with his brandy in less than two minutes. The thunderstorm was so intense now that Verraday was obliged to open his umbrella just to make the ten-yard dash from the store to his car without getting soaked. Even with his umbrella held close above him, the rain pelted his shoes and jeans from the knees down. When he reached his car, he set his brandy on the roof and slid his free hand into his jacket for his keys. Still holding his umbrella in his left hand, shoulders hunched, he fumbled around for them, finally locating them wedged crosswise in a corner of his pocket.

He was prying them loose when he was suddenly blinded by an intense white light.

He looked up to see a Seattle Police Department SUV parked across the lot, partially hidden behind a dumpster, with its high beams trained on him. With the whoop of a siren and a flash of red-and-blue lights, the SUV crept toward him. Verraday couldn't make out the driver until the vehicle had pulled up close enough to him that he was even with the door. The rain-slicked driver's side window slid down, revealing the officer within: Bosko. Verraday gave him a sour look.

"Nice of you to come out in such lousy weather just to pay me a visit, Officer. But then again, you've been spending so much time hanging around my house you must be getting used to it by now."

Bosko returned Verraday's disapproving expression.

"I don't know what you're talking about. I'm just here doing a routine stakeout for the Drunk Net program, looking for DUIs. Liquor store seems like a logical place for it, don't you think?"

"Are you kidding me? On a night like this?"

"Oh, you'd be surprised at what kind of lowlife come out in this kind of weather. You know, pissheads who'd rather get drenched than go a night without booze."

"I should have guessed it was you who's been following me around, Bosko."

"I'm not following you around. I'm just here in this parking lot doing my job."

"Do you really think you can get me to drop my lawsuit by fucking with me, leaving my gate open all the time, putting a dead rat on my doorstep?"

"Doc, I don't know anything about your gate or any dead rat. And I don't know how much time you psychologists spend around crazies, but I'd suggest you cut back on your hours. I think the nut jobs are starting to rub off on you."

"Oh yeah. Deny, deny, deny. It's the oldest trick in the playbook."

"Have you consumed any alcoholic beverages this evening, sir?"

"Yes. Two glasses of wine. If you have reason to suspect I'm lying, I'll be happy to blow into a Breathalyzer. Otherwise, I'm a free citizen going about my lawful business, and if you want to continue this conversation, I'll go ahead and call my lawyer."

"Two glasses of wine, huh? Okay. You're free to go. Have a good night."

Verraday was completely soaked from the knees down now. He pulled out his remote and unlocked his car, fighting a losing battle against the pelting rain. As he lowered himself into the driver's seat, he closed the umbrella, then cursed as a cascade of cold rainwater ran down from it onto his crotch. Fuming, Verraday put the key in the ignition and started the car.

He looked out the window to see Bosko gazing at him quizzically, motioning with his chin to get his attention. Verraday lowered his window.

"What is it now?" he snapped.

Bosko gestured to a point just above Verraday's head.

"Don't forget your bottle, Doc."

"Fuck," whispered Verraday as he realized that, rattled by the confrontation, he'd left it on the roof of his car.

Bosko raised his window and backed the patrol SUV across the parking lot into its lair beside the dumpster so that it was invisible from the street. As Verraday climbed out to retrieve his bottle of brandy, even through the rain, he could see Bosko shaking his head, a derisive smirk on his face.

CHAPTER 30

At Verraday's request, he and Maclean met in his office at Guthrie Hall instead of at the café to review the evidence. Between the previous evening's confrontation with Bosko and the photos of the trophies in North's apartment from the murdered women, he wasn't in the mood to deal with anybody's bullshit. He was feeling pretty jangled, though he took pains to hide it from Maclean.

He poured some strong dark roast coffee and milk from a thermos into two cups and handed one to Maclean. She took a sip. He noticed that she closed her eyes for the briefest instant as she tasted it. This was a woman whose life only allowed for fleeting pleasures.

"Mm, this is good. Thanks."

"So? What's the score?" asked Verraday.

"They've got the champagne chilling down at headquarters, all set to pop the corks. The captain of homicide and the chief say they're both ready to hand the case over to the DA if I am."

"What do you think?"

"I think it would make a lot of people happy. But we never did turn up any evidence connecting Cody North to Alana Carmichael. So it doesn't get Cray off the hook. And it doesn't expose Fowler as the fraud that he is. Unless I'm wrong, and the Alana Carmichael case isn't related to this one."

"Why are you suddenly doubting yourself?"

Maclean absentmindedly rotated her coffee mug on the desk, a nervous reaction that Verraday noticed was extremely unusual for her.

"I'm wondering why we only found trophies from Rachel Friesen and Helen Dale at Cody North's apartment. None from Alana Carmichael. What if Cody North *didn't* kill her? What if I've blinded myself to that possibility, lost my objectivity because I hate Fowler so much? And swayed you as well. Plus Fowler would love for me to be wrong. If I don't have all my ducks lined up, and soon . . ."

"I know what it will mean," said Verraday. "And you know what I think?"

Maclean stared into her coffee. He didn't wait for her to answer.

"I think you're a good cop. And a decent person. And because you're a good cop and a decent person, you're questioning yourself and your motives. But you have good instincts, and you're one hell of a detective from what I've seen. Your gut is telling you that something's not adding up here. And I think your gut is right."

She looked up from her coffee, but didn't speak.

"So, Detective, what are your instincts telling you right now?" asked Verraday.

"That it's very strange that we haven't found any trophies related to Alana Carmichael."

"Putting your feelings about Fowler aside, do you think she could have been killed by someone other than whoever killed Rachel Friesen and Helen Dale?"

"It's possible, but I'd say it's unlikely. I agree with your assessment of Cray, your profile of him, and I still don't think he killed Alana Carmichael. Plus there were no other murders with this MO. I just can't figure out why, if Cody North did it, he would want souvenirs of Rachel and Helen but not of Alana. As a psychologist, can you think of a reason a murderer would have one particular victim whose personal effects didn't interest him?"

"No. I can't."

"Then why would we find trophies from two victims, but not from all three?"

"To determine that, you also have to determine what Rachel Friesen and Helen Dale have in common that's different from Alana Carmichael."

"They have almost everything in common. All three are of the same type physically and aesthetically, and they all traveled in the same circles. There's only one thing different that I can think of: as far as any member of the general public or even the police department knows, there's already a suspect in custody who's confessed to killing Alana Carmichael. And that the only thing standing between that suspect and a conviction is the trial coming up next month."

She paused.

"James, only you and I know that we're looking for somebody who also killed Alana Carmichael."

"So whoever the real killer is, he thinks he's off the hook for the Carmichael murder. He's only worried about getting caught for killing Rachel Friesen and Helen Dale," said Verraday.

"Yes, and that would mean that he did it by framing Cody North, killing him or having him killed, then making it look like a suicide to tie a ribbon on the whole thing," Maclean continued. "But why frame Cody North? Why choose him?"

"Because whoever did it was smart enough to realize that Cody North had the right profile to be believable as the killer. And that it was also believable that he'd commit suicide rather than go back to prison. Who do you know who would know all that about North?"

"Son of a bitch. Griffin sponsored Cody North and brought him to Seattle just before Alana Carmichael was murdered!" exclaimed Maclean.

Verraday nodded agreement. "And he kept him around as insurance against the day that he'd need a scapegoat for the murders."

"Plus they're the same age and race," said Maclean. "Someone looking for a person with Jason's profile could easily fall for the sleight of hand and be directed toward Cody instead."

"Jason Griffin planned this very carefully. He probably looked through the profiles of hundreds of ex-felons before he found just the right one."

"But how do we prove any of this?" asked Maclean. "How do we know we're even right? There's not a shred of Jason Griffin's DNA on any of the bodies."

"We've got to shake him up," said Verraday. "Jason thinks he's smarter than everyone else. He thinks he's outwitted us at every turn. So we have to throw him off balance, find his Achilles' heel. He's got to believe we've got so much on him that there's no point in putting up a fight. And we've got to figure out how to do it as quickly as possible before there's time for the shit to come down on you for openly questioning whether Fowler got it right."

"There's something you said early on that's stuck with me," said Maclean.

"What's that?"

"That whoever the perpetrator is must have committed killings before to be this good at it. Since there were no bodies fitting the killer's signature found in Seattle before Alana Carmichael was murdered, we have to assume that if Jason Griffin is the killer, he committed his previous murders somewhere else. So what happened in Jason Griffin's life that would have changed his MO? Made him started killing the way he's killing now?"

"He said his father died last year. He was the head of the business until then."

"Yes," said Maclean, "which means that now, Jason can use the hangar as the kill and cleanup site. It's perfect."

"He would have had to take his victims somewhere else to dispose of them," said Verraday.

"But where?"

"Robert Pickton's family owned a forty-acre farm in Port Coquitlam. That's how he was able to hide the bodies of so many women."

"There was a picture of Jason with his mother at the controls of a floatplane," said Maclean. "Professor Lowenstein mentioned that they used to fly floatplane charters."

"Right, and if the Griffin family had a lot of money at that time, it wouldn't be unreasonable to assume they had a vacation property some place."

"I can do a search of land titles. It's all electronic nowadays. It'll only take a few minutes."

Verraday vacated his seat so that Maclean could come around and use his desktop computer. She punched in the surname and a string of properties came up, both for ones currently owned and ones sold within the last several years.

"Look at this," said Maclean. "There are only three recent property transfers in the state listed for a Fred Griffin. One is the family home in Fremont, which, as you can see, was transferred from Jason's father to Jason's mother when they divorced four years ago. Fred also owned a condo that Jason inherited after his father died last year. The third one is a twenty-acre waterfront vacation property up on Suquamish Island, in the San Juans. It was sold off less than a month before Fred died."

"You know anything about the San Juans or Suquamish?"

"Never been there. Let's check it out."

Maclean Googled it and in seconds had some results.

"No ferry service to Suquamish," she said. "And no airstrip. The only way in is by private boat or—get this—floatplane. Only about thirty full-time residents. Very lonely, very remote. The kind of place where something terrible could happen to you and nobody would ever know. Fred inherited it from his father, so his ex-wife couldn't touch it as part of the divorce settlement. But as next of kin, Jason would have been in line for it. *If* his dad hadn't sold it first."

"But then the father dies suddenly a few weeks later. I wonder if the new owner has received any generous offers from mysterious strangers wanting to buy it?" asked Verraday.

"I'll check on that," said Maclean. "And I wonder what he died from. The obituary suggested a mental health organization for donations."

"Suicide?"

"If that's the story, I'm going over that coroner's report with a fine-toothed comb, and if anything's out of place, I'll have the case reopened. I want to find out if the father had any help dispatching himself. And I'll speak to the new owner and the real estate agent," said Maclean, "find out if Jason's tried to buy back the property. There's something else I've been wondering too."

"What's that?"

"When you asked Jason Griffin if the numbers matched on the engine and frame of his Dodge Charger, I saw a flicker of something on his face. I'm going to run Jason through the DMV registration system, make sure that car's registered in his name. And if it is, I'm going to find out if that's the original engine. You're the vintage car expert. The VIN code would indicate what the original engine is, right?"

"Yes, it would."

"If it's not the original, we should get the serial number off it and find out where it came from. Might be hot.

Now, how about Cody North's death? What are your thoughts on it? Forensics says there were no fragments of skin or clothing under the fingernails. Jason's lawyers will use that."

"If Cody North was close enough to the edge of the trail to go down without a fight, or to not see it coming, then if there was someone else there, it had to be someone he trusted, someone he'd let get close to him. Someone like Jason."

"But Jason was in Port Angeles. He's got the proof. Unless he hired someone to kill Cody for him."

"Not necessarily," said Verraday. "I was thinking about that. Port Angeles is only two and a half hours away by car. He would have had just enough time to call Cody, arrange to meet him, drive down, kill him, and drive back in time to fly that plane into Seattle at eight AM."

"But he had the car rental contract that showed only twenty miles on the odometer."

"You know, if I was looking for an alibi for where I was when someone was killed, and the place was driving distance from where that killing took place, I would order a bottle of wine from room service. Then I would take a glass down to the beach in front of the hotel where everybody would see me. Then just to be really certain I'd been noticed, I'd leave my rental car parked as close to the office as possible, so everybody could see it too, see that it was parked there all night."

"And then?"

"Do they have more than one car rental agency in Port Angeles? There's no law against anybody renting more than one car, is there?"

"You're saying he rented a second car in Port Angeles, then drove it down to Issaquah and back?"

"It's possible."

"You have a devious mind, James."

"I try."

"Okay. I think it's time for me to head downtown, access the DMV registration system, and make a few calls to Port Angeles."

CHAPTER 31

Jason Griffin sat on the other side of the desk in interrogation room number six. He had an earnest, serious expression on his face, like this was all just some terrible misunderstanding that could be quickly cleared up so he could be on his way. If Griffinair was in financial difficulty, it wasn't evident from Jason's choice of attorney. Rod Tarleton was an eight-hundred-dollar-an-hour defense lawyer who had expensive tastes and a reputation for pulling rabbits out of hats. Griffin had called him so quickly that Maclean had barely had time to read him his Miranda rights.

Maclean had a small Bluetooth earpiece that allowed her to hear Verraday, who was watching via a Skype link from behind the two-way mirror. Maclean would have liked to have him in the room. But if anybody had noticed his presence—and chances were good that in the interrogation rooms, either the chief, the homicide captain, Fowler, or one of his cronies would see him—the effect would have been explosive. This case was volatile enough as it was.

"Mr. Griffin," said Maclean. "I've done a lot of research on you during the past day, and there are some things I don't understand. Why didn't you tell me before that you your father committed suicide?"

Jason looked at her gravely. "Because it's still a very painful memory for me. It's not exactly something that's easy to talk about. Besides, it didn't seem relevant."

"Didn't seem relevant? Doesn't it seem odd that people who are close to you have a habit of committing suicide?"

"Detective, there's no call to speak to my client that way," said Tarleton. "He has suffered a great deal in the past year."

"That's okay," said Jason. "She's just trying to do her job."

Then he turned to Maclean.

"Yes, it's true that I've had more than my fair share of tragedy. First my father, then Cody. But my mother always taught me to believe in myself and in the value of hard work. So I'll get through this, just like I got through the trouble with the family business."

"Well, here's another detail for you to consider. We've examined the coroner's report regarding your father's death. And I've gotten a second opinion. My ballistics expert thinks the coroner missed some important details. The powder burns and the angle of the bullet are right on the edge of what would have been impossible for anyone to do themselves without having had help. Bottom line is that it was sloppy work by the coroner. And by the killer, whoever that was. So we've reopened the case."

"Are you suggesting that I killed my own father?" asked Jason.

Tarleton touched him lightly on the arm. "You don't have to respond to this line of questioning, son."

"Okay, time to unglue him," whispered Verraday. "Mention the land now."

"Well you certainly had a reason to," said Maclean. "Your father was running the business into the ground. That was why he sold the twenty-acre retreat that your family owned on Suquamish Island. For cash flow. But you had an even more important reason for not wanting him to sell it, didn't you?"

Jason sat there with an uncomprehending expression on his face.

"You see," continued Maclean, "I checked with the new owner of the land, an Ellen Williams. She told me that a realtor has been calling her every three weeks with an offer to buy. So I asked her who this realtor was, and I spoke to him to find out who he was representing. Are you going to make Mr. Tarleton guess who the mystery person is, Jason, or should I just tell him?"

Jason Griffin shrugged. "So I put in an offer. I grew up there. I have a lot of fond memories from the family cottage."

"Nail him!" whispered Verraday.

"I bet you do. And we're going to dig up every one of those fond memories of yours until we have all the evidence we need to put you on death row."

Jason Griffin smirked, his personality suddenly shifting to belligerent. "You don't have shit," he said.

Maclean brought out a photo of a border collie.

Griffin looked vaguely amused. "What's with the dog, Detective?"

"I'm glad you asked. This is a cadaver-sniffing dog belonging to the State Patrol. His name is Torch. He's successfully located bodies that have been buried for more than two decades. He's also found remains as small as a single vertebra."

Maclean pulled out another photo, this one an aerial shot of a heavily treed island. "I think you'll recognize the island in this aerial photo. Shouldn't be hard, since by your own admission, you have so many fond memories of it." She pointed to a large waterfront parcel of land marked off with red ink. "This is the recreational property that your father sold to Ellen Williams. We flew Torch and his handler up to Suquamish Island this morning to start looking for your other victims. The ones you used to fly out there in your floatplane before your father sold that too, along with the island property, so shortly before his conveniently timed 'suicide.'"

Tarleton looked apoplectic. "This is outrageous," he thundered. "You don't have proof of anything, Detective. Just circumstantial evidence for crimes that you can't prove even exist."

"Really? Well then let's talk about that Dodge Charger Hemi instead."

"What?" snorted Griffin.

"You said it was at an upholstery shop."

"That's right."

"You're lying, Mr. Griffin. I had a patrol car do a drive-by of your mother's home this morning. What do you think they found?"

Jason didn't answer.

"There was a covered vehicle carrier in her driveway," continued Maclean. "One that was exactly the right size to have a Dodge Charger in it. So we got a warrant and executed that warrant right before we picked you up, so you and your mom wouldn't have time for a little emergency conference. And what do you suppose was in that trailer but a vintage Dodge Charger worth a lot of money."

"Detective, that vehicle is lawfully registered to my client. Where are you going with all this?" asked Tarleton.

"Hold on, Counselor. I think you'll find this interesting. So Jason, you lied about the car being at the upholstery shop. It was at your mother's house."

"That's not a crime," said Tarleton. "He probably just didn't want you and your horde pestering his poor mother."

"No, Counselor, I don't think that was the reason. I think it had more to do with the fact that the VIN number, which I checked this morning, indicates that your car came equipped with a 318 V-8, not a 426 Hemi?"

"So what?" sneered Griffin.

"So the engine serial number of the Hemi now installed in your car indicates that it originally came from a 1971 Dodge Challenger down in Eugene, Oregon. Apparently two men came to test drive it a few months ago. Since the car was worth almost $100,000, the owner, one Paul Schmidt, quite understandably wanted to ride along. For some strange reason, instead of leaving their own vehicle at the home of the Challenger's owner, one of the men test drove the car while the other man followed behind in their vehicle. An hour later, when Mr. Schmidt hadn't returned home, his wife became concerned. And apparently she had reason to be, because Paul Schmidt's body turned up a week later, in a backwoods canyon, burned beyond recognition. The Dodge Challenger was never recovered."

"Look, I bought that Hemi in good faith from somebody Cody knew. I had no idea it was hot or I never would have bought it."

"Well, here's the thing," said Maclean. "The wife of the owner was watching from the kitchen window when her husband went out to meet these two young men. She couldn't get a good look at their car or plate number, but there was something about them she didn't like. She's already identified Cody as one of them. And she has agreed to be flown up here to pick you out of a lineup. In fact, she's here as we speak. Now, your mother had your car with the stolen engine stored at her property. That makes her an accessory."

"This is bullshit," said Jason.

"My client is right, Detective. This is ridiculous."

"Well, the judge didn't think so, because he's issued an arrest warrant for your mother. And she's in custody right now."

Jason's jaw tightened.

"Keep working him over about his mother," whispered Verraday. "That's the first time I've seen him flinch. She's the way in."

"I looked in on her right before this interview," said Maclean. "There are some pretty nasty crack whores in that holding cell with her, let me tell you. And a Criplette who seems to be taking quite an interest in her. We'll try to keep them separated, but it's pretty full in there today. Hard for the jailers to keep an eye on everybody, you know? Could take a while to process the papers before she can post bail and head home."

Jason looked angry now. "Leave my mother out of this. She doesn't know anything."

"Only one way to find out," said Maclean. "We'll have to keep her here for questioning."

"I'm about to send you a text," whispered Verraday. "You know what to do."

Maclean's cell phone buzzed. She pulled it out and checked the display.

"Just got a text from the search site. That dog that you think is so funny? It found a hot spot up there on the property your family owned until very recently. So we'll be bringing a backhoe in on a barge tomorrow morning. It will cost the taxpayers hundreds of thousands of dollars, but we'll find every last one of those bodies, I promise you, Mr. Griffin. And the more money it costs the taxpayers, the more likely it is that the district attorney will go for the maximum penalty. That means that unless you decide to tell me the truth now, the only decision you'll have left to make after you leave this room is whether you'd prefer to be executed by hanging or lethal injection. It's your call. And by the way, I'm going to subpoena your mother as a witness. I want her to give me a little tour of the family retreat, so when the bodies of your victims start coming out of the ground, she can see what her precious little boy has done."

"That's enough!" said Tarleton testily. "You don't have a single shred of hard evidence."

"Oh, and one other thing, Jason. You showed me a rental contract for a car up in Port Angeles. Only twenty miles on the odometer when you brought it back the next morning. The manager at the Red Lion noticed it parked just outside the office all night. He says you spent about an hour down by the shore, watching the waves roll in. Said you looked like you had the weight of the world on your shoulders."

"I told you about that already."

"I know you did. You made sure everybody saw you drinking your wine before going back into your room. And you made sure they saw your rental car parked there all night. Right by the main entrance to the hotel. I'm wondering if there was something wrong with that car?"

"Where is this going, Detective?" asked Tarleton.

"Patience, please, Counselor. This won't take much longer. Mr. Griffin, was there something wrong with that rental car?"

"No."

"Then why did you rent a second car? One from a place right in town, not from the agency at the airport where you rented the car you parked at the hotel? And since you're so careful about claiming expenses for the company on your Visa card, why did you pay for the second car with cash? Was it so that there wouldn't be an electronic paper trail? Because the only way I found out that you rented a second car was by calling every car rental agency in Port Angeles and e-mailing them a photograph of you. Fortunately they had all the records on file, including the in and out mileage on the odometers. The nice young woman on the counter told me that you put a lot of miles on that car for a one-night rental. Two hundred and ninety-four miles to be precise. Exactly the distance from Port Angeles to Issaquah, with a little stop-over at Cody's apartment to plant the evidence after you lured him to that trail and pushed him off the edge. So despite what you wanted people to believe, you were not in your hotel room all night, Mr. Griffin."

Jason Griffin put his hand on Tarleton's arm. They whispered to each other, then Tarleton turned to Maclean.

"Would you bring in the district attorney, please?"

★   ★   ★

District Attorney Kirk Weder arrived and before he'd even settled into the seat next to Maclean, looked directly at Tarleton.

"Okay, what's the offer?"

Tarleton leaned forward. "My client is willing to plead guilty to the murders of Helen Dale, Rachel Friesen, Alana Carmichael, Cody North, Paul Schmidt, as well as five other Jane Does, whose bodies he will locate for you on Suquamish Island, on the condition that you do not seek the death penalty and that you do not charge his mother as an accessory or subpoena her to be a witness."

Weder leaned in toward Maclean. They exchanged whispers. He turned back toward Tarleton and Jason Griffin, who was now staring at the floor.

"Deal."

CHAPTER 32

The Bellingham was busy that night, and it was only by calling ahead and saying that it was a special occasion that Verraday was able to reserve the two wingback chairs by the fireplace. Out of sheer curiosity, he had arrived four minutes before the appointed time. But as he looked down the length of the bar, he could see Maclean's Burberry coat already draped over the back of the chair. How she always arrived first was one mystery that he'd have to wait for another occasion to solve.

Maclean smiled as she saw him approaching. She looked more relaxed than he'd ever seen her before. She was wearing a cowl-neck sweater dress over black leggings, and her hair was down. She was definitely off duty. The same waiter who had served them the other night came by their table as Verraday took his seat.

"The usual, folks?" he asked with that easygoing, confident smile.

Maclean nodded. "Please."

"Sounds good," said Verraday, happy to be recognized and treated like a regular on his second visit.

"Coming right up," said the waiter as he left to get their drinks.

"So?" asked Verraday. "You look like the cat that swallowed the canary. You have stories to tell. And I want to hear them."

Maclean grinned broadly.

"Well . . . the captain and chief are pretty pleased. I'll be doing a press conference with them tomorrow morning to announce that Jason Griffin has confessed to the killings. And they're already talking promotion."

"Well, they should be. You're the best homicide detective they've got. Congratulations. Did Jason have anything more to say?"

"Yeah. I pumped him for everything he had to make sure that the confession stuck. He was even more devious than I realized. That empty apartment had been empty since the day that Cody arrived in Seattle. Jason kept it as a dummy address so that he could stall if anyone ever tried to interview Cody. The apartment we searched was Cody's real home. Though all the evidence was planted there only after Jason killed him. He didn't miss a thing. When Helen Dale pleasured Cody in the cockpit of the plane, it wasn't just a generous boss handing out employee benefits. He retrieved the semen from the tissue that Helen used to clean up and put it on Rachel Friesen's panties so that he could implicate Cody if he ever needed a scapegoat. As for Alana Carmichael, Jason had the Cupid's arrow hidden away just like you said he would. The kill room was the office. Soundproof and quite chic looking, as you are aware. He had a Berkley horse with soft leather restraints hidden in the ceiling.

And the radiator repair tubs were where he washed his victims. Then he used the van to dump their bodies afterward. End of story."

"And thank God it is," said Verraday. "Well done."

"You too. Great work, James. You're a mind reader."

"You flatter me, Detective. But I'm no mind reader. Just a neurotic, hypervigilant guy who's found his niche."

The moment he said it, he regretted uttering those words. He realized he didn't want her thinking of him that way, even in jest.

"I don't believe you," she said, smiling. "Not completely anyway. So what's up for you after this?"

"Got the big midterm exam coming up," replied Verraday with a hint of sarcasm. "And that's about it in the way of excitement. Things are going to seem dull going back to university life after being around you. Other than that, you know what they say about academia. It's publish or perish. I'm doing some new research on psychopathy and memory. I'm wondering if a psychopath's memory function works differently than it does for the rest of us. I'll have to devise some tests, then find some willing psychopaths. Fortunately or unfortunately, there's always a ready supply of them on hand. So that's my life. What about you? After the press conference, what's next for the newly promoted Detective Maclean?"

"I don't have any new cases. Not as of tonight anyway, and I hope it stays that way at least until tomorrow. But working with you on this has piqued my interest in some cold cases. We have three hundred on file. I think I'll dust a few of them off and see what I can find out."

"What about Fowler?"

"Word is he's being bumped off homicide. They're going to do a Robson with him, bury him someplace in the department where he can't cause any trouble. Some minor administration role. I would have preferred that he'd been kicked off the force, but that's not going to happen. Not yet anyway."

"Well, it's a start. Maybe there's karma after all. So does your mom know that you busted a serial killer?"

"I sent her a quick e-mail to tell her we'd cracked a big case. I'm going to see her tomorrow after the press conference. I'll give her the details then."

"She'll be proud of you."

Maclean laughed, almost shyly. "Oh, yeah. Everybody on her floor at the hospital will hear about it. That's my mom."

"You two are close."

"Yeah. I see her at least once a week. She's one of my best friends. How about you and your dad?"

"I don't see him that often," said Verraday. "It's hard to explain, but he keeps a distance between himself and everybody else. I mean, we love each other, though he's not the type to say so. He's old school, you know? He was never the same after my mom was killed. I mean, he kept it all together. Made sure that Penny got physio and that we both went to school and had lunches and clothes and everything. But he became withdrawn. Spent most of his evenings drinking down in the man cave. Still does."

Maclean nodded.

"He must have loved your mother a lot though, for it to have affected him so much."

"He never talks about it, but yeah, I guess you're right."

"How about you and your sister?"

"We're close. Though she does the 'big sister' routine with me a bit, you know? But she means well, and she's smart as hell. Got her own place. Plays wheelchair basketball. Won a regional archery championship last year."

"She sounds interesting. I'd like to meet her some time."

"You'd like her. You have any siblings?"

"No," replied Maclean. "Maybe that's why my mom and I are so close."

"She must be a strong person to have held it all together like that after your father died," said Verraday.

"Yeah, she is. My mom is amazing. There's nothing I can't talk about with her."

"You're lucky."

Maclean took a sip of her drink then looked up at him thoughtfully. "Thank god we still have who we have," she said.

"Yeah," agreed Verraday quietly.

Maclean raised her glass. "Here's to the ones taken from us too soon."

Verraday raised his glass and thought about what Maclean had said. "And here's to the ones who carried the extra burden and kept the lights on," he added.

Verraday and Maclean clinked glasses and took a sip of their drinks. Verraday resolved to call his father the next day and find an excuse to get together.

Maclean was gazing into the fireplace. He watched her silently, not wanting to disturb the moment. He enjoyed seeing the firelight playing across her cheeks and the tiny constellations of light reflecting in her eyes, eyes that somehow seemed to be both faraway yet fully present.

At last, Maclean looked away from the fire and turned to Verraday. "In all the excitement, I forgot to ask. Did you tell your dad about Robson?"

"Not yet. Kind of trying to figure out how. Penny and I are still strategizing."

"How did she handle it when you told her?"

"It was . . . interesting."

"Is that all you're going to tell me?"

"We visited Robson's gravesite up in Everett."

"Holy shit, that's not something you hear of victims doing very often. Let me guess. Penny's idea?"

"Yeah. I didn't want to at first, but she talked me into it."

"What was it like?"

"Actually, it was kind of cathartic. We both pissed on his grave."

Maclean burst out laughing, covered her mouth with her hand, not quite quickly enough to stop a line of vodka and soda from dribbling out.

"Hey, not fair to tell me something that funny just when I'm taking a sip!" she said, wiping away the rivulet. "Don't you know that's illegal?"

"What, making a cop laugh when they're drinking?"

"You know what I mean," said Maclean.

"Well, I didn't want to lie to you about it," Verraday replied. Then he leaned forward. "Hold still. You missed a spot on your chin."

Maclean held her face motionless while Verraday reached over with his index finger and gently wiped away the droplet.

"There you go."

"Thank you. Lucky for you, Everett is outside my jurisdiction. Making me laugh while I'm sipping a drink, however, is not."

Maclean signaled for the check.

"Well, it's late," she said. "I should go. The press conference is at ten in the morning, and I don't want to be too foggy for it."

The waiter brought the check and began to hand it to Maclean.

Verraday signaled for it and took out his wallet.

"My turn, Detective. But only because they're not paying you overtime."

CHAPTER 33

Maclean pulled up at the curb in front of Verraday's house.

"Well, Professor, it's been interesting working with you."

"Same here, Detective. You've had an intriguing life. And dare I say it, you've even changed my opinion about cops. At least about some of them."

"And you've changed my opinion about psychologists, Doctor."

Verraday smiled, suddenly feeling bashful.

"They're even crazier than I thought," she said, laughing.

"Thank you," said Verraday. "I'm glad to have been so edifying."

"Well, I guess this is it," she said.

Transitions had always been difficult for Verraday. Maclean was right. This *was* it. They had done what they set out to do. Jason Griffin was behind bars, would stay there for the rest of his life, and would never have the opportunity to hurt anyone ever again. But Verraday would miss the time he had spent with Maclean.

"Yes, I guess it is," he replied, trying to conceal his awkwardness.

"I'll keep you posted and make sure you get proper acknowledgement for helping solve the cases too," said Maclean. "Once I've smoothed the path with the chief."

"Thanks," he said. "Maybe we could even work on something again some time."

"I'd like that," said Maclean.

"Well, until then," said Verraday.

Maclean held out her hand, something she hadn't done since that first morning when he had agreed to meet her and work with her. She shifted sideways in her seat so that she was facing him. That was something she'd never done before when she'd dropped him off either, thought Verraday. She'd always faced forward. He thought her pupils were dilated. Was it just the way her eyes looked naturally, adapting to the shadowy interior of the vehicle after she'd turned the headlights off? Or was it something more? He couldn't be certain.

He took the hand that she offered. It was that same grip he remembered from the day she'd met with him. Strong and confident but gentle. It felt good. So good that he held her hand just a moment longer than was customary. When she didn't withdraw it, his heart began to race. She didn't speak. Didn't move. Just gazed into his eyes. Was he imagining it? He leaned toward her very slightly. She shifted, moved almost imperceptibly forward. When she still didn't withdraw her hand, or speak or pull away, he slid his free hand around her. He felt her relax into his touch. He leaned forward and gently pulled her toward him. An instant later, his lips were on hers. She released her grip from his hand, and a moment later, he felt her reaching around him, drawing him closer in return. Her other hand caressed his cheek. He felt her tongue responding to his gentle probing. Her hair smelled good and felt wonderfully silky to the touch. He stroked it as he kissed her and breathed in her intoxicating scent. He felt himself getting hard and pulled her even more tightly against him. When she responded in kind, he felt like he was having an out-of-body experience. Yet at the same time, he had never been happier to be in his flesh.

He had no idea how long they were there. It could have been five minutes, or it could have been twenty. This was one situation where his expertise in the field of memory was of no use to him. But gradually, following some subtle series of signals, they slowly disengaged— not fully, but just enough to gaze into each other's eyes and speak.

He thought about inviting her in. But he didn't want to seem too aggressive. She'd already mentioned the morning press conference. He didn't want her to be tired the next day for her big public appearance. Nor did he want to jump the gun. Underthinking relationships had been his downfall in romance. Then he had the maddening realization that overthinking had been a problem for him too. He saw her looking at him, just expectantly enough to signal that she wanted him to provide the lead.

"Well," said Verraday. "I should let you go. You've got that press conference in the morning. And I've got a lecture too."

"Right," said Maclean.

She straightened up. Verraday thought he saw something, a microexpression, some flicker of disappointment cross her face. He suddenly felt afraid of losing her.

"But if you're free on the weekend, there's a new Thai restaurant on East Madison that's supposed to be great. I want to hear about the rest of your week. Unless you'll be too big of a celebrity by then to be hanging out with lowly academics."

"Sure," said Maclean, laughing slightly. "It's a date."

He leaned across, held her, and pressed his lips against hers one last time, lingering for a long moment before he withdrew. He hoped it was enough to signal genuine interest and not leave her wondering if he was just beating a polite retreat.

Then he opened the door slowly and stepped out. Verraday stood on the sidewalk, still watching her. He couldn't read her expression. He felt wistful and was momentarily frozen, unsure how to extract himself. She was returning his gaze.

She lowered the passenger's side window, smiled, then said, "You know how this works, right? I hope it hasn't been *that* long. One of us has to look away."

"Okay. You first," said Verraday.

"No. You're forgetting that I have those protective instincts I mentioned. I need to see you enter your domicile and lock the door safely behind you, sir. And really, you should get a security alarm. I wasn't kidding about that."

He laughed. "All right, Officer. I'll go straight home and I won't talk to any strangers. I'll call you later in the week to sort out a time for dinner."

Verraday grinned like a teenager, knew he was doing it, and for once didn't care. He reached for the gate handle and noted that it was closed and latched, which pleased him. For all Bosko's bluster and protests of innocence, Verraday had called it right. Confronting the meat-headed patrolman had worked. He'd put Bosko in his place and sent him packing. Maybe this would be the end of it all now.

When he arrived at the front steps, he reached into his jacket for his keys. He fumbled for just a moment then mercifully, felt them in the bottom of his pocket. He knew Maclean was still watching him and was relieved that for once he had remembered where he'd left his keys, enabling him to make something resembling a smooth and suave exit.

He put the key in the lock, opened it, then turned and stood in the doorway. He could see Maclean now only in shadows, silhouetted by the streetlights. He waved to her, and she returned the gesture. Only when he backed into the house and slowly began to close the door did he see her put the vehicle in gear and pull away from the curb.

He locked the door then kicked off his boots and hung his jacket up on the hall tree. He turned on the gas fireplace and poured a brandy for himself, plunking down happily on the sofa. He took a sip of the amber liquor and savored the warmth of it spreading through his body as he felt the welcome glow of the gas fireplace on his skin.

He was filled with a sense of well-being he hadn't experienced since . . . well, he couldn't think of when. He smiled inwardly, thinking of how good Maclean's body had felt against his when they kissed. Her breath was gentle and warm, her skin pleasingly soft, though he could feel that her arms were lithe and athletic beneath the sleeves of her Burberry trench coat. As he raised his brandy to his lips, he caught the scent of her perfume on his sleeve, something exotically floral with an almost imperceptible musky note.

He debated calling her, finally gave in, and picked up his cell phone. He was about to speed dial her, but suddenly felt awkward at the prospect of exactly what he'd say. If he invited her to come back, it would force a response, and if that response was "no," it would introduce an awkward note into what had been a heady, if brief, start to their romance. He decided to text her instead. A text would give them both a bit more leeway. There would be no awkward pauses while she was forced to say yes or no. If she didn't want to come back, she could even pretend she'd had her phone turned off, and they'd both save face.

He flip-flopped a few times and finally settled on writing, "I should've invited you in. If you're awake and not up to anything, come on over." Simple yet functional.

He hit send before he could change his mind. An instant later, he castigated himself for sending such an inarticulate note. But the matter was now out of his hands. He began reading again, but had only gotten through three more pages before a wave of fatigue hit him. The adrenaline and exhaustion of the last week, he suspected, had finally caught up with him.

He felt a craving for sleep so powerful that he went upstairs without even turning off the gas fireplace. He'd nap for a few minutes, he told himself, and then if Maclean did come back, he wouldn't be a narcoleptic dud.

★   ★   ★

Verraday awakened in the dark. He had no idea how long he'd been asleep. He thought he'd heard a thump. Or had he? He couldn't tell if it was a real sound, or just a muscle spasm from him relaxing, something from the subbasement of his unconscious mind. The thud, if it was real at all, was over by the time he'd awakened, and for a moment, with the house so quiet, he wondered if it had just been something he'd dreamed. He lay there on the bed for a moment. It could have been raccoons knocking over the garbage can outside. Or a gate, his or someone else's, banging in the wind. But he saw that the shadows of the tree branches on his bedroom wall were motionless. The air outside was still. And the sound, it seemed to him, had been closer. He had an urge to fall back asleep, but then realized how bad it would look if Maclean had returned and knocked on his door, and he hadn't answered.

He wondered if she had responded to his text message. Then he recalled that in his haste to lie down, he had left his cell phone in the living room. Still fighting to shake off the fatigue, he made his way across his bedroom, surprised to find himself unsteady on his feet. As he crossed the threshold of the bedroom doorway into the hall, he saw a faint flickering of orange light from downstairs and realized he'd forgotten to turn the gas fireplace off.

In the next moment, a searing sensation shot down his neck and arm. He felt like his breath was being squeezed out of him, like hot, stinging tendrils had plummeted through his shoulder blade toward his chest. He stumbled forward and hit a bookcase, then collapsed backward onto the carpet.

It took a moment for Verraday to grasp what had happened. Someone was moving in the hallway behind him. He was unnaturally groggy and in excruciating pain. He looked at his shoulder and saw the blood now seeping out onto the floor.

But even through the waves of pain, he was stunned to the marrow when his tormentor stepped out of the shadows, identity now revealed: it was Jensen, the mousy-looking student, the one with the unfashionable glasses who seemed to live in a bulky sweater and baggy jeans. Only she no longer looked anything like the girl who sat quietly in his classes four times a week. She wasn't wearing glasses. Her black hair wasn't pulled back in the usual way that made it look short and severe. It hung loose, and Verraday could see that it was much longer than he'd realized. Neither was she wearing the bulky sweater and baggy jeans. She was dressed in black leggings and a clingy sweater under a motorcycle jacket. If she hadn't been standing there right in front of him, he would never have believed the transition. She had transformed into a lithe vixen who wouldn't have gone unnoticed for more than a second in any crowd.

"Jensen, what are you doing?" he croaked.

"Isn't it obvious? I'm killing you."

"Killing me?"

"Well, I didn't start out the evening with that idea. I originally came by to seduce you."

"What would possess you to do something like that?"

"Because I know how much you like me and how much you're attracted to me."

"What are you talking about?"

"Come on. All those times you looked at that Bettie Page site?"

Verraday felt hopelessly confused by this new information. His brain was foggy, and the pain from the knife wound was so overwhelming that Jensen's statement sounded like a puzzle wrapped inside a non sequitur.

"That site you kept going to. I made it up. There's no fucking Bettie Page exhibit at the MoMA. Those thumbnails you kept looking at were of me."

"I have no idea what you're talking about. I don't know about any Bettie Page exhibit."

"Don't lie to me!" shouted Jensen. "I have your IP address from our e-mails. And it turned up on that fake web page I made. A whole bunch of times. Each one of those photos had a code encrypted in it. And I know from it that you even looked at the pictures of me more than you looked at Bettie Page."

"Pictures of you?"

"Yes, the thumbnails? Where you couldn't see her face. All of those were me. And you loved it. I know you did because you clicked on all of them. Over and over. You were hot for me. So don't deny it."

Through the dim light of his memory, Verraday now realized that Jensen had concocted an elaborate test for him.

"You went to my site seven times this week. Seven fucking times. Do you know how good that made me feel, when I saw that you clicked on those thumbnails and knew that you were fantasizing about me? That you kept coming back to see *me*? Not even Bettie Page, but *me*."

"I didn't know it was you," said Verraday.

"But you wanted me. Whether you knew it was me or not. You were obsessed with me, Professor. And you could have had me too. But you screwed everything up."

Even through his stupor, he could see that Jensen was becoming agitated. She was pacing, making jabbing motions at him with the hunting knife. He tried to placate her. "It's not surprising that I was attracted to you," he said. "You're an extremely beautiful . . ."

"Girl? Is that what you meant to say? Girl? Fuck you. Don't try to talk your way out of this. You had your chance and you chose someone else."

"I don't know what you mean."

Jensen's voice rose with anger. "Like hell you don't. And not just anyone, but a cop. A fucking *cop*. So much for all your anti-authority bullshit. And to think I even killed for you."

"What do you mean, killed for me?" asked Verraday, alarmed. He had a sudden horrifying fear that she might have done something to Maclean.

"Robson. Do you really think he died in a gun-cleaning accident? Do you have any idea how much work went into that? I drugged his whiskey, just like I drugged your brandy. And when he saw me coming for him, he looked at me helplessly, with this stupid expression on his face. Like he was so fucking surprised. He couldn't believe that he was a big bad cop and he was about to be killed by a girl."

She glared at Verraday.

"Robson was a coward. That's why he ran away from what he did to your family when you were a kid. He couldn't face up to what he had done. He was the worst kind of killer. Weak. Gutless. Disgusting. When I made him hold that gun in his own hand and turn it on himself while I pulled the trigger and blew his brains out, I had the biggest rush of my life. And I haven't lost a moment's sleep over it. He deserved everything he got and more. Don't you agree? I would have shot him in the spine and let him spend the rest of his life in a wheelchair, if I'd been able to figure out a way to keep him from ever saying who did it to him. Can you even imagine someone wanting so badly to make you happy that they killed for you? Because that's what I did, James. I killed for you. I would have done anything for you. *Anything.* But instead, you had to ruin it by kissing that *cop.* Do you have any idea how I felt when I saw that?"

"You were watching me tonight?"

"Of course I was watching you. I've been watching you for weeks. I even broke into your house a few times to find out how to make you happy. I went through your files so I'd know what you liked. I found the photos of that girl—I think she's an ex? So I bought lingerie like that to wear for you. Then, to test it, to make sure I was right and that I wouldn't disappoint you, I left those flyers on your doorstep. I came back later and saw that the only flyer you kept was the one for the burlesque show."

Verraday's head was swimming. He couldn't believe that anyone had been in his space and he hadn't noticed. That she had repeatedly violated his inner sanctum and he hadn't noticed. So much for his powers of observation. "I went to so much effort to please you. Because I loved you. But you tore my fucking heart out. You were the only one I invited into my world. The *only one*. And you betrayed me. We could have been such a force. Taken down so many assholes together."

Verraday tried to buy time. Maybe if he could just calm her down, he might get a chance to disarm her.

"Maybe it's not too late," he said. "Now that I realize it was you."

"Of course it's too late. I offered myself to you on a platter, and you rejected me. I had to sit there in the dark like an idiot tonight watching you kiss that woman, holding her body against yours. Throwing yourself at her. You hurt me to the core. And now you're going to die. Slowly."

"Please don't do this," said Verraday weakly. "I didn't mean to hurt you."

"And yet you did. But don't worry. Even though you hurt me, I won't make you feel that much pain. I put Ativan in your brandy. A lot of it. I know you always have brandy before bed. And I know that you have a prescription for Ativan. You should be more careful what you put in your recycle bin. The police department could use something like that to discredit you. I saw them going through your bin once, you know, while I was watching you. Fortunately, I'd already taken out your empty prescription bottle so there was nothing much for them to see. They're morons. But what do you expect from a cop? I mean, who could possibly be interested in fucking a cop except for some pathetic piece of shit."

Verraday saw the hunting knife coming at him. He tried to move but his legs felt leaden. The blade sank deep into the long muscle of his thigh, and he screamed. He tried to grab her wrist, but the Ativan had made him slow, and she leapt out of the way.

"What you said in class, about Wall Street psychopaths? You're wrong, you know. Those hedge fund managers might be psychopaths, but the rush they experience is just a substitute for what I can do. I know because I fucked a few of them. For seven hundred dollars a pop. And you know what? They're so sublimated it's pathetic. Look at Donald Trump. What a needy asshole. He's begging to be respected, so he builds these fucking monuments to himself all over the place because he can't face up to what he really wants to have: power over life and death. So because of his programming, he finds a substitute instead. I, on the other hand, already have what I want: the ability to totally dominate another human being. I don't need all that money to make me feel powerful. I *am* powerful."

"No you're not," said Verraday. "You're dead inside. That's why you need to do things like this."

"Well, it's irrelevant for you, because you're about to become dead inside *and* outside. You're going to bleed out very slowly. And there's enough Ativan in your system that you won't be able to do one thing about it."

She put the hunting knife aside and pulled out a long stiletto. Verraday's hope sank at the sight of it.

"I've always been curious to see how many of these punctures it would take to kill a human. I've used this on dogs and cats. Once even on a raccoon that was foolish enough to walk into a trap at my parents' house. I was going to use it on that rat I left on your doorstep, but this doesn't leave much of a mark, and I didn't want you to miss any details."

He raised his arm to block the stiletto and felt a wave of agonizing pain as it punched through the palm of his hand and emerged out the back between his tendons. He grabbed at her with his other arm, but she was quick and leapt backward out of the way.

"You know, I could just plunge this into your liver or your heart. That would kill you pretty much instantly. But what would be the fun in that?"

He winced as the stiletto sank into his abdomen. He felt the warmth of the blood rolling down his side under his shirt and blackness closing in around him.

★   ★   ★

He came to with the terrifying sensation that he was drowning. There was water in his nose and throat, and he couldn't breathe through his mouth. Verraday tried to move his lips but realized that Jensen had sealed his mouth with gaffer tape while he'd been unconscious. He coughed desperately trying to dislodge the water in his nose.

"Don't worry," came Jensen's voice from behind him. "I won't let you drown. Yet. I'm going to keep you alive a little longer."

She moved into his line of vision now, staying far enough away that she knew he wouldn't be able to grab her in a sudden lunge, even if he were able to rally the strength. She was holding a pitcher of water.

"You were disappointing as a lover, but you're quite amusing as a playmate. I like to think of this pitcher as half full, not half empty."

She laughed sardonically and dumped the water onto his face. He felt it going into his nose and down his windpipe. He began to choke and started to black out again.

"Ah-ah-ah, Professor. Come back. I'm not finished with you . . . yet."

He felt her straining to turn him over on his side. She thumped him on the back and the water dribbled out his nose. He gasped for breath. He felt her finger on his jugular vein and wondered if she was now about to administer the coup de grace.

"I can see why our security agencies waterboard people," said Jensen. "Your pulse is nearly one hundred and sixty beats per minute! You're exhibiting a full-on panic reaction. But don't worry. You won't drown. I need to keep you alive just a little bit longer. Now where were we? Oh yes."

He felt the cold steel of the stiletto tip against his belly.

"If I've calculated correctly, and if you hold very, very still, this will miss all your major organs. Here goes!"

He screamed as she once again plunged the stiletto into his abdomen.

Verraday felt the world slipping away again, but then, as if from the bottom of a well, he heard faint but frantic knocking from downstairs and the persistent ringing of his doorbell.

Jensen put her finger to her lips.

"Shhhh! Be a good boy and don't make any noise."

He attempted a grunt anyway.

"You're not listening to me," she hissed at him.

Jensen balled her gloved hand into a fist and swung it down hard. He felt an explosion as the cartilage of his nose cracked and the blood immediately began running out of his nostrils. At the same moment, just as he was about to drift off into darkness, he felt the floor vibrate heavily under him. Despite the excruciating pain and the sensation of his skull being on fire, he knew the tremor was too heavy to be anything that originated from within him. It was help on the way. He rallied himself to stay awake. He heard the crash of his front door erupting in splinters, the clatter of broken window glass spraying across his foyer. Then he heard Maclean's voice.

"James! Where are you?"

He was choking now on the blood running from his nose into his throat.

Jensen leaned in toward him, an angry, caustic expression on her face. She whispered, affecting an imitation of Maclean's voice.

"'James'? You're on a first-name basis with that bitch now, are you? You cheating bastard."

She kicked him hard in the ribs. Despite the air being stomped out of him, Verraday managed a tortured grunt.

"He's upstairs," Maclean shouted.

Jensen backed away from Verraday's face, to his feet. She reached into her gym bag and drew out a throwing knife.

Maclean hurtled up the stairs, taking them two at a time. Verraday tried to shout a warning to her but all he could get out was a faint gurgle. Jensen raised her right hand, holding the serrated blade of the knife between her thumb and index finger as she chambered it, preparing for the throw. Verraday's legs and arms felt like concrete. He watched in horror and frustration, time slowing to a crawl as, in his peripheral vision, he saw Maclean's face emerging from the gloom, Glock service pistol raised in front of her.

In the shadows, Jensen grinned and took careful aim. Verraday summoned the last of his strength and despite the grogginess and waves of pain surging through him, kicked with his one good leg at Jensen. He caught her hard on the shin, heard her groan with pain, felt his kick throwing her balance off an instant before the knife left her hand. He watched it tumble end over end toward Maclean as she emerged onto the landing.

Maclean saw it at the last moment, the realization so sudden that her face didn't even have a chance to register surprise. Jensen's aim had been thrown off just enough that when Maclean dropped down to the left, the knife whizzed past her cheek, missing her by a hand's width. The uniformed officer directly behind Maclean never saw the knife coming, and he didn't have time to react. The blade caught him in the throat, less than three inches above the top of his bulletproof vest. Verraday saw the look of surprise on the officer's face, then his hand going up, almost in disbelief, feeling where the knife had penetrated. It was Bosko. Or so he thought. He wasn't certain if he was hallucinating now from shock and blood loss.

Jensen ducked through the doorway of the study. Maclean was still recovering her balance but managed to fire off a quick volley from the Glock. The light in the hallway was dim, and though Verraday was partially blinded by the muzzle flash, he saw wood splinters fly as Maclean's shots tore through the door that Jensen was slamming shut and locking behind her. He heard Jensen moan, then from within his study, the sound of a window shattering. Maclean sprang at the door, breaking it open on the first kick. He saw Maclean enter his study, pistol at the ready. She returned to the hall a moment later and pulled out her handheld radio.

"Dispatch, this is Detective Constance Maclean. I need EMS and backup. I've got an officer down with a knife wound, a wounded civilian in the home, plus a wounded suspect outside on the front walkway."

From where he was lying, Verraday could see that Bosko was losing blood rapidly through the gash in his throat. Maclean leaned down to Verraday, pausing just long enough to pull the duct tape back from his mouth.

"Where did she cut you?"

"In the shoulder, hand, abdomen, and leg. No major arteries or organs though, I don't think. She was trying to take her time."

"Okay, hold tight," said Maclean. "I'm going to get you out of here."

She was already sprinting toward Bosko. She knelt beside the downed officer and applied compression to the wound in his throat. It was bad. Bosko had bled so much it had soaked through the carpet and was beginning to pool on top of it. Bosko's eyes were closed now, his face expressionless. Probably unconscious from loss of blood, thought Verraday.

"Stay with me, stay with me," he heard Maclean say. "Help is on the way. You're gonna make it. You're both gonna make it."

Verraday felt a tingling sensation that started in his feet and quickly spread through the rest of his body. It was pleasant. It was, he realized, the sensation of the blood coursing through him. He wasn't sure if it meant he was living or dying. He felt fear now, not just pain. His heart began to race. He felt it miss a beat, recover its rhythm, then miss another beat. He didn't know if he was drifting into life or death. He pushed that thought away, focused on his breath, drew it in, counting the numbers off slowly. He heard distant sirens then felt his consciousness slipping away. The darkness began to envelop him. He released his breath one last time, closed his eyes, felt the tingling warmth. Whatever was happening, he'd resigned himself to it. He let go and allowed himself to be carried away into the void.

CHAPTER 34

Verraday gradually, reluctantly became aware of a bright light, so bright that even with his eyelids clamped shut, it seemed to penetrate directly into his optical nerves. He tried to raise his hands to block it, but found that he couldn't move them. He tried to turn his head away but discovered that he couldn't do that either. In fact, his body seemed to have taken leave of his consciousness. Maybe this is what people meant by "going into the light," he thought.

The light grew in intensity as he gained consciousness, which, through his tightly closed lids, created the effect that he was staring into an orangey-red color field. He tried to speak but his tongue was thick and heavy. He felt like his throat was lined with sandpaper. So he groaned his annoyance instead.

"He always this happy to be alive?" a male voice asked.

"I'm not sure. I've only known him for a couple of weeks now," replied a female voice archly. He recognized it and began to smile. Despite the blinding light, he struggled to open his eyes so he could see the face that went with that voice. When at last he had managed a squint, he saw Maclean and a doctor in a white medical coat silhouetted against a bright afternoon sky in an airy hospital room.

"This is Dr. Wellesley," said Maclean. "He's the surgeon who saved your life."

"Thank you, Doctor," said Verraday. "Figures, the one sunny day we've had since September, and I slept through most of it."

"You slept through two sunny days, actually," said Wellesley. "I put you under heavy sedation. You've managed to accumulate quite a collection of holes, Professor. You were leaking pretty badly when your friend here brought you in."

"Strange, I don't remember that part," said Verraday.

"The good news is you'll recover completely. The girl who did this to you was highly selective about where she placed the perforations."

"Some guys have all the luck."

"Indeed they do, Professor Verraday. And you're one of them. Another inch in any direction on those abdominal wounds, and you'd be somewhere nice and dark. Forever. Now if you'll excuse me, Professor, I've got to take care of some genuinely sick people. So I'll leave you to Detective Maclean. Later."

"Thanks, Doctor," said Verraday as Wellesley headed out the doorway.

Verraday turned as much as he could to look at Maclean. "You okay?" he asked.

"Sure, I'm fine, thanks to you."

"And I dodged God knows what, thanks to you. So I guess you got my text?"

Maclean smiled. "Yeah. I decided losing a few z's wouldn't make that much of a difference at the press conference. Thought maybe all those love hormones you're always talking about would make up for the lack of sleep."

"How did you know something was wrong?"

"You didn't answer when I rang your doorbell or when I knocked. I thought you'd gone to bed but then I saw the light from the gas fireplace. That seemed strange. I called and you didn't answer your cell or your landline either. So I took a stroll down the side of your house. Saw that the phone line had been cut. So I called for backup and decided to go in."

"What about the patrolman who got hit with the knife? Was I hallucinating from blood loss by then, or was that really Bosko?"

"It was Bosko. He was doing a stakeout at the liquor store a few blocks from your place when I called for help. He was there in under a minute."

"He was bleeding pretty badly. Did he make it?"

"It was really close. He flatlined in the ambulance on the way to the hospital, then once more in the ER. But he's still with us—so far at least. In critical but stable condition in the ICU. They think he'll pull through."

"Did he know it was me that you were going in for?"

"Yeah. I thought he deserved to know. He told me the two of you had a run-in the night before. Said you accused him of being a stalker."

"Yeah, he stopped me in the parking lot of the liquor store. We had some words."

"I know. He told me about it as we were going in. He said if you really did have some nut job stalker in there with you, maybe we should just leave you two alone together to sort it out because you're such a pain in the ass."

Verraday smiled weakly. "Yeah, that would have been convenient for him."

"He was kidding. He agreed with me that there was no time to wait for more backup. He was the one who broke down your front door."

"Well, tell him I have an eight-hundred-dollar deductible. That ought to give him some consolation."

"I'll mention it when he comes around."

"You can mention something else too. Tell him I'm dropping the lawsuit against him."

"You sure?"

"Yeah. How can I sue someone who took a knife in the throat trying to save my life? But I'm making it conditional on him taking an anger management course."

"I think he'd rather take the lawsuit and the knife in the throat."

"Okay. I'll drop the suit against him. No conditions. But I'm not dropping the one against the city and the SPD. They're the ones who are really responsible for it. That's where the orders came from."

"Word is they want to settle out of court with you, James. You've just helped them close a lot of cases. They don't want to be seen to be making an enemy of you. They want to treat it like an unfortunate misunderstanding."

"What about Jensen? What happened to her?"

"Now there's a piece of work. One of the shots I fired through the door got her in the arm. Even then, she had no intention of giving up. She jumped right through the window of your study. Hopefully your insurance will cover that, too. I looked out and saw her lying facedown on your walkway. I thought she was dead, and I knew you and Bosko both needed my immediate attention. Tempted though I was to leave the duct tape on your mouth, I was afraid you'd choke on your own blood. And I knew I'd lose Bosko for sure if I didn't get some compression on that knife wound. So I left her out there while I tended to the two of you. When the backup arrived, they asked what had happened to the wounded suspect who was supposed to be outside. She was gone. A patrol car spotted her in an alley three blocks away. She had a broken ankle but she was halfway through hotwiring a car for a getaway. This girl's done her homework."

"She's a deeply disturbed individual. And trust me, I've met a lot of them."

"Yeah, I'm getting that. But she was sane enough to realize she didn't have a chance when a second patrol car showed up and sealed off the alley. So she surrendered. She's been charged and is in custody. No bail."

"That's reassuring."

"When we checked her dorm room, we found a kill kit she'd put together: knives, box cutters, syringes, a mask, garbage bags, and plastic handcuffs. She kept a diary that she wrote everything down in. She's been researching you since she was in high school. Had every single article you'd ever written bookmarked on her computer. She wanted to learn everything that you could teach her about profiling so that when she started killing, she'd know what to do to throw investigators off her trail. Then once she became your student, she developed a romantic interest in you. An obsession, really. She kept a diary. She wrote about you in it. A lot."

Verraday knew he wouldn't want to hear what was in Jensen's diary, and he wished there was some way that Maclean hadn't seen what was in there either. But he knew that in the course of her investigation, she would have had to read every last embarrassing word.

"Jensen fantasized about you constantly. She dreamed that the two of you would become a dynamic duo, killing together and then making love."

Verraday said nothing. He felt embarrassed. He wondered if Jensen had written about the pictures she'd taken of herself and mentioned that he'd looked at her photos online. It would be just his luck if, at the first blush of romance, Maclean had come across something humiliating about him in Jensen's notes.

"Killing the rat, killing Robson, it's all there," said Maclean. "She also mentioned torturing and killing animals and taking pictures of them back when she lived with her parents in Tacoma. She had planned to kill her roommate too. And some other student named Koller. Any idea who that is?"

"Unfortunately, yes. I'm familiar with him," said Verraday.

He fought to suppress a laugh, only because it hurt so much.

"I wonder what triggered all this in her?" he mused.

"Wait 'til you hear this," said Maclean. "Jensen was adopted. Born in Serbia. Spent the first year and a half of her life in an orphanage there. According to her adoptive parents, the place was a hellhole. Cold. Wet. Leaks in the ceiling. She'd been kept in a steel crib, no contact with any other kids, and only about two minutes a day of adult interaction during feedings and diaper changes."

"I've read about those orphanages," said Verraday. "In spite of the shit those kids go through, most of them turn out okay once they're adopted. Human beings are resilient. But that's the nature of psychopathy. If the condition pre-exists in a child raised under the best of circumstances, with loving parents in a nurturing environment, that child might grow up to be a corporate lawyer or a hedge fund manager. Under the worst circumstances—like being left in a crib for the first year and a half of your life with no love, no warmth, no bonding—you get a serial killer."

"It's sad, really," said Maclean. "Her parents told me that when they got her, she was so developmentally stunted, she didn't know how to walk or even smile. They eventually got her physically healthy, but the other part of her, that inner part, never seemed to heal. They said she never seemed to bond with them either. Not really. They bought a few family pets over the years but stopped because the animals always died mysteriously. They tried taking her to a counselor. You can guess the rest."

"Psychopaths are extremely good at appearing normal when it suits them," said Verraday, "and they can be very charming when they want something. Counselors get fooled all the time. It takes years of training—and really good instincts—to detect one."

"The adoptive parents hoped that going away to university and getting a career would straighten her out. They're feeling pretty guilty about what happened. But they said there was never enough evidence to do anything serious, and they loved her in spite of it all."

"It's human nature," said Verraday, "irrational as it is. It's an evolutionary development. Parents love their kids and want to protect them no matter what those kids are like. Otherwise most of us would probably have been strangled in our cradles."

"I like it when you let your romantic side show like that," quipped Maclean.

Verraday began to laugh but felt a searing pain in his shoulder and abdomen. Once it had subsided enough for him to speak, he continued.

"By the time they took her out of the orphanage, it wouldn't have mattered what her adoptive parents did. No amount of kindness would have changed her. The jack-in-the-box handle was cranking away inside her head, and it was just a matter of time until the lid blew off."

"I'll tell them you said so. Except for that jack-in-the-box part. Maybe it'll make them feel better. Anyway I don't want to monopolize your time. The doctor says that until you're stronger, you can only have visitors for half an hour a day. Penny's waiting out in the hall. With your dad."

"My dad? Did I hear you correctly?"

"You just said it yourself. Parents love their kids."

Verraday nodded. "Listen, before you leave. You still up for going to that Thai restaurant with me next weekend?"

Maclean frowned. "Sorry. I don't think that's going to happen."

Verraday had an anxious, sinking feeling, and he didn't want to push Maclean for a reason. Maclean had read Jensen's diary. He could only imagine what Jensen must have written in there. Probably something about Verraday checking out the thumbnails of her in lingerie. It was excruciatingly embarrassing, and no doubt it would have extinguished any budding romantic feelings that Maclean had toward him. He resigned himself to it. What could he expect? He was an idiot to have taken Jensen's bait, and the Internet was a merciless public arena that didn't allow you to conceal any lapses in judgment. He might as well have set up a Twitter feed to announce his sexual tastes and lack of common sense to the world.

"That's too bad" was all he could muster by way of a response. But he didn't push it, because he really didn't want to hear the reason she had changed her mind about going out on a date with him.

"For one thing," Maclean continued, "the doctor says you won't be out of here until next week. And I'm not really into Thai food, so I'll have to pass."

"Sure, I understand," said Verraday, trying not to sound dejected.

Then Maclean grinned at him mischievously. "But I heard there's a Bettie Page exhibit on at the MoMA. Could be fun. What do you say?"